ALEX y ROBERT

Also by Wena Poon

Lions in Winter (MPH Publishing, 2007; Salt Publishing, 2009)
The Proper Care of Foxes (Ethos Books, 2009)
The Biophilia Omnibus (BookSurge Publishing, 2009)

ALEX y ROBERT
WENA POON

SALT

LONDON

PUBLISHED BY SALT PUBLISHING
Acre House, 11–15 William Road, London NW1 3ER United Kingdom

© Wena Poon, 2010

The right of Wena Poon to be identified as the author of this work
has been asserted by her in accordance with Section 77
of the Copyright, Designs and Patents Act 1988.

Printed and bound in the UK by CPI Cox & Wyman Ltd

Typeset in Bembo 12 / 13.5

The publisher is grateful to the National Arts Council, Singapore,
for their support with this book.

NATIONAL ARTS COUNCIL
SINGAPORE

ISBN 978 1 907773 08 2 paperback

1 3 5 7 9 8 6 4 2

Contents

ACT ONE

The Act of the Spears

THE TRACKS WERE CLEAN, narrow, intimate. A man could lie down, stretching with his toes and fingers, and spread himself across both sets of tracks. He could stop two trains going in opposite directions if he wanted to.

There was low fog on the ground that night. In the east, planes lay helplessly on the airport runway, unable to take off.

She walked along the tracks, feeling the sharp new gravel under her sneakers. Finally, a whistle, like an old musician gently trying out a chord on a harmonica. It was the Missouri-Pacific railway, a bulk goods train that lovingly threaded itself through the urban fabric of the city. She stopped and listened.

Phhumm-mm.

It was a vintage sound, about far away, about railway tracks stretching for hundreds of miles in all directions, away from this city to all corners of the country. It was a sound about distance and nearness and carried with it all kinds of strange purpose.

She stepped closer. A lone dog barked.

She shut her eyes at first, then decided against it. She opened them and looked right at the yellow spot that began to grow ever larger. The tracks were still quiet, but

1

the earth deep beneath her feet began to purr. One glowing, blurry spot became two, then four distinct lamps. This was where the tracks straightened out, where the train ran at its maximum speed.

She took a deep breath and squared her shoulders, flexing her damp hands. If she even began to think, it would all be over. Logic was infallible. She was the only variable.

Then it came — all its thousand tons of clumsy, hard, angry iron, spewing in catastrophic wrath. She had expected everything but the immensity of the noise — the thunder in the ground, the deep bellows of a giant's church organ blasting all at once, the shriek of hot metal wheels being dragged in protest across cold iron, the sudden, arresting constriction of her heart — but then it was over, it was over so quickly, she was left with nothing but ringing ears and a lingering numbness and the soft batting of tiny midges on her face.

She stared at the echoing dark for a long moment.

"*Fuck*," said the girl quietly, unclenching cold fingers.

Now it was done. She was cured.

The clock was reset.

Austin, Texas. It was May, after finals week. The billiards bar on Sixth Street was jammed with sorority girls. One of them leaned against the plate glass windows, looking intently across the street.

Balls clacked and scattered smoothly. "Your turn, Alex."

"Yo, Alex!"

She looked round. "I'm done. I can't play billiards."

"Oh, c'mon!"

"Don't be chicken!"

"I can't, I'm no good at it, it's boring." She turned back

and stared out the window. The object of her scrutiny was a statuesque draft horse the color of cinnamon. It was blinkered. Its fate was to wait, motionlessly and meaninglessly, outside the Driskill Hotel, yoked to a painted carriage with leatherette seats and garlands of plastic flowers. The driver stood before the horse, smoking a cigarette, bored. Man and animal seemed bound in a wretched, useless duty. Because there was nothing else to do, the driver kept turning round and combing the horse's thick mane with his fingers, looking for tangles that were not there. The simple act moved Alex deeply.

"Does your cellphone work in Spain?"

Someone was talking to her again. She was getting on a plane tomorrow; her sorority wanted to send her off with this billiards party. She replied, "Yes, I think so."

"Want another mojito? Their mojitos rock."

"Can you videochat with me from Spain?"

"Are the mojitos better in Spain? Are mojitos *from* Spain?"

"Where is your summer program, exactly? Barcelona?"

"No, Valencia."

"Where?"

Alex shouted above the din of the crowd, "Valencia!"

"Where is that?"

"Is that where oranges are from?"

"Why Spain? Isn't there enough Spanish history here? Whaddabout south of the border?"

"I'm doing my senior thesis on Spanish architecture," said Alex. "The buildings are in Spain, not Mexico." The horse had not moved at all. Even its tail was still. How long had it been standing there?

If set free on the plains, how fast could it gallop?

Do draft horses, with their legs heavy like pillars, also yearn to run? She made a mental note to look it up.

"Why this fascination with Spain?"

She replied, "My father was from Spain originally."

"Really. I always thought you were from Me-*hi*-co."

"Or Puerto Rico."

"Or Cuba."

"Which part of Spain was your family from?"

Alex tore her eyes away from the horse. "Barcelona," she lied. Why bother. That was the only city in Spain they could name anyway, besides Madrid.

"Have you ever been to Spain?"

"Yes."

"Have family there still?"

"Sure."

"Hey, Alex! Heard you were going to Spain! Chase the bulls for me!"

"Very funny," said the young woman, rising to make space for another girl. Alex was tall. She was the only girl in the party in a long-sleeved white shirt and denim jeans in spite of the heat. She settled back down while the waitress took a new round of drink orders. They'd been here all evening. The music was looping. "Light My Fire" by the Doors came on again over the sound system, this time partly drowned by the conversation of the growing crowd. More girls came and joined their table.

"Hey, Alex! You're going to Spain? For how long?"

"Six weeks."

"Nice!"

"You get credit for going to a summer program in Spain?" asked a guy from the next table. Alex recognized him from the gym. He was always trying to talk to her when she was on the treadmill. He had told her his name on different occasions, but she never remembered it. It was something generic, indistinguishable—Scott, or John, or Dave. The girls of her sorority told her that he was known at the gym for always going after the Hispanic chicks; that he had some kind of fetish for brown girls.

"Yeah, it's part of the Spanish study abroad program," she said. She kept her distance. She noticed his fingers tapping on the table unnecessarily; he was self-conscious.

"What a scam. I'm in the wrong major." He had a funny way of twitching the area around his mouth after each sentence. He waited for her to ask the next obvious question. Such was the ritual courtship of a university bar.

She baited him with disinterest. "What major are you in?"

"Engineering."

"Good for you." The drinks arrived. She reached for a mojito and raised it to him, "Have a good life working for Dell."

The girls drowned out his reply with a sudden toast. "Here's to Alex and lots of tapas!"

"And paella!"

"And running with the bulls!"

She waited for them to run out of the three facts they knew about Spain. But there was a fourth.

"Hey, is Valencia where they throw tomatoes at you? Someplace they throw tomatoes at you."

It was two in the morning when the billiards hall booted them out. Cars raced by. Drunk boys hung out of the windows and called out at the girls sauntering down the sidewalk.

"What did he say?"

"He said nice ass, Nicky," said Alex.

Her roommate looked delighted. "To me or to you?"

"You, of course."

"Naw."

"I'm being generous," said Alex. She looked at her watch. The horse outside the Driskill had not moved for four hours. She called out at the girls stumbling in front of them. "Hey! You guys go on ahead. I'll catch up with you later. I have to go to the ATM. Bye, Nicky."

"Later."

She peeled away from the crowd and the noise, waited until they piled into cars and roared off, then jogged alone across the darkened street. The driver was now fast asleep in the carriage. The horse moved its huge head slightly when it felt the pressure of her hand on its neck.

"Hey," she said to the man. "You available?"

He woke and pushed his hat back on his head. "Waiting for you all our lives. Where would you like to go?"

She leapt up into the seat beside him. "Just down to Town Lake and back. Circle a bit. Give him some exercise."

They clattered down the now empty street. The driver asked, "Where you from?"

"I'm from Austin. I've been watching your horse all night from the bar. What happened to Tom Wilson?"

"He moved to El Paso. I'm new. So's the horse. Feeling sorry for us, were you?"

"He's the first Belgian I've seen in town. This is a beautiful animal."

"Ah, you're a horse woman."

"I live on a ranch."

"Well, Jake here sure appreciates you noticing him."

She leaned back in the seat, grinning. "I have a special rate with Tom."

"And what might that be?"

"Twenty bucks."

"All right, since you're a horse woman. The boss'll have a fit if he knows."

"I ain't tellin'."

Since moving to Austin for freshman year, she had ridden the hotel's ceremonial horse trap whenever she could. Nobody else seemed to. She hated the sight of the horse standing for hours in the heat, blinkered and unmoving, while the traffic roared around him. She was never sure if her small act really did the horse any good.

"See you again next weekend?" said the driver cheerfully when she paid him at the end of the ride.

She did not answer him. She had buried her face in the horse's neck, absorbing its sorrow. Then she waved and ran back to her car.

❋

Plaza de toros. It is known by the same name in every town.

Do not hesitate. Say it breathlessly, authoritatively, the way they say it in Spain: *PLA-tha-day-TOR-os*. Even saying the words brings the warm waft of manure, sand, and cigarette smoke.

In the airplane, she sat behind a row of young girls with identical chestnut hair and olive skin. It had been a long time since she saw people like that. A new palette of colors began to assert itself that would slowly creep over her reality. She was almost there.

❋

"Tomas?" called his wife from the hallway. "It's UT for you."

"UT? The school?"

Shelly hung around anxiously as he picked up the phone.

"What is it?" she asked quickly when he hung up.

"She didn't show up in Valencia."

"I knew it!" said Shelly. "Five thousand dollars! I'll kill her."

Tomas began to laugh. "I thought we discussed this. We said okay to let her go back to Spain, didn't we?"

7

"I said okay *if she took a course for credit*. You know what she's gonna do, don't you?" Shelly's eyes narrowed. "You have been secretly hoping she would do it! I give up. I give up. One day the girl will be dead and you will have a lot of people to answer to. Including me. God knows why I care so much about someone who isn't even my daughter. God knows. I'm sick of you . . . Latin people."

"Where are you going?"

"I need to go for a drive. Or find a psychotherapist. Or both. I can't bear the thought of her in that country—"

"It's her country!"

"— *bullfighting*—"

"You don't *fight bulls*, you *torear*. Some words just cannot be translated."

"— getting *killed*—"

"But you let her go to matador school in San Diego."

"But you were with her! She's out there alone, in Spain!"

"It's her country," said Tomas stubbornly. "She has to learn."

"I—you know—if anything happens—forget it. I'm going out. I need to go to a movie, or something. Since I can't do anything about it, I have to get it out of my mind."

She slammed the screen door. Tomas opened it again and called after her, "Hey, we're out of toilet paper. Can you stop by HEB?"

All he heard was an angry, short scream. He smiled, shaking his head. In his mind, he was completely without fault. After all, it was Shelly who first told Alejandra Herrera that she could grow up and be anything.

At the Valencia train station, the young American

woman headed directly for the ticket counter and asked for the train to a small town. It was a town so small that Alex couldn't buy the tickets in advance on the Internet, because it wasn't even available. It was off the tourist map. Each time she arrived at Valencia she half expected the girl at the window to tell her that San Martín trains had been discontinued.

"San Martín?" said Alex warily.

"Ida?"

"Si."

There was only one train a day. She had many hours to kill before it arrived. She stepped out in the sunlight, into the bustling traffic as tourists and travelers bypassed her hurriedly, trundling suitcases over the pavement. It was almost high noon; the sun beat down. She turned to her right, slowly. She could already smell it.

Valencia's bullring was silent at midday. It was right next to the ornate train station. The two iconic buildings had stood, side by side, for the better part of a century, like a pair of salt and pepper shakers. Bullrings were to Spanish cities what baseball stadiums were to American ones, except that baseball stadiums didn't smell like horse dung. The only bullrings Alex had seen in America were rough wooden pens, familiar to those who went to the rodeo or the county fair. The architecture of the Spanish bullring, in contrast, came from the functional brutality of classical Rome, of the Coliseum, in which bull and human sacrifices were made. There was nothing about the Valencia bullring that would have prepared a tourist for the delicate tendrils of Gaudí that were to come just a few decades later. As a child, she had looked at pictures of Spanish bullrings on the Internet and imagined their shadow, their heat, their smell. They reminded her of old Hollywood movies of gladiators in their strappy leather sandals, of biblical stories of slaves being thrown to the lions.

Alex walked round the façade of the red brick building, noting the names of matadors appearing in upcoming bullfights. Impossibly, bullfights here were still advertised with nineteenth century posters. Alex remembered the first time she saw them. She had thought they were simply vintage posters on display for tourists. On closer inspection, she saw that the dates were current. Every single one of the matador names was of living men, or in some cases, boys. She would never get used to this deliberate anachronism.

At every entrance of the bullring, old ushers smoked dourly and stared back at her through the iron gates.

"The box office is that way," said one of them in Spanish gruffly.

Alex replied quickly in Valenciano that she wasn't here to watch the bullfight, that she was just killing time before her next train.

His eyes sparkled when he realized she could speak his language. The usher began a cautionary tirade about young American tourist girls coming to watch the bullfight and leaving halfway in tears.

"There's at least one every fight," he said, chucking his cigarette and looking her up and down. "Coming out traumatized, hugging her friends, crying, saying poor bull, poor animal, so cruel, and so on. Why do you guys even come. You won't enjoy it. It's not for tourists."

Alex smiled and said she was familiar with the bullfights and had watched them many times. She nodded at the nearest poster and said, "You guys looking forward to Roberto de la Torre?"

"Ah, you are a fan, I see," said the usher, lighting a new cigarette. "The dames like him. I prefer El Rivera. There is just no comparison." He turned and pointed to his favorite matador's name on the poster, and kissed his fingers in admiration, as if describing the best food he had ever eaten. "As for De la Torre, I'm afraid you're out of luck. Tickets are all sold out."

"Oh, I got one already," said Alex airily. "From America."

The usher scowled. "How?"

"The Internet!" She straightened her backpack and strolled back towards the cool foyer of the train station, before the usher could say something rude back to her.

The child psychologist was well-known in town for grief counseling. Alex was an obedient child and dutifully attended every session. She liked the doctor and the cheerful pink and white room. There was a large, fluffy white teddy bear on the coach.

"What's this for?" she pointed at a box of tissues, which was encased in a pale lace doily.

The doctor had a gauzy cloud of auburn hair and interesting earrings. She merely smiled. Alex picked up the teddy bear and put it on her lap. Her small arms immediately went confidently around it. She smiled back.

"What did you do in school today?" asked the doctor.

Alex told her.

"And what birthday present have you picked out for your friend's party?"

Alex looked at the ceiling. "I was thinking maybe . . . beads. But Shelly says books make good presents. I have ten dollars."

"You could buy a good book with that."

Alex said nothing for a long time. Then, point-blank — "Can I ask you a question?"

"Sure."

The little girl chewed her lip. "Shelly said I should tell you. It's this dream I've been having."

The doctor folded her hands on her lap.

"I'm living in a big house. There are lots of people. My grandma's there. And uncles, aunts, cousins, and people from all over, visiting. That's my dream."

"Is there anything else?"

"Yeah. So, in my dream, everyone's getting ready for a party. There's tons of food, and stuff. And we're all putting on nice clothes. And the people downstairs keep yelling up the stairs, *Come down! Hurry up! Are you ready?*"

The doctor waited patiently. Alex swung her feet to and fro above the floor, intoxicated by her own rhythm, her hands clutching the edge of her seat, her eyes looking out the window into the quiet parking lot.

"My grandma lives in a house with five stories. In Spain. It's a really neat house. She's got a lot of old things in it. Anyway," Alex flicked her hair from her face self-consciously, trying her best to sound like an adult, for after all this lady was a doctor and had no time for nonsense. She had better be quick, too, for Shelly said this doctor charged by the hour, "we're getting ready, with my mom, and my dad's already there, waiting for us in town, and we have to go join him. And Mom's putting on my clothes for me. It's really hot. It's like a hundred degrees outside. And there's something really important going on that afternoon, and we can't be late. Roberto is fighting the bulls and we're all going to support him. And Dad's already there, with my grandpa, and we're running late, so I'm telling Mom to hurry up 'cos she's taking so long. Mom's finally put on my clothes, and I'm running downstairs. Then I wake up. Everyone's gone to this big thing and I missed it."

Later on that day, the psychologist rang Shelly. "Got a minute?"

"Yes. What do you think?" asked Shelly, swiftly ducking into her home office and shutting the door.

"It's not unusual. She's remembering a trip to Spain

with her parents, her cousins and uncles and aunts. You should take her to Spain more to see her extended family. The more you can expose her to her relatives, the more it would help. What about taking her there during the summer holidays?"

"Well, it's hard for us both to get away from the ranch. And you're mistaken. She's never been to Spain with her parents. She just went on her first trip with my husband last month, that was the first and only time. It was to meet her grandma."

"Are you sure?"

"Absolutely. Her parents always meant to take her to Spain when she was old enough to behave on the plane. But she was only three when they died. And she has no cousins, uncles or aunts. If she had more relatives, of course, we would try to go more often."

"Interesting. She mentions someone called Sofia."

"That's her grandma."

"What about Roberto?"

"That doesn't ring a bell."

"Strange."

"She makes things up sometimes. She's got imaginary friends. She talks to the animals and gives them names. You remember we live on a ranch. I'm not too worried about it, I was a farm kid myself. She's got lots of real friends at school. She's popular."

"Good to know. I'll like to see her once a week."

"Okay."

"What are you doing?" asked the boy suddenly.

Nicky set her phone down hastily. "Nothing."

The naked frat boy slid off her. "You were texting someone while we were having sex?"

"Was not."

He grabbed her phone and checked. "Jesus Christ. They said you were an SMS addict, but this is ridiculous. I'm out of here." He pulled on his clothes hurriedly.

"Hey! Come back here!" Nicky pulled the duvet off her futon, wrapped it around herself and limped halfway out of her room. She called down the corridor, startling a couple of students, "Andy! I wasn't texting about having sex with you!"

His voice came ringing down the dorm hallway. "Whatever!"

"I was texting Alex, my roommate, she's in Spain! Oh, screw it." Nicky kicked the door shut, tied her hair up in a scrunchie, and crawled back into bed, naked, texting furiously. She then went over to her desktop PC and tapped a few buttons, calling Alex on Skype.

"Hey Alex! I can talk now! How are you? You're really in Spain? Omigod, I am so jealous! I've always wanted to go there and take pictures. Did I tell you my dad finally got me a Nikon D3?"

Alex's voice came over the speaker. "Nicky, you're naked. Your webcam is on."

"Oh, shit," Nicky reached for a T-shirt and continued talking to the PC, the lower half of her body still bare. "What's the weather like?"

"Hey, Nicky, listen, I just want to tell you where I am in case something happens to me, okay? Can I trust you?"

"We took a blood oath in freshman year, remember? You're the only person who knows I'm still a virgin. Well, at least, I almost succeeded tonight, but I was texting you and he ran off. You remember Andy? He's that guy in my photography cla—"

"Listen, Nicky. I'm not in Valencia. I'm in a small town called San Martín. Pretty soon UT's gonna know that I skipped the program and disappeared, I don't want you to freak out, okay?"

Nicky's smile faded. "Are you gonna be all right? Are you running away? Are you coming back to UT? What's going on?"

"Remember all the bullfighting stuff I told you about?"

"Uh-huh?"

"I'm gonna do it in Spain."

"Okay? Like, try out the rodeo? That'll be fun. You always look so cool in those pictures riding horses on your dad's ranch."

"Well, if they let me in the bullring."

"Why not?"

"Have you ever seen a woman matador?"

"No. So? It's Europe. Anything goes, right? Aren't they all, like, liberal?"

"What I'm going to try to do may get me in a lot of trouble. I just don't want you to be freaked out when the school reports that I never showed up here."

"Um-kay? Like, what kind of trouble? Are you gonna get arrested?"

"I don't know. I might get injured in the bullring."

"Did you get travel health insurance?"

"I'm pretty sure bullfighting's not covered."

"Anyway that rodeo stuff, it's all fake, right? At least it was fake when I saw it here, as a kid. You can wear, like, some kind of protection, right? And the bulls are all trained?"

"Yes, yes," said Alex. "Listen, I gotta go. I got my cell-phone to work here, but roaming's expensive. You can SMS me. It's cheaper than emailing."

"What about your stuff?" asked Nicky, looking around the dorm room.

"Don't worry, I took what I needed."

"Can I borrow your clothes when you're gone?"

"Take my clothes. Just take whatever you want."

"Can I read your magazines in the mail?"

"Of course."

"Cool! I'm like so jealous you are running away to Spain. How long are you gonna be gone for?"

"Long."

"You sound like you're not coming back for senior year, my friend," said Nicky, getting up and rummaging in Alex's closet. "You have the best jeans — can I wear this? Alex?"

Nicky padded back to the computer, but the connection had been broken.

"In the end, I blame myself," said the old lady.

With every visit, her grandmother seemed smaller and more wizened, like an olive left out in the sun. Alex wondered if old people really shrank, or if she herself had grown. On the window, a portable wireless played old Cuban love songs, inexplicably interspersed with fragments of Mozart's "Requiem". A tendril of grey-white smoke curled into the air from a basement window.

"It's not your fault, Grandma."

"It must be Tomas's then."

"How is it his fault? He's from Mexico. He's never been to Spain, even. He's only seen bullfights in Mexico City."

Sofia sank back in her chair, tearing up. "I sent Angel away just so that he would never even hear about bullfighting. Do you know what it's like to send a three-year-old away?"

Alex leaned against the disheveled trellis that hugged the side of the porch. She was thirsty.

"I wanted you to grow up completely American."

"I *am* completely American."

"Who would have thought that your parents would die and you'd be raised by a Mexican who's crazy about bull-fights?" Sofia unfurled her fan and flapped it in front of her face. "I should never have told you about Pedro. I must have been out of my mind. Can we never get away from the bulls!"

"Grandma, all your efforts didn't save Dad. Think of what he could have known about our family before he died. He would have been so happy if he had known Grandpa was famous. He never knew anything about Spain. He married Mom, who couldn't speak Spanish and didn't give a fig about Europe. They could never tell me anything about where I was from, and they were gone before I was old enough to ask properly. If it weren't for Tomas, I would've grown up just like all the other American girls."

"But you were raised Catholic. And they made sure you learned to speak Spanish."

"I'm not talking about that stuff. I needed more. You did the right thing telling me about Grandpa. It just confirmed what I already knew."

"How did you know?" asked Sofia suddenly. "Is it true, what we have always feared, that there is such a thing as bloodlust, and that it is passed on from generation to generation?"

Alex noticed the smoke from the kitchen, which had only increased. She got up and walked the length of the porch. The enormous juniper tree in Sofia's garden was still there. The guidebooks cited it as the oldest tree in San Martín. In the fifties and sixties, English tourists would come and peep through the bars of Sofia's wrought iron gate, hoping to catch a glimpse of the tree in the court-yard; these days nobody came. The guidebooks about San Martín were long out of print.

"Don't talk to anyone here about bullfighting, Alejandra. You'll cause trouble. Becoming a *torero* is hard enough for the boys. For you it would be impossible. And unthinkable."

"You always say that. I've waited a long time, Grandma. I can't wait anymore. I'm nineteen! Tell me where Grandpa's swords are."

Sofia shuddered at the mention of swords. "No."

"I'm not leaving without them."

Sofia sighed. "San Martín already has Roberto de la Torre."

"He's my age, Grandma. In fact, he's two weeks younger than me. What can he do that I can't? Weren't our grandfathers famous matadors together?"

"Alejandra, you are a girl."

"In America, we don't call nineteen-year-olds girls."

"You are the first in our family to go to university. I won't have it."

"It is precisely my education that caused me to want to do this."

"It is not possible for a woman to be a *torero*. Other cities maybe, but not San Martín. And they're always these lower class types. They say there is a *torera* in Andalucía —she works as a postman on the weekdays. It's completely ignoble. We are from a nice family. We don't gamble. No Herrera woman would do something that ridiculous. And —may I remind you—your grandfather's money is for your education."

"This is part of my education."

"If you really want to understand our culture, why don't you take up *flamenco* dancing instead?"

"*Flamenco*'s ridiculous."

"What! It's our tradition."

"So is the *corrida*."

"Why can't you just do the American rodeo? I talked to Tomas about it."

"Grandma, the rodeo in Austin is the opposite of the bullfight. Have you ever seen it? It's where the largest possible man wrestles the smallest possible baby cow. It's over in ten seconds. And it's set to rock music. Even Shelly knew better than to suggest that to me."

"At least it's safe."

"No question." Alex shook her head. "I'd rather be buried alive."

"You were such a difficult child to raise. When you were sent to figure skating class, you wanted to compete in ice hockey."

Alex tried to hide a sudden smile.

"When you were sent to ballet, you practiced bull-fighting moves in front of the mirror and scared the children."

"I live on a ranch, Grandma. If you wanted me to learn ballet you shouldn't have bought my father a ranch."

"It's a ranch of bulls—ornamental bulls—that you breed for shows, you don't kill them. I made that very clear to the lawyer at the time. It was not my fault. Angel wanted to stay in Austin, he wanted something gentlemanly to do. But he didn't want to work in an office. He wanted to be in the country and ride horses."

It was becoming tremendously smoky in the back yard. Alex said suddenly, "Is your house burning down?"

"Maria is burning orange wood to make paella. Just for you."

"Oh my God," said Alex, as ash-grey smoke poured from the basement windows. "It's already such a hot day."

"It's worth the trouble, you'll see." Sofia flapped her fan listlessly. "Alejandra, why do you never listen to me? Women have never been accepted in the world of bull-fighting. So many have tried."

Alex retreated to a cool spot in the yard. "Where I'm from, a closed door is an invitation to knock."

"It's not proper."

"Tell it to the nineteenth-century nuns who were the first women *toreros*."

"Nuns were never involved in bullfighting! Where did you hear that?"

"You didn't know? There's a rich history of women in the ring, you just haven't read about it. Franco probably suppressed it."

"Who said so?"

"It's all over the Web."

"The *Web?*"

This was a familiar quarrel. It never changed, and there was only one outcome. Alex always won. "Where's Grandpa's stuff, Grandma?" Alex picked up her backpack and went into the house. "Who are you saving his things for? I'm the only grandchild you have left. Unless you're planning on selling them on eBay."

Sofia said she didn't know what eBay was, and that she preferred to continue the discussion after lunch. She went into the kitchen. "Why don't we eat first?"

"I'm not eating until I see what I've come for," said Alex, trudging up the stairs.

"It's *paella de marisco*," called Sofia from the kitchen. "Tomas says you have paella in Texas, but I refuse to believe it is the same."

"I already ate."

"But I specifically told you not to have lunch before you come!"

"I couldn't help it, I had to kill time."

"Where did you eat?"

"In the train station's video arcade."

"What kind of lunch can one have in the video arcade of a train station?" asked Sofia, astonished.

"Donut."

"Donut!"

"No lunch before I see the goods, Grandma. Maria! I'm finally here! Where can I find a bath towel?"

Sofia hobbled slowly out of the hazy kitchen and stared at the wall in the hallway, at an old family portrait. She crossed herself, whispering a prayer.

❊

"Ha!" Shelly looked up from her laptop. "I just sent you an email."

Tomas lowered the volume on the television set. He was watching the NBA Finals. "You know I don't read emails."

"I sent you a link to a BBC news article about how animal rights groups are getting EU officials to consider a bullfighting ban. In Spain, Portugal and France."

"This is old news. Anyway they should mind their own business."

His wife looked up, tucking a wild white strand of hair behind her ear. "*Popular opinion polls now show the majority of Spanish people are anti-bullfighting.* This article says that we're at a tipping point, that there will be a big crash. Imagine — all those breeders, matadors, bullrings — all gone! It'll be like our dot com crash, except this phenomenon and hype has been building for more than a few years. It'll change a whole generation."

Tomas watched the television placidly, wondering what was going on with Alex in Spain. Unlike his wife, he trusted his ward completely, so he didn't try to call her.

"Did you hear me?" Shelly threw a fragment of popcorn at him.

"Yes, I heard you. So, shut it down. It'll go on in South America. All of the matadors will emigrate there, and it'll be better for me. Cheaper too. Who cares about the EU?

I prefer the Mexican fights anyway. *Viva la fiesta brava! Viva México!"*

❀

Her long hair was damp and curly from the shower. Alex wrapped a towel around herself and walked down the gloomy old corridor. It was flanked on both sides by framed black and white photographs, all slightly askew, of weddings and christenings of relatives and friends long-dead. The top floor of the house smelled of smoke, baked tiles, and humid timber. There was a folding staircase that led up to the attic. She pushed open the trapdoor.

She found the light switch. It was attached to a ceiling fan that whirred and cast a flickering, intermittent light in the small, dusty room. Grandma's house was a bourgeois townhouse built in the eighteenth century; the attic was put in much later and was considered "modern", as in 1920. The first time she visited as a child, she loved the crumbling, five-storied house and its mystery. With each subsequent visit the enchantment faded. Her points of reference shifted. The house became normal, then obsolete. Now, as an adult, she would come to San Martín and feel as if she had stepped into a foreign-language film. A period piece. White subtitles were going to come on any moment, marching across the bottom of her vision.

She sneezed. Why was everything so bloody backward? Elsewhere, if the Spanish newspapers were to be believed, there were wind farms, high tech industries, the world's best infrastructure companies. But not in San Martín. San Martín always had an uncanny way of reminding her of every decade except the current one.

Grandpa's matador suits were hanging in a carved wardrobe with mirrored doors. The mirrors were old with bloom, like gelatin prints gone wrong. She pulled one of his suits out and removed its plastic cover. The suit twinkled in the light from the single, naked light bulb.

Slowly, she held up the suit against her body and stared in the mirror. She continued rummaging in the closet. Besides the stiff jacket, there were pants and yellowed undergarments, quivering with cotton laces. She imagined she could still see the form of her grandfather in them —the curve of his calf, the muscle of his arm. Finally, she dragged a chair over, stood on it, and felt the top of the wardrobe. There were several boxes. She opened each one expectantly.

"Why did the Minotaur want the girls?" asked Alejandra. She was seven years old, curled up on Tomas's lap on the rocking chair in the wide porch of the ranch house.

"Um, he was just a really bad bull, he liked to lock them up," said Tomas, turning the page of the book quickly.

"What did he do to them when he locked them up?"

"Well, they were just bad kids, you know. If you're naughty you get sent off to the Minotaur and he locks you up."

"Forever?"

Tomas's wife, Shelly, looked up from her laptop. She was tall, blond, and came from hardy German ancestors who had settled in the Hill Country. "Could we breed British longhorns?"

"What's wrong with our American ones?"

"I just read an article about the British ones fetching a lot more money. Apparently they're fashionable now in England for decorating castle grounds. We could start a new fad here."

"Can we have a zoo?" said Alex, looking up from the book.

"Make up your mind, honey. Do you want to go to college, or be a bullfighter, or be a zookeeper? Remember, pretty girls can do anything!"

"Bullfighter."

"Okay then, be a bullfighter. And don't believe what Tomas tells you, honey, about the Minotaur. He doesn't just lock them up."

"Maybe we should read another story," said Tomas, closing the book. "It's too scary."

"The truth about the Minotaur, Alex," said Shelly, continuing to type furiously on her laptop. She was making spreadsheets and going through the ranch's finances for the month, "is that he asks for virgins from the villagers as a form of sacrifice."

"What's a virgin?"

"Pure, nice, innocent young girls."

"What does the Minotaur do to them?"

"He tortures them and then he eats them."

Alex let out a little yelp. Tomas chided his wife.

"Why do the daddies and mommies give him their daughters to eat?"

"Because it's their tradition. Because if they don't, the Minotaur will destroy their village. Because they have no choice."

"I *hate* the Minotaur!" cried Alex contemptuously, slapping Tomas's lap for emphasis.

"Now look at what you've done," said Tomas, sighing. It was always like that with Shelly. He often wondered what it would have been like if she had agreed to have children, back when they were younger. "You better leave her with something nice to think about, otherwise she'll have nightmares."

Shelly looked up, grinned, and put away her computer. "Come."

The kid got up and crawled up her lap. "Is there any more to the story?"

"You betcha. One day, the villagers prepared a new virgin to be sacrificed. She was a very nice young lady — tall, kind, beautiful, and very intelligent. Everybody loved her. There was not a single dry eye in the village the day it was her turn to be sacrificed. Her name was Alejandra, just like yours."

"Oh, Shelly," said Tomas, lowering his newspaper.

"Why do they want to safri — safri-kise her?" asked Alex in a whisper.

"You see, she was the very last girl left in the village. There was nobody else. It had to be her." Shelly hugged Alex close and stroked her hair. They looked out at the setting sun across the undulating scrub. "When the time came, Alejandra told her mother and father not to cry. She said they didn't have to worry at all. So they put her in the ceremonial white robe, and they marched her deep into the woods, down, down the tangled path, to the entrance of the cave that was the mouth of the labyrinth. And all this time, Alejandra pretended to be asleep on the funeral bier that they carried her in. They left her at the mouth of the cave. One by one, weeping, the villagers kissed her goodbye and left. The last to leave were her father and mother. But soon, they, too, had to go. Darkness fell. Alejandra did not move. She lay, as if asleep. She kept very still. Soon, there was a strange moaning sound, like a soul in pain. It came from deep within the earth. Then — *thump, thump, thump* — you heard the heavy hooves of the Minotaur. He was half-bull, half-man, and he was so tall that he had to stoop to emerge from the entrance of the cave."

"Was his top half a man or a bull?"

"Oh, his *bottom* half was definitely that of a man," said Shelly, winking at Tomas, who groaned and buried his face in the newspaper. "The Minotaur had the head of a bull.

But not the orange and white longhorn bulls we have here, in Texas. Not those. His head was black, deep black like the night, and he had a thick, fat neck and a huge bulging forehead. He had short, white horns that gleamed like crescent moons. His eyes were so small and black that you can't see them, lost in the darkness of his shaggy fur. And he had a large, wide nose that breathed steam and fire."

By this time, Alex had curled up tightly against Shelly, her dark eyes sparkling with anticipation. Shelly smoothed the child's dark hair over her forehead.

"He bent over Alejandra. His breath made her white dress ripple. But Alejandra was not afraid. No, she had prepared her whole life for this moment. She had seen what had happened to the other girls. Unknown to her mommy and daddy, she had concealed beneath her white robe a long, long sword made of the strongest steel. *Come closer,* she said to the Minotaur, hiding the sword under her dress. He licked his lips and came closer. And when he was very, very close, Alejandra leapt off the funeral bier with a cry and plunged the sword right into his neck. The Minotaur roared in terrible anger, and all the trees and rocks around them shook in fear. But Alejandra held on to her sword, sinking it deep, all the way, until all you could see was the hilt. And it was only then that she let go of the sword. And that was how Alejandra killed the Minotaur."

"She keeled him?"

"She killed him, indeed. And saved the village from harm, forever."

"All right," said Tomas briskly, getting up from his rocking chair. "Bed time."

Alex slid sleepily off Shelly's lap and allowed herself to be herded indoors.

"I'm pretty sure I've never heard that version before," said Tomas, leaning down to kiss his wife goodnight.

"Make sure she brushes her teeth," said Shelly, opening up her laptop and resuming her accounting work. "Can't slay dragons if her teeth are bad."

"And I thought I was the crazy one, teaching her how to fight little calves."

"Well, you do your bit, and I'll do mine. I don't want her Spanish grandmother accusing us of not raising her properly."

"We're raising her *Americana*, that's already not raising her properly."

"Oh, go to bed. I'll never finish this otherwise."

"But if there were enough women, you wouldn't have had to retire." Alex was in her UT sweatshirt and sweatpants, wearing her bluetooth headset. Nicky was in the bathroom singing "Beautiful Liar" by Shakira and Beyonce at the top of her voice.

Alex was listening to the person at the other end of the phone. She stared out of the window, lost in thought. "Yes, ma'am. I understand," she said in Spanish. "No, really, this has all been very valuable to me. I am honored that you spoke to me. Please don't tell anyone else. I need to figure this out myself. I know the odds. I'll find someone else to be my sponsor. Oh, he's famous all right. No, I haven't asked him. But we'll see. One day, though — there will be so many of us that this wouldn't be a problem."

The caller at the other end asked a question. It was a difficult one. Alex chewed her lip. "I don't know how it will end. I'm not planning to die. It'll end when I run out of money. You don't understand — I've been planning for this my whole life. I won't call you again. But thank you. Thank you very much. Goodbye."

Nicky burst out of the bathroom, her hair in a towel,

belly dancing. "Hey, who would you rather be, Beyonce or Shakira? Check out this move," she caught sight of Alex's laptop screen. "Who *is* this dude?"

Alex shut the screen window hastily. "Friend of a friend."

"Nice website. What is he, in a band?"

"You ready to go down for dinner?"

"Sorry, pal, I got a date with Andy Morris."

"That guy in your photography class?"

"Get this — he's also on the cycling team, he's got such a hot butt." She showed Alex a photograph she had shot of a recent bike race. "This is going in the campus newspaper."

"Your dad bought you a five thousand dollar camera so you can shoot guys' butts."

"Shut up."

"Nobody straight is on the cycling team, Nicky."

"Shut *up*!" She swatted Alex with her towel. "You wanna join us on a double date? I'll set you up."

"It's okay, I've got a paper to write. It's due tomorrow and I haven't even started it."

Nicky poked her head out of the bathroom door. "Um, if I come back with Andy?"

"Just text me beforehand, I'll get out of here. I'll take my laptop to the library."

"Thanks!"

"Aren't you glad I'm going to Spain? God, you could turn this apartment into a love nest."

"That is my plan, my friend."

"*Toro!*" cried the little girl, shaking her white handkerchief.

Tomas had his foot on the lower rail of the wooden fence, chatting with a rancher.

"Yours?" asked the rancher.

"No, no, this is little Miss Alejandra Herrera."

"Did they only have one kid?"

"Yes."

The rancher lowered his voice so the child could not hear. "Good thing she wasn't in the car at the time."

"I know. They were in Napa for their wedding anniversary."

"Was that where it happened? I didn't know that. What a tragedy."

"They have these tiny roads there, you know — no central dividers, cars coming in both directions, tourists in rental cars, people drinking good wine." Tomas shook his head. "We had promised them to babysit her. Little did we know. It's going to be the world's longest babysit. Not that we mind, of course. We were already her godparents."

"Poor thing. What did you tell her?"

"My wife told her that her parents went to visit relatives in Spain, and that she could go when she was older," said Tomas sadly. "Well, that's what the child psychologist said to do since she's so young. We'll tell her when she's older. We're in touch with Angel's mother in Spain. She'll help."

"Ever think of moving her back to Spain?"

"Oh, no," said Tomas, sticking his leg out so that Alex didn't wander off. "The lawyer says the estate will be taxed heavily if it is moved out of the country. We're her trustees. We have to protect it for Alejandra when she grows up."

"*Hay, hay, toro!*" shouted the little girl again, sticking her arm through the railings in the fence and waving the handkerchief in front of the bull. Tomas picked her up hurriedly.

"Watch it, kiddo!" cried the rancher, laughing. "Who taught her that?"

"She was watching some videos with me of bullfights in Mexico City." Tomas touched her nose fondly. "The white handkerchief is only for spectators. Do you want to be a spectator, Alejandra? Or *torero*?"

She learned forward towards the bull, her arms outstretched. He let her climb and sit on his shoulder.

"Get her a little matador costume for Halloween," said the rancher, pinching her cheek.

"Oh, don't encourage her. She already made my wife buy the Superman costume so that she could rip the red cape off and shake it in front of the dog." Tomas nodded. "Gotta go. See you next week!"

Tickets for Roberto de la Torre's tour in Valencia had sold out weeks in advance. He was a rising star. The bullring was built to hold seventeen thousand people and was packed to the gills that night. Even the spots in the unbearably hot sun section were full. Alex had purchased one of the most expensive tickets so that she could be closer to him. She had never seen him perform live until that night.

He was lucky; the bull was a splendid, intelligent animal. It responded brilliantly. Roberto ended a flawless *faena* with a swift kill. The bull dropped like a stone. As it lay dying, the matador went up to it and patted the great head in somber gratitude. He did not smile. The delighted crowd was on its feet, shaking white handkerchiefs vigorously, faces turned to the president of the *plaza*, hollering at him to award ears.

"Hey, Roberto!" cried Alex when he walked past her at the end of the night, raising his victory trophies. As a reward for his performance, the crowd gave him two ears off the dead bull. They flapped like flimsy old purses in his hands. He shook them at the crowd proudly, like a kid who had won a game of marbles.

"Roberto!" yelled Alex. "Catch!"

He caught the paper airplane she tossed at him, and threw it back to her, as was the custom.

"Why doesn't he keep the presents they throw him?" asked Alex when she was little, turning away from the television set.

Tomas was making cornbread from a mix. He rummaged in the kitchen trash. "Shit, I dumped the box and the instructions. Hm? Oh, you mean the things the crowd throws him? He touches them and blesses them, then throws them back."

"Like the Pope?"

"Well, no, the Pope only blesses bibles and rosaries. Not panties and fans."

Shelly came through the front door. "Are you guys still watching bullfights? I'm starving. Is dinner ready?"

"No!"

Hankies, hats, cheap lacquered fans rained down on Roberto as he did his victory stroll around the ring.

"No, you idiot! Read it!" shouted Alex, pushing through the throng to throw the paper airplane back at him. "I'm not one of your fans, don't throw it back! Read the damn thing!"

Thick with ecstasy, glowing with delight, Roberto didn't hear her, but she noted with satisfaction that one of

31

his *banderilleros* now held on to her airplane. Maybe he'd look at it. If not she'd try some other way. She didn't want to have to go through Sofia.

❁

It was Halloween.

Alex, age five, was dressed in a makeshift matador costume in the backyard of the ranch. There was a party at her house. The grown-ups were indoors. She was surrounded by a ring of older Mexican kids dressed as pirates, ghosts, witches and devils. She had a box of Kleenex under her arm. Solemnly, she handed out a white tissue to each.

"Wave it like this!" She demonstrated. The kids waved their white tissues obediently.

"Okay. Follow me."

They followed her to the bottom of her yard in a tangle of costumes, trailing brooms and pitchforks.

Wielding a plastic sword from a knight's costume kit and a red cape from her Superman outfit, Alex began shouting at a large Australian Shepherd, who trotted over and sniffed her cautiously. She fixed a stern glare at the dog.

"Do it like the other day!" cried the little girl, stamping her foot. She reached into her pocket and flung him a treat, then began trailing the red cape across the yard while the dog chased it. She flicked the cape expertly over its head and taunted it again, one arm cocked behind her back and her feet held tightly together. She bent backwards and jutted her chin out. "Come on!" She rewarded the dog with treats every time he performed properly.

"You say *olé* when he does this!" she yelled to her friends, caping the dog.

"*Olé!*"

"No, say it only when he goes under the red cloth!"

The kids simmered down; then, as Alex caped the dog, they cried, "*Olé!*"

Finally, the dog fell down, exhausted, and rolled over to its side. Alex poked it gently between its shoulders with the plastic sword. "I killed it. Now you shake the hanky." She then paused and turned to look back at the older kids, who shook their white tissues in unison.

"You say, *valiente, valiente!*" she commanded.

"*Valiente, valiente!*" they shouted. "I want to try! I want to try!"

The dog got up hastily and ran off. The kids gave chase.

❁

The morning radio show played "Ave Maria". Maria the housekeeper was softly singing along as she did the dishes. Sofia was at the table reading the newspapers.

"He's good, he's good," said Alex, pacing back and forth in the kitchen. "But I'm better." She disappeared into the passageway outside the kitchen.

Sofia could hear the sly creak of a rusty hinge of an old armoire.

"What are you looking for, my dear?" called Sofia.

"Nothing."

❁

"Hello? May I speak with Miss Alejandra Herrera?"

"Is that you, Rob?"

He sounded wary. "Hi. I didn't know you spoke Spanish."

"Yeah, so laugh at my accent. Where are you?" Alejandra left the dinner table abruptly and went out into the balcony. She saw Sofia staring after her, so she shut the French windows firmly. Her grandmother lived in the oldest neighborhood in San Martín. Her townhouse formed one side of a tiny plaza. Across from her in the narrow alleyway, a neighbor hung her clothes out to dry.

"In a hotel in Madrid. I'm on tonight."

"You're on in Las Ventas tonight? Sweet! So, you especially nervous?"

"One is always nervous before a fight."

"Break a leg."

"Excuse me?"

"Never mind. When or how can we meet?"

"Is it really true that you're training to be a bullfighter?"

"Yeah, are you going to send a hit man after me?"

"No. Why would I do that?"

"Isn't all of Spain against women bullfighters?"

"I don't have a view. Well, not one that can be conveyed in the fifteen minutes before I get ready for the fight. My manager's coming to get me any minute. I'm not supposed to talk to people on the phone. I'll email you my tour dates, you can decide which city is best for us to meet. My schedule's fixed, I'm afraid. How long are you here for?"

"I know your schedule. It's on your website. You know, the one that makes you look like you're in Menudo."

"I didn't design it." He sounded uncertain. "When we meet, what do you want to talk about?"

"Did you see that YouTube link I sent you of our grandfathers' bullfights?"

He was silent for a beat, then— "Why do you think I called you?"

Alex checked a crumpled printout from her pocket. "You're back in Valencia next Thursday. I'll go to the fight and meet you after. Call this phone number, it's my cell in Spain, and tell me where to meet. What's that playing in the background?"

"Oh," he sounded sheepish. "It's *Halo 3*."

"You play videogames before a bullfight?"

"Please don't tell anyone."

"But what if you get killed in *Halo* before your fight? Is that a bad omen?"

"I've never thought of that before. I don't want to talk about it, please. You're making it worse." He added, "My mother says you're like a cousin to me. Because of our families. I don't trust anyone who isn't a relative. If you tell the press anything about me — personal things like that — I'm doomed."

"What's so strange about a guy your age playing *Halo*?"

"Because I'm a professional matador, Alejandra."

"I get it. We need to keep up the macho mystique."

"There's a lot of money in this business. It's not all about me. I have responsibility to a lot of people. You won't understand. Your dad left you money. I have to work to pay off my debts."

"All right, I get it, okay? See you next Thursday. If you survive."

"I'll be all right, Alejandra."

"Good luck. And call me Alex, please."

"Thanks. Alex." Then he blurted, "Isn't that a boy's name?"

But she had hung up.

"What's this tape in the video camera? Can I erase it?" asked Tomas, pressing a button.

"I don't know. Samantha was babysitting Alex yesterday, I said they could go next door for Colin's birthday party. Sam took it along for fun."

Tomas' eye was glued to the view finder. "Come look at this."

"What?" asked Shelly warily.

Tomas lowered the video camera suddenly, staring into

the distance. He had a strange expression on his face, as if he was in a trance. Then he took the tape out and looked hastily around the room. "How do I play this on the TV?"

"*You* had the manual."

"Come on, where is the cable that hooks up to the — ah. Okay. Watch." He paused the tape and looked up. His wife had disappeared in the kitchen. "Shelly! Can I please have your attention. Five minutes."

She came back out, a wooden spoon in her hand. "What's she doing? Oh God, did you teach her to do that? Oh, God. Barbarian."

"She's playing with their golden retriever with a dog treat and a bath towel. Look! She's got him charging at her. She's got him by the nose. Look, he's completely spellbound. This is amazing."

"I'm not watching the dog, I'm watching the people at the pool," said Shelly, sitting down with the kitchen towel on her lap. "Look at them staring! Look at their faces! We should charge admission for this."

After the video clip ended, Tomas asked Shelly where she kept the leftover wood from the corrals they built last summer.

"Why do you want it? Oh, no. No. *Not* in my back-yard."

"Hi, Rob."

"Alejandra?"

He had called out her name even before he got up and turned around.

"How do you know it's me?" she asked.

"Nobody in this country calls me 'Rob'. How did you know I was here?"

Alex held up her phone. "Twitter."

Roberto looked startled, excused himself from his table, and walked to the back of the bar with Alex. They stood furtively in a dim corridor outside the restrooms. "I was going to call you when this was over—" he broke off as a corpulent man squeezed between them to use the restroom. "We always have to come to this bar after the bullfight, it's not where I wanted to meet you, there are too many people. What do you mean, anyway, by Twitter? What's Twitter?"

"One of your fans is in this bar and told the whole world he saw you here. Seventeen minutes ago." She held up the phone for him to see.

"Oh, God, one of those things," he said, glancing at the screen. "Well, since you are here, let's go quickly. I'll make an excuse. Come on."

They pushed through the crowd of men wearing dark blazers and suits. The cured hams hanging from the ceiling gently sweated the smell of oily, salty pig—a strange, moist perfume that rose above the bitter, dry smell of cigarette smoke. Hands reached out and gave Roberto congratulatory shoulder pats. They were always old men—they touched the matador, as if trying to feel again the electricity of youth. Roberto greeted them with humility and respect. A few people took pictures of him as he passed, but paid no attention to Alex. Roberto appeared in public with a different young woman every night, so they'd stopped photographing his arm candy years ago.

He signed a few autographs and then they were on the curb.

"Get in the car, quickly."

"Why?"

"The photographers."

"Where are we going? Which hotel are you at?"

"No, no, not the hotel—there are even more photographers there. I know of a good spot to talk."

At the traffic light, he looked at her curiously. "I've never met a Herrera before. You look so American."

Alex stared at him evenly. "I've never met a De la Torre before. You look so Spanish."

If he had a sense of humor, it escaped her. She was curious about him. Over the years, Sofia had spoken so often of the De la Torres that Alex just assumed they were related. It was only recently that Sofia said that they were not, that they were in fact just long-time neighbors. In those days, when living spaces intermingled to a higher degree, people had a different concept of privacy. A neighbor was as good as kin. She asked Roberto if he knew her grandmother.

"Yes, of course. Everyone in San Martín talked about you guys when I was growing up," he said. "My mother still knows your grandmother even though we moved when I was born. You were the ones who went to the United States. Nobody else we knew went. Of course, she had to do it because of the curse."

Roberto's car was new and fast; he drove recklessly. Fortunately the streets were small and winding in the old part of Valencia. One couldn't pick up much speed. She checked her seat belt discreetly and said, "I've heard different variations of the curse. What's your version?"

Roberto shrugged. "Our grandfathers were best friends, born in San Martín practically next door to each other, went to bullfighting school together. In the fifties, San Martín was a poor, crappy small town. People went hungry during those years. The pair of them was so successful that they made the town proud. They actually became rich from bullfighting, which was unheard of. One in a million. Pedro Javier Herrera and Juan Carlos de la Torre. I was so proud, as a kid, seeing their pictures in the bullfighting museum in San Martín."

"I know," said Alex quietly.

They pulled up at a red light. The couple in the next car stared at Roberto, then started waving excitedly.

"Know them?"

"No." The light changed and he stepped on the gas. In the rearview mirror, Alex saw the woman lean out of the window with her cellphone, taking pictures.

Roberto had a careless, soft lisp and an almost monotonous voice. He never sounded like he cared about anything he was saying. "Herrera was the older of the two. He was always looking after De la Torre. De la Torre had a bad manager. He lost a lot of money. After that he trusted no one except Herrera with his career and his family affairs. One day, in 1959, De la Torre got badly injured in a bullfight in Madrid. Herrera was up next. It was his job to go into the ring and kill the murderous bull. But—as the superstition goes—if De la Torre died from his injuries, then it would also end badly for the matador who killed his bull. Sure enough, Grandpa died, and within a few months, your grandfather also died in another bullfight. So in a single season, San Martín lost its best fighters, went down the rankings and has never produced a brilliant bullfighter since."

"Until you came along."

"I'm doing it for my parents. They see themselves as responsible for San Martín and for upholding Grandpa's name."

"*That's* the reason you're doing it?" She was surprised.

"Yes. Don't you know by now? People who don't leave San Martín, that's all they have—the family name, bullfighting. That's all they know. They're not going to become teachers or politicians or directors of big companies. Their world is so small. You've been to San Martín, haven't you? There's nothing there! Nothing! A fistful of townhouses and plazas squeezed around a cathedral on a hill. Do you know what it's like growing up there? No wonder all they care about is breeding bulls and the annual *corrida de toros*."

"They? What about you? You don't care?"

Roberto shrugged. "I am who I am because my father failed to become a *torero*. So the burden has passed on to me. You don't know what it's like to grow up in this kind of family."

"Why do you say that? Aren't the Herreras a bullfighting family too?"

"Yes, but unlike our side, your grandmother decided to put a stop to it. She shocked everyone. She thought she could erase the family obsession with the *corrida* by doing so, and the curse along with it. She took all of your grandpa's money and invested it well. She didn't want anyone to fight bulls again. *Leave while you're winning*, she was famous for saying. Well," Roberto pulled up in a driveway, "until *you* came along."

"I wouldn't have known if she hadn't told me. She started it."

Roberto turned off the engine. "Why did she tell you?"

"When my parents died in the car accident, she thought I should learn something about my culture. She regretted sending my dad away. She wanted to reconnect with me. She thought that I was raised completely American by my adoptive parents so there was no danger that I would be interested in bullfighting. My mom wasn't even Spanish."

"No, Alejandra," he said gently. "She thought there was no danger of you ever becoming a bullfighter because you're a *woman*."

"You know what the problem is with bullfighting? You kept alive a nineteenth century custom. And you kept the social attitudes of that time along with it. You know what you need, Roberto? A good dusting."

He looked unhappy with her criticism. She got out of the car and looked around. "Where the hell are we?"

But Roberto was polite, after all. She noted with amusement that the instinct to treat her like a guest, to show her around, was strong. "It was supposed to be a public library commissioned by the city of Valencia," he said. "They were renovating an old palace. They ran out of money because of the recession, so it's unfinished. It's quite abandoned. It's peaceful inside. I used to practice here. No photographers." He reached into the trunk of the car and pulled out a duffel bag. "Come on."

The construction site was full of rusty iron rods, bags of cement, heaps of torn down brick. On one end rose a ghostly eighteenth century façade partly covered with graffiti. All the glass panes were broken; many windows were boarded up with criss-crossed wooden beams to support the crumbling structure.

"Beautiful. Eighteenth century? Might be beyond rescue," said Alex, looking round.

"They've torn down too many things already. I'm glad they're saving this one. Look. The roof's gone, but the newspapers said that they were going to leave it open like that, build a glass atrium within the gaping roof and air condition the interior. From the outside it'll look like a ruin, but inside it'll be all modern and cool." Roberto picked his way through the wheelbarrows and orange construction cones. They came to the center of the old palace. Moonlight fell in a single shaft from the broken roof. Pale frescoes still adorned the walls, speaking of an earlier time. Their footsteps stirred up smoky plaster dust.

He set his bag on the ground and pulled out a magenta and yellow cape. He handed it to her. "Go ahead. Show me."

For years she had eagerly anticipated the first moment in Spain when she would show off in front of a professional matador. She had always thought it would be at a bullfighting school, or at a novice fight, before the watchful eyes of a crowd. Always, the crowd had jeered or applauded, hooted or stamped in approval. Sometimes fans and flags would rain down, sometimes flowers; other times they would throw stones at her telling her to go home.

So, this was it. In an abandoned construction site, at midnight, in front of a boy barely her age, who now settled back in the shadows, his boot against a low wall, watching her with intense concentration. She hardly knew him. She had seen him in hundreds of clips on the Internet, on the news—but always at a distance, always in his full costume. Now, in a T-shirt and jeans, he seemed whittled down to the teenager that he really was—with long, thin arms and legs, and shoulders that still bore the trace of childhood. But for his height, which everyone said was a distinct advantage when it came to bullfighting, he looked just like a typical Latino neighborhood kid from back home.

All he had said, simply, was *show me*.

When she finished, she looked at him defiantly.

"Not bad. Who taught you this?" he asked.

She named a number of instructors she had consulted over the years. Tomas had to sell a few prize longhorns to get them to train her. "The rest from watching TV."

"They're televised in America?"

"Are you kidding? Only on the Internet."

"Don't you go to school?"

"Yes. I'm in university."

He looked impressed. "But have you killed any bulls?"

"Yes. Practicing privately. There is a matador school in California. I go in the summers. It's mostly Portuguese American kids. A few crazy white guys. We can't kill any bulls in California—it's illegal. But we have training trips to Mexico and we get to kill bulls there sometimes. I've trained with bulls, steers, and cows. We re-use them some-times."

"That's suicidal. Once it knows you, it'll charge at you instead of the cape."

"Better training. Look, we make do with what we have. Sometimes it's better, isn't it? It's like learning to drive stick, in an old car with bad clutches."

"It's more like driving an old car with no clutches at all . . . downhill . . . along the side of a cliff."

Alex began peppering him with questions. She wanted to know how bullfighting contracts worked, how much money did each *corrida* cost to stage, and how to hire a manager.

Roberto brushed away her queries. "Who lets you do all this? You'll kill yourself."

Alex grinned. "It's America. There are no rules."

Privately, Roberto began wondering what it would be like to see her fight. He entertained a small spark of inter-est about whether her unorthodox training in America made her a better matador. "I'd like to see you do it someday. You would either be gored right away like one of those silly boys in the street running with the bulls, or you would surprise everybody."

"I can get them in the right spot with my killing sword. That's the thing that I'm best at. Why that look? Sur-prised?"

"That's the thing you're *best* at?" he asked, trying to sup-press his astonishment.

"I'm not good at cape work. My *veronicas* suck. We don't know how to do it properly back home."

"Ah. That's important."

"I know, I know, the art, the flair," said Alex, grinning. "Remember, my recycled bulls are smart. They charge at me, not at the cloth. So the part that I practice the most has been just the last part, the killing part. My grandfather was always good at that, too. I've watched his *recibiendo* a thousand times."

"Of course," he said thoughtfully. "How long have you been training?"

"Since I was about ten."

"I started at the same age, too," he said. "Are you serious about doing it as a profession?"

Alex was taken aback. She didn't think that far. "Didn't Cristina Sanchez retire because the men won't let her fight?"

"Ignore whatever you heard. I'm asking you again, is this what you want to do, for real? Seriously?"

"Yes."

He began to laugh. She, too, had been prepared for this moment, but it didn't make it hurt any less.

Roberto stepped out of the shadows and took the cape from her. "You're the first girl I've ever lent this cape to."

"I earned the right to use it. Don't laugh at me."

"I'm not laughing at you, I'm laughing at myself," he said quickly. "It just occurred to me that for as many years as I've been trying desperately to get out of bullfighting, that you have been trying desperately to get *in*."

"Get out? Why? Don't you like it?"

"I did at first, but this has been going on for too long. I graduated to matador long before I was ready. My family pushed me. They say I'm not even at the height of my career yet. They want me to do it for ten, fifteen more years. I'm not yet twenty, but I feel like I'm forty. I spend my days in hotel rooms playing video games, working out at the gym. I live in hotels, Alejandra. The rest of the time I'm in minivans being shuttled from city to city, doing television interviews, talking to old men and bullfighting officials and bull breeders, and all they talk about are bullfights. When I travel abroad, I only get to go to bullfighting countries. Last year, my father decided to start me on the international circuit. This means that I spend the winters in South America, the summers here. I am in bull-fights back to back, without stop, all year round. Last August, I killed *forty* bulls in one month. It's going to be the same this season. Every Sunday, and every other day in between, almost. What do *you* like to do on Sundays?"

He had not moved from where he was sitting, but by the end of his outburst Alex felt the distant heat of a temper.

"But it would be the same if you were a professional athlete," she said coolly. "Or a concert pianist. It's good training."

"I don't see it that way," he said abruptly. "It's different with you. I've been performing publicly since I was twelve. I never kept up with school. I'm a drop out. I can't speak English like you. I have no friends my age, except other junior matadors, or those who are desperate to be bullfighters themselves. If they ever called me or emailed me, all they talk about is bulls, bulls, bulls. I grow quickly —I'm tall—but every time I outgrow the *traje*, my parents make a whole set of new ones. I'm in this for the long haul. Do you know how it feels?"

"But you've finally made it up the ranks. Why stop now?"

"You're only as good as your last fight. You can never make a mistake. One small slip, and they'll begin to tear you down. They'll hasten your decline. I've seen it happen to friends. I can't take it any longer. Don't get me wrong. I love the art, I love the bulls, I love performing. I'm no longer afraid of dying. But this is a profession in which you become a legend only if you flare like a firecracker and explode. Our grandfathers were famous because they died in the ring at the height of their fame. Don't you know that? But somehow I didn't inherit that death wish. Nothing changes the fundamental fact that in this day and age, being gored by a bull is a stupid way for a man to die. It's time someone said so."

She chewed her lip, looking at her shoes. This was not what she came to Spain to hear. "You're just trying to discourage me, like my grandma."

"No! I'm not! Join the ranks! By all means! But I'm done. I *will* be done. Soon. I don't care what *you* do."

"What do you mean you're done?" said Alex, aghast.

"Last year, a young matador died in Barcelona. Manuel Luis Martinez — you heard of him? He was my age. We went to the same bullfighting school. He died of a small wound. So small, no one expected it. Even modern hospitals couldn't save him. When I heard that on the radio, something in me just snapped. I've decided to retire after the next season."

"What! You can't! You're nineteen!"

"I'm getting out. I haven't announced it yet. My parents don't know. Don't tell them." He folded the cape. "Why did you come to Spain, Alejandra?"

She shrugged. "I just want to fight once. And not just anywhere. I want to fight in Las Ventas."

"Why?"

"Because it's the most important bullring in the world. Don't smile. Don't give me that look. I am the granddaughter of Pedro Herrera. It's not so crazy that I would want to come back to fight."

"There's so much you don't know."

"I tell you what I don't know. I don't know my grandfather. I never knew him, my father never knew him. We never knew Spain. We were raised American. I have come home to change all that."

"You sound just like those American tourists who come here trying to look for their family connections. Cultural tourism."

"No. You're wrong," she said fiercely. "I was born to do

this. I can't change the way I am. Every fiber of my being is like this. I am sure I am a *torero*, as much as you are sure you are a man. I have wanted to do this ever since I could walk, Roberto de la Torre. Do you know what that's like?"

He thought he knew. He remembered feeling that way about the *corrida* as a child, reading the news clippings that his parents had saved of his grandfather's bullfights, marveling at the newspaper photos of the great arc of Las Ventas, and congratulating himself, at age five, that he had the same last name as the famous matador. *D-E L-A T-O-R-R-E* he would spell, over and over again, touching the newsprint that his father had lovingly laminated. He remembered counting on his fingers when he could be Grandpa's age, and thinking that it was a terribly long time before he could grow up and fight in Madrid.

"But women aren't interested in bullfighting," said Roberto finally. "I don't know a single woman who is."

"I don't know about other women. I don't *care* about other women. I just know I am a woman, I am a *torero* and no one can tell me I'm not. This is the hand I've been dealt with. I don't have a choice."

"The *aficionados* are not going to like an American woman coming in. They'll think you're being a tourist, just like all the other foreigners who have tried, or talked about trying. It's a closed world, Alex. They — everyone, the matadors, the ranchers, the fans, the news critics — they will eat you alive. Especially because you are a woman."

"But you haven't," grinned Alex. "You didn't seem surprised when I first called you. And you let me use your cape."

"That's because nobody was looking," said Roberto, getting up and dusting himself. "If you got us individually, we'll all probably agree with you that it is possible that a woman could learn to bullfight. But not when you ask us in a group. Look, I don't know how you're planning to do this, but there's not much I can do publicly to help you except say a few words of encouragement."

"You could get the president of the Madrid bullring to give me a bull to fight."

"Alex, I'm a matador, I'm not God."

"Aren't they the same thing in this part of the world?"

He shook his head. "I can't."

"You know, John Steinbeck said that matadors aren't really that brave outside the ring."

"Who's John Steinbeck?"

"An American writer. He said for all the valor in the ring, matadors are cowards in real life, they wouldn't take a stand in politics or speak up for the poor."

"Would you?"

She was taken aback. "Well, I'm not the one who rests my self-esteem on my courage."

"Do you think I do?"

She shrugged.

"You think you know me, don't you? But we've only just met."

She shrugged again, defiantly.

He studied her. "Come on, get up."

"Why?"

Roberto unfurled the cape and shook it authoritatively. "Your cape work is not as bad as you think, but it's not great either. I'll show you."

"What's the point of getting better if I can't fight?"

"What's the point of anything, Alex? Come on, it's late. The restaurants are closing. What else are you going to do tonight?"

He held out the cape and assumed a pose. She mirrored him. For a brief moment, they each remembered a famous photograph of their grandfathers posing together. It was the first thing that greeted visitors in the entrance of the

San Martín bullfighting museum. It was a large black and white photo. Only Alex and Roberto saw it in color. As children they had admired the suits of light hanging in unused closets.

Herrera, who was taller, always wore midnight blue. De la Torre — the reckless one — always wore bright red, to tempt the bull even more.

❁

The attic ladder descended with a crash. The housekeeper let out a yelp of alarm. "Oh my goodness! It's you!"

Alex came down, cobwebs in her hair. "Sorry."

"What are you doing up there? It's only junk."

"I'm, um, cleaning it."

Maria said, suspiciously, "What are you looking for? Perhaps I can help?"

"Grandpa's matador things."

"Sofia keeps them all up there. She never looks at them. Didn't you see them all?"

"Yes, but—"

"Something missing?"

"It's okay, I'll ask Grandma."

"Suit yourself. I'm off to the market. Want anything special? They have good melons."

"I'll come with you. It's my last day. I'd like to see the market before I go back to Texas."

"Nothing much to see, it's only San Martín! For sight-seeing you should go to Valencia's central market. I'm leaving soon."

"I'll come now."

When the two women left the house, Sofia went to the telephone and dialed a number.

"May I speak to Cristina de la Torre please? It's Sofia Herrera."

Sofia waited, leaning against the table for support, and closed her eyes. She heard the phone being put on hold, and another picked up somewhere else.

The voice at the other end was weak. Sofia had not seen Roberto's mother for a long time. Cristina had been suffering from diabetes.

"Cristina?"

"Is that really you Sofia?"

"How are you? How is your health?"

"I'm fine, thank you. Thank you for your flowers."

"Would you like me to come see you?"

"I'm in bed a lot. I used to go around in a wheelchair but I've had a bad month."

"I'm sorry to hear that. Listen. I'd like to go get Pedro's things."

"Oh. Wait a moment."

Sofia heard the woman at the other end asking someone to leave the room.

"All right, it's safe now. What do you want them for? Do you know I've never told my husband or Roberto? If you hadn't raised this, I fully intended to die not telling anyone where they are."

"I need to give Pedro's swords to someone."

"What!"

Sofia imagined the weak woman so stirred that she was sitting upright in bed for the first time in weeks. "I know, I know. It's just that I—"

"Who?"

"It's a long story."

"Well, come by this afternoon. The whole family would be at the bullfight. We'll go get it together from Molina."

"Okay, I've set up your account. You're RobT1988. I'm AlexH1988. No one will guess who you are."

Because of the paparazzi, they met under the cover of night, or in the early hours of the morning, in deserted parks, in broken-down barns, in silent construction sites.

"It's as if we're the droids in *Star Wars*," said Roberto doubtfully, looking at his phone.

"You don't like it?"

That night they were beneath the Puente del Mar in Valencia. It had started to rain. The soft bed of pine needles in the park absorbed the sound of raindrops. They pulled their bags out of the car, ran, and ducked under the stone bridge in the empty park. The bridge dated from the sixteenth century. Its massive arches provided ample shelter and space to practice in.

"I'll have to get used to being a number."

"Now, download this app on your phone. You'll be able to IM me faster this way. I'll write back if I'm awake."

"But why would I write you? What would I talk about?"

Alex put her phone away. She went to one of the nooks in the thick wall where she had stowed her bag. She took out her cape. "I don't know," she said teasingly, her eyes wide, backing away from him and unflaring the heavy magenta cloth. "*What* could we possibly have in common?"

AlexH1988 became his secret friend who lived inside his phone, like a genie. For the first time in his life, he had a hidden channel to the outside world. Even though he felt that she was using him, that she was only getting close to him because she wanted to partake of the world that he was in, for the first time in his life Roberto had a friend whom his parents and his manager didn't know about. Despite the time difference, she usually wrote back whenever he sent her a greeting, whatever time it was. He suspected she slept with the phone, and that it must be a thing that American university students do. They seem to abuse everything: drugs, alcohol, the Internet.

She downloaded his new bullfight tour schedule in South America in the winter months, and would send him a cheery SMS in the long, dreadful mornings and early afternoons before the fight. He grew accustomed to checking into the hotel room and charging his phone in anticipation of the little green balloon that would pop up, with a greeting from her. He wasn't allowed to socialize much during the day, before the bullfight. He was used to being shut up in his hotel room for long hours, where he was expected to pray to his saints to keep him safe. But now, even if his manager was outside his door, he wouldn't hear Roberto talking to anyone. The nature of SMS communication was silent and discreet. He achieved a curious privacy by setting himself free on the endless prairies of the World Wide Web.

Shelly flew out of the house, screen door banging, and ran towards the cab pulling into the long driveway.

Alex stepped out of the cab and hugged her tightly.

Tomas came down the porch steps. "We'll kill you later. After dinner, maybe. You hungry?"

"I'll pay you back the summer tuition money," said Alex, hoisting her backpack and trudging up the driveway. "I swear."

"Forget it," said Shelly, holding open the screen door. "It's your dad's money anyway. I really thought something bad was going to happen to you. What happened? You going to tell us? Did you go see Sofia?"

"I went to see Roberto de la Torre."

Tomas gave a great shout of triumph.

"Who's that? Juan Carlos's son?" demanded Shelly, following her into the house anxiously. "I can never keep track of all these *la la* names."

Tomas said, "No, it's the grandson. The famous one, he just graduated to professional matador status a couple of years ago. He's her age. This is exciting! What's he like? I haven't been following his fights, he's not in the top ranks yet, but what did you think?"

His wife elbowed past him. "Why," said Shelly through gritted teeth, following Alex into her bedroom, "did you go see De la Torre's grandson, Alex? Is that what all this was about? You could have given us some warning. I was so scared that you were going to get into some bullfights when you were there. You didn't, I hope?"

"Could you get into a bullring? Did he let you? What was it like?" asked Tomas excitedly.

"I can't get in, I have no way in. He won't help me. Yet," said Alex. "This is going to take a shit load of time."

"Forget it, just do the rodeo. Forget about Spain," said Shelly. "It's a waste of time. They're a bunch of savages."

Alex looked at Tomas. "You were right. I should start in Latin America. It's easier to get in there. Start there, then work my way to Madrid."

He nodded. "Yes, let's call Luis in San Diego and tell him, we can work out a schedule for you in Mexico City for the *novilladas*—"

"What, what, what?" cried Shelly. "What about college?"

"She'll do it in the summers. We've had this conversation, Shell," said Tomas.

"Last time I checked, her parents had appointed us *both* as her guardians, not just you, you . . . you stupid, bullfight-obsessed Mexican cowboy!" said his wife angrily.

"Why is it that it's always the women who object to bullfighting?" said Tomas, folding his plump arms. "First

Sofia, now you. With the exception of this one, of course," he pointed to Alex.

"Didn't you say the De la Torres did it for the money? Why are you forcing Alex into this? We don't need the money, we're not the savage, low-class brutes like that other family. Putting little *kids* in the bullring, for God's sake. I've seen the photos."

"It's not the money, Shelly, it's *honor*."

Alex cut between them. "Guys, don't do this. My heart is breaking to hear you guys fight. You never fight except because of me. I'm going to move out if you do this."

"I just have one question," said Shelly finally. "Are you going back to start senior year?"

"Yes. I'm going to get my degree," said Alex, darting Tomas a look. "I'll keep training at the bullfighting school, though."

There was silence as the three of them stared at each other.

"Fine. Finish your college education," said Shelly. "Then you can do whatever the heck you want. Seriously. I wash my hands of you both as long as you get your degree."

This was a new move, a tremendous concession on Shelly's part. Originally she had wanted Alex to go to business school before she was allowed to become a bullfighter. By which time, of course, nobody in her right mind would still be interested in the bullring.

"Sounds like a plan," said Tomas approvingly. "Now, tell me, what was he like in the ring? I want all the details. Did he do the *banderillas* himself, too?"

"Does this hotel have Wi-Fi?"

"Yes, it's twenty dollars a day."

"Does it really work?"

"Yes, yes," said the receptionist. "I promise you. Here's the password."

Roberto was about to go when she pushed a photograph shyly across the gleaming countertop at him. Before she even asked, Roberto had signed it dutifully. He then turned and said to his manager, "I'm going to be in my room. Praying."

"Okay. Meet down here in three hours. And call your mom."

"I will."

He wore sunglasses in the elevator. Most of the time Mexicans would not recognize him in ordinary clothes. Those who did often expressed their surprise that he was "so small", "so young".

They always stayed at the same few hotels in each city, the ones that welcomed bullfighting people. Once or twice, somebody would screw up a booking. He and his father would then have to stay at a chain hotel while the rest of the team slept in the car. In Mexico, the American businessmen at the bar would mistake him for a bus boy and ask him for the check. When he was younger he was angry; he conceived certain ideas of English-speaking people. Meeting Alex that past summer was a shock. It seemed inconceivable that the great Pedro Javier Herrera of San Martín, who couldn't speak English, could have a granddaughter who was a college student in America. Even more inconceivable was how she taught him to rely on the Web to keep in touch with her upon her return to Texas.

In 1889, a great fire swept through the city of San Martín. It was started in the middle of the night by the unlikeliest of culprits—mice. A small mouse had gotten hold of a box of matches and dragged it into the wainscoting of a townhouse belonging to a rice merchant and his family. Matches spilled all over the interior of the walls. For a few weeks, as the summer intensified, hundreds of mice ran busily all over the matches on their various nocturnal errands. Nothing happened. Then, one night, when the driest winds were blowing and people tossed in their hot, sticky beds, a small mouse scurried over a match and by chance dragged it against the dry side of the matchbox. The match flared and very quickly ignited the other matches. The flames spread quickly in the paper-dry interior of the walls and up the timbers to the roofs.

The great fire that ensued wiped out two narrow streets of crowded eighteenth century townhouses and killed forty people. Because of the fire, the homes were never rebuilt. Instead, the local authorities demolished that street and built a wide, tree-lined boulevard in its place.

History is like mice, and men and women merely matches. It was only a matter of time.

"This thing is like a drug," he wrote, tapping gingerly on the phone. He couldn't type fast enough. "I like writing you even though I have nothing to say."

AlexH1988 wrote back, *What do you think about before a fight? Aside from* Halo?

Roberto lay back on the bed and considered. He could hear the traffic from the street below. The hotel maid trundled her supplies cart down the passageway, knocking on doors.

"I think about how painful it would be if I get gored in the nuts."

No kidding. Can't you wear something?

"Not allowed."

I know it's not allowed but who would know?

"Are you saying all this just to annoy me?"

So practically every day you worry about getting neutered?

"And the animal rights people say it's stressful for the bull. At least he only has to go through this once."

Have any lofty thoughts?

"You mean about Death, God, all that? Yes when I was younger. But when Manuel Martinez died, I started thinking about things like going to college, getting a job. Normal things."

What kind of job?

He typed back slowly, "Is this an interview?"

Yes.

"It would be fun to work on animation, like for movies and videogames. I'd like to learn how to do that."

Sorry, pal. When matadors retire, they just open ranches and breed bulls.

"I know. That's what your dad went into, didn't he?"

Yeah, we never could get away from bulls. Except ours are different. We breed and sell them as fancy pets. They win awards. We don't kill them or sell their beef. Here's a picture of Maxine. She's got the longest horns on the ranch.

"What a freak. Did you grow up fighting that thing?"

No. But I have fought younger bulls and cows with shorter horns. Would you fight longhorn bulls?

"Absolutely not. How do you even get close?"

They're really docile. You can ride some of our steers like a horse.

"That's not the same as our fighting bulls."

I train with whatever I get. I think your chances of surviving a goring improves if their horns are straighter, don't you think?

"I try not to think along those lines."

I notice that if their horns are curved, you get stuck on them and you can't come off. But if their horns are short and straight, you slide off. It's only when you're stuck that you get killed, right?

"I really try not to think about it."

Hey, isn't it time for you to get ready?

Roberto looked up in a panic. Time had a way of evaporating whenever he was messaging Alex. He almost thought he was with her in America; he imagined they were in the same room together, at her university, chatting. Life was almost normal. But now he woke up to the old nightmare. He signed off quickly. Before he turned off the phone, she popped up with a final greeting, in English. She no longer said *break a leg*, or even *good luck*. They hadn't learned yet to say goodbye, knowing that each goodbye could be the last.

TTYL.

He held on to those four letters as emblems of an exotic hope. A knock came on his door. The team had come to watch him dress for the ring.

"Aren't you excited about the Lima festival?" asked his father. "We leave day after tomorrow. You'll be well trained by next season in Spain because of the South American fights. You can build up your following. I've got a new television network interested in covering this, did your manager tell you?"

Roberto winced as they cinched him into the suit of lights. He had checked the weather report on the television. It was one of those unbearably hot days. He would be drenched in the stiff costume within minutes, then stand in his own sweat for hours.

"What's that sound?" said his father, looking around.

"Nothing."

"I heard a beep, like a pager. Or is it one of your videogames?"

"It's nothing."

Roberto winced again as his father prodded the side of his suit. "What's this? What's this you got tucked in here?"

It vibrated gently and went *boop*.

"Your phone? Why is your phone tucked inside your *traje*? Are you insane?"

"Might stop a horn killing me," said the matador coolly.

His father dug it out of his clothes and tossed it onto the couch. "Don't be unorthodox. I let you play videogames, but this is too much. You can't have anything in your suit." He motioned for the assistants who held up the final piece of the suit, the jacket that sparkled rigidly in their hands like the useless carapace of a crayfish.

❁

RobT1988: *I have been thinking about your technique.*

Alex was out running. She slowed down and sat by the riverbank, smiling at her phone. Some ducks waddled up to her, looking for treats; she pushed them away.

You're still too much on the defense to pay attention to your cape work. You need to train with good, proper bulls. You need the time to let the animal get to know you and coax it into doing what you want. And anyway it's safer.

AlexH1988: "So I suck. I already know this. And I'm already nineteen. I'm so old compared to people like Joselito Rodriguez. He even made the Austin newspaper today because he's the youngest to cut two ears in a *novillada* in Las Ventas. When he puts on his *traje* he looks like Little Lord Fauntleroy! Screw the kid."

Don't despair. It's not too late. The key is just to train with as many live animals as you can, even bad ones. By the way, you can't tell others the stuff I tell you. And please don't ever say anything about my views on bullfighting to the press.

"Why are you so paranoid I'd tell reporters? I don't know *any*."

They're always asking me for opinions. I have to be careful. I always just say very boring neutral things. Never my real thoughts. I trust no one.

"All right, all right. Do you think I have a chance?"

It depends.

"I've been practicing my cape work. But I still suck. I've enrolled in bullfighting school again. In California we stick the bulls with Velcro darts. It doesn't kill them."

How American.

"Hey, hey."

It's like how Americans like potato chips without any fat.

"So, get me into a real bullfight."

I've been thinking. You need to ask one of the top matadors, not me. I'm too junior.

"Who should I ask?"

I can't think of any who wouldn't want you to sleep with them first.

"Thanks. Good to know."

Sorry.

"Name, please?"

"Sofia Herrera."

The nurse looked up quickly. She was new and didn't recognize them. "You here for Dr Molina or Dr Rodriguez?"

"Molina," said Sofia. "I did call in advance."

"His office is just through those double doors. Do you need help?"

"No, I can push her. Thank you."

The nurse held down a button as Sofia wheeled Cristina in her wheelchair slowly through the automatic doors.

"Ladies, what a pleasure," said Dr Molina, appearing

at the door. He was fatter than ever. "Come into my office."

They settled down and discussed Cristina's latest medical problems. Then—

"You have it?" asked Cristina.

"Of course I have it. In fact, you remember, it was in this very office nearly fifty years ago where we hatched the plot."

The two women watched as the portly doctor dragged a chair to a corner of his office, got up on it with some difficulty and, with a wooden ruler, carefully poked at a loose panel in the ceiling. It parted, showering him with dust.

"It's probably very dirty," said Molina apologetically. "There are pigeons inside the roof. We are due for a renovation."

Pulling a large, soiled handkerchief out of his pocket, he wrapped his hand and reached in.

First to emerge were the two leather cases holding the numerous killing swords belonging to each matador. Then, with great effort, he carefully extricated a heavy, pale blue suitcase holding the capes.

"All in good condition," said Molina. The three of them stared at the opened containers. He bent down and unzipped an interior pocket in the yellow silk of the old suitcase. "Even the patron saints and charm bracelets are here."

Nobody tried to touch the objects. Sofia remembered the day she last saw them. The womenfolk of the De la Torres, the Herreras and their neighbors were present. That day, the young Sofia thought that everything would end. That families would end, lives would end, bullrings would end. And here they were, fifty years later, and the bullfights went on more or less as they did before. Pedro's and Juan

Carlos' deaths had been so small, after all. Two deaths in two centuries of bullring deaths.

Cristina turned to Sofia, "Are you doing the right thing?"

Sofia said tiredly. "Yes. Wild horses will not drag her away from the bullring. She wants to fight."

Dr Molina's lower lip protruded doubtfully. "She should consider taking up *flamenco*."

"I have to give her Pedro's things," said Sofia quickly. "She will never forgive me if I keep hiding them. I will lose her if I don't give them to her."

"You'll lose her if you do," said Cristina. She was hardly fifty, but her feet were already bandaged from diabetes, and her eyes were all but sunken in her red, puffy cheeks.

Dr Molina folded his handkerchief, waited for the appropriate moment, then asked mildly, "So, Sofia, you taking one box? Shall I put Juan Carlos' things back up there?" He proceeded to reach for it, but Cristina's walking stick fell quickly on the suitcase. He was surprised.

"I'm taking them," said Cristina crisply.

"You are? But I thought you always said—"

"Sofia is giving Pedro's swords to Alejandra. That means I have to give Juan Carlos' swords to my son. We shall face the inevitable. Let the young people kill themselves if they want, but let them have a go at it. Let it be their decision, not ours."

Sofia nodded at the doctor. "Give these things a good wipe and we'll be on our way."

There was a gentle buzz and the phone went *bing*.

Nicky looked up from her desk where she was online shopping on her desktop PC. Alex had woken up early that morning for track practice and was already sound asleep on the couch.

RobT1988 said something in Spanish. She looked at the gently glowing green balloon on Alex's phone.

I have your ... the last word was something Nicky, with her limited high school Spanish vocabulary, could not recognize.

Rob, huh, she thought. Rob must be Alex's new secret boyfriend whom she met in Spain. The one with the Menudo website she was always surfing. Some guy in a Spanish band. Alex didn't talk about it, but there were just some things you couldn't keep from your roommate.

Nicky carefully snapped a close-up photo of Alex sleeping and then emailed it to RobT1988. She typed, in Spanish, *Alex is sleeping*. She could at least compose that sentence. She was so proud of herself.

Chuckling, she set the phone carefully back on Alex's desk, took a swig from her two liter bottle of diet soda, and went back to comparison-shopping for a new zoom lens for her camera.

"Where are you going?" Roberto's father gripped his arm.

"Back to the hotel."

"Some people came all the way from Spain to Lima to see you fight. Stay and say hi to them."

"But it's late. I'm tired."

"You all right?" His manager hovered anxiously. "You're going to be all right for tomorrow?"

Roberto had been knocked down by the second bull that evening. There were no open wounds, but he had been severely bruised. He didn't freak out in the ring and made a quick recovery and an excellent kill. The crowd roared with approval. He was awarded two ears. The

63

doctor pronounced him fine for the next day's fight, but he wasn't so sure.

His manager drove him back to the hotel. His father, in a sudden spurt of generosity, had decided to book a large suite for him. It was dark. The suite was like a large apartment with two bedrooms, a living room, and a study. He counted four televisions scattered throughout the suite, but didn't turn them on in case he saw footage of himself being tossed by the bull. Sometimes the news in Peru would run such clips again and again, often in slow motion and from different angles. They would even highlight glee-fully, on the screen with an electronic squiggle, the entry of the bull's horn into the matador's body. In soccer, they repeated clips in slow motion when you scored a goal. In bullfighting, thought Roberto humorlessly, they appreciated your moment of failure and ignominy.

He showered and put on his bathrobe, then sat sullenly at the long dining table of wrought iron and polished glass. The table had twelve chairs — whatever for? he thought darkly. He typed an SMS carefully to Alex.

I have your killing sword.

The message came back almost immediately, startling him. It was a photograph. Her eyes were closed. *Alex is sleeping.*

He was puzzled at first, then realized someone else must have sent it. He wondered who it was, and panicked a bit at the thought of who might be reading his messages. Then he calmed down and remembered she was always talking about her roommate. It must be her. A prank. It was clear that he couldn't write any more. He couldn't risk someone else reading what he had to say.

She looked so peaceful in that photograph. He wondered if she had slept through the tumult of that evening. He raised the phone to his face to see if he could smell her.

They got into the car. It was stifling hot that night. Roberto blasted the air-conditioning as they turned into the street.

When he pulled up to her hotel, he said, "You always smell of cake."

"What?" she was startled.

"Whenever I drop you off in my car, you leave behind a smell of cake. Like icing." Roberto began to laugh at her expression. "I'm not being rude, it's a compliment."

She sniffed the back of her hand. "It's a lotion. My roommate gave it to me. Lemon cupcake or something. Sorry."

In bed, Roberto felt his ribs carefully and counted the bruises.

He once saw a documentary on the television about a famous tightrope walker. The man wore a camera on his chest and walked across dizzying heights — a rope between two skyscrapers, a rope between cliffs. He couldn't look back, or he would fall. But if he looked straight ahead, there was no end to the long rope. All he could do was put one foot in front of another with agonizing slowness. It was awful. Roberto turned off the documentary before it ended.

❀

RobT1988: *I thought of you today. A news magazine asked me why women think they can become matadors. I didn't know what to say.*

AlexH1988: "Tell them it's because we think our asses look better in those damn tights than yours."

Austin, Texas is a wet city on a dry plain. It is a gem-green bud of aloe vera ripening on limestone the color of bleached coral. Beneath the limestone is something called the Edwards Aquifer. Think of an aquifer as a silent, vast, underground lake that bubbles up, in some places, to form wells of spring water. It was this water that allowed the first Spanish missionaries to thrive in central Texas. It is this water that punctuates all of Austin's existence. The town is riddled with tiny, tepid creeks. Many homes and businesses — as the locals will tell you glumly — are on a permanent flood plain. Because of flood plain zoning, some buildings were built top heavy, like old dames permanently picking up their skirts and standing, with blue-veined pale knees, in anticipation of a deluge that never comes.

Nicky needed a new swimsuit.

"Come and try on swimsuits with me."

"No."

"You are like totally breaking the roommate bond."

Alex sighed, pulled her lanyard and room keys off the table, and trailed after Nicky.

By the time Nicky finished trying on clothes at the store and they headed back to campus, the cafeteria was jammed with students. It was peak time. They stood in a long line. Alex reached for her phone and began tapping at it restlessly.

"So, what do you think I should get? Pink or black?" asked Nicky. "Are black bikinis still in?"

"Just get both," said Alex absently, checking her messages.

"No way. $69.99, I only have cash for one pair. Hey, look, it's Dave."

"Who's Dave?"

"Captain of the cycling team, omigod, he's looking our way."

"Where?"

"Two o'clock, two o'clock."

"Don't look at him then."

"He's totally coming over to talk to us, it's pathetic."

A guy sauntered up and pushed his baseball cap back on his forehead. "We're over there if you guys would like to join our table."

Nicky said, "I got your email about night kayaking. Sounds good."

"Yeah, but you haven't signed up."

"Still thinking about it."

The boy darted a look at Nicky's roommate. "Are you okay?"

"I've got to go," said Alex abruptly, picking up her backpack. "Sorry."

"Don't do this to me, Alex," said Nicky, half-laughing.

"No, I'm serious, I — I forgot something."

"You eating?"

"Go ahead. Catch up with you guys later."

She ran all the way up three flights of steps, dialing Roberto. His phone was engaged. Of course. During 9/11, she remembered Shelly frantically dialing her aunt in New York. Nobody's cellphone worked.

Once in her room, she went directly to the news website. No news. She went on a bullfighting fan site. Someone had uploaded the clip already from a cellphone. It was a blurry image. The bull had drawn blood from under Roberto's arm. The clip was only fifteen seconds, filmed after the goring. She saw Roberto take his shoes off so that he would not be standing in shoes filled with his own blood and slip. He walked into the ring barefoot while the crowd cheered ecstatically. As was expected of him, he did not pay attention to his wound, nor did he flinch, stop, or check for blood loss. It was as if it never happened. He looked at the bull and raised the cape and waited. He stared with sovereign willfulness at the animal, jerked his head back and shouted fiercely. There the clip ended.

She didn't know who to call, so she called home.

"Tomas? Roberto's been gored. Only just," she said breathlessly. "In Lima. I'm trying to get the news but I can't."

Tomas was in the middle of making dinner and sounded like he didn't want to be interrupted. "Oh yeah? Is he okay?" he said, knocking tongs against the side of a steel pan. "Hey, do you know where Shell keeps the spaghetti? I could have sworn I bought a whole box of it last time from Costco, how could we have run out already?"

Alex's heart contracted. Through the years, she had thought they were on the same side, that they understood each other perfectly. But now, hearing Tomas' voice, she realized he was always only a spectator. The fact that Roberto had been injured, may be dying, only invoked in Tomas the mild, slightly-excited curiosity of a distant fan. There was a reason why Tomas was content to watch bull-fights all his life on television. When she was little, he built her a training ring in the backyard as a hobby, as a joke. When it became serious, he delegated her bullfighting training to the schools. He did not get involved in her aspirations except as someone who loved to watch from the periphery. She had arrived at one of those classic moments in adulthood when she suddenly saw the people who raised her as behind her, rather than always in front of her.

She remembered suddenly that Tomas had never met Roberto in person. Perhaps one should never meet a matador, let alone be their friend, let alone exchange SMSs with them long-distance, late into the night. She had been imprinted by Roberto.

She hung up on Tomas and dialed Roberto again. She kept getting the standard Spanish recording, a woman repeating robotically: *This number is not available. You can leave a message after the tone.* She grew to hate that calm voice.

An hour later, more clips appeared on the Web. She couldn't bear to read the excited fan commentary that accompanied the amateur videos. People analyzed his goring on bulletin boards. Finally, someone—a French fan—posted the actual few seconds of the goring itself. As usual, the moment of contact between man and bull was so unexpected—even the matador, the person closest to the animal, didn't see it coming. The audience always noticed it a split second after tragedy struck. He was hurled into the air and then slammed into the dust. A horrified roar went up across the stands.

He got up so quickly that his suit wasn't even dirty. He continued the fight for fifteen more agonizing minutes. It was a bad kill. Roberto's costume was completely drenched with blood. Eventually Roberto and his team had to slay the bull. No major trophies this time, even though a scattering of his die-hard fans shook their white handkerchiefs dutifully, hoping the president of the ring would award him with one ear just for holding up like a man. He got nothing. She couldn't see his face in the clip. He walked calmly out of the ring, as if the wound wasn't there, and his manager clapped him on his back and poured water over his head, as if in benediction. When the

Spanish news television interviewed him, he said a few perfunctory words about how the crowd was tremendously supportive. His face in the close-up was white, his lips bloodless.

"Why do they make him talk to the camera when blood has been gushing out of his side for *twenty minutes*?" whispered Alex to the computer screen. Her eyes began to smart. She had not cried in a long time.

Fate has a way of striking so great a blow, so unexpectedly, that we quiver with indignation. Blood surprises us — there is so little in our tidy lives. Most of our waking hours we go about our everyday routine, confident in our ways, making the right decisions, impressing people. And then something so random, so terrible happens — a drunk driver crosses a divider on a highway, a matador moves the cape a fraction of a second too late — and we marvel, even in our shock, at the impact.

She felt with surprise her shaking shoulders, her heaving diaphragm, her tears wetting the cool wood of her desk. It was a new sensation.

Pedro had died in the morning.

When you had lived long enough, memories had a way of turning slyly round a corner, never to come back. But Sofia still remembered that morning. A particularly fine morning it was — crisp, cool, around 6 a.m., before the traffic started, before the sun got too hot.

After that, it was in his office that she, Dr Molina, and the local priest (who had died long ago) made a grim decision that her three-year-old son was to be sent to live with friends in America, to get away from the curse forever. It was also here, a few days later, that the two widows of De la Torre and Herrera decided that the swords of their husbands were to be hidden, away from the bullfighting clubs and museums who had demanded their release for exhibition and adoration. Wealthy businessmen from Madrid offered money for the collectibles. The widows lied and told the public that they had burned —perversely, out of pure grief and classic female incomprehension of sacred bullfighting memorabilia—all of the trappings of their husbands' careers, except for the suits, which they asked to keep in memory of their husbands.

Molina had been a young doctor, fresh out of medical school. He practiced surgery by sewing up the wounds of matadors. He had been the one who banned the bullfighting clubs from coming into the hospital when Pedro lay dying, and stopped them from taking photographs of his dead body for the press. Terrible things happened in those days. Sofia saw what De la Torre's wife went through when he died. She was convinced that if they had been allowed to, the fans would have exhibited the bloody sword in the local matadors' pub, and burned Pedro and drank his ashes out of admiration.

"Alex. Alejandra!"

"Did you look in here?"

"I thought you already did?"

Tomas pushed open the stable door.

"They're not coming back from Spain, are they?" asked the little girl in the shadows.

Shelly stepped into the stable and cried in alarm. "Jesus Christ! You're bleeding! Tomas, call 911!"

The girl picked herself up from the straw and dusted herself. Her face was swollen from crying. "It's not my blood. I killed the calf. I'm so sorry."

"Calf! What calf! Which calf?" asked Shelly.

Tomas put away his cell phone. "It's her practice calf. Everybody calm down, please."

"I left her out there," said Alex. "She was too heavy —"

"I'll bury her, don't worry."

Alex was in a pink shirt and purple dungarees. She was covered with blood and bits of straw. She drew her knees up and buried her face in her arms. Her small frame shook with grief.

Shelly knelt and hugged her tightly. "Come on. Let's go inside, honey. You're a mess."

Alex stood up and shrugged off Shelly's embrace. She wiped her face with the sleeve of her sweatshirt. "I feel so sad for her."

"Yes, honey."

"She reminds me of me." Her face scrunched up again.

"Hush, don't say that."

"Please let go of me." She shook herself free from Shelly's hug, handed Tomas her dirty sword and left the stable quickly without another word.

RobT1988: *Are u there?*
AlexH1988: "Yes."

I'm alive.

"How do you feel?"

Freezing. They can't seem to turn down the A/C in this hospital room.

"How many stitches?"

Twenty.

"Are you going back to Spain?"

No. The season isn't over. We're going to Mexico City tomorrow morning. I've been terribly unlucky this time in South

America. All the bulls are preternaturally smart. They're uncontrollable. My manager lodged a complaint.

"How can you fight when you're injured?"

I can raise my arms. I can't get out of it now.

"Who cares? Didn't you say you're pulling out after next season?"

Yes, precisely. I have to finish this season and the next before pulling out. By that time I would have paid off all the money we owe.

"This is ridiculous."

It hurts to type on the phone.

"If it hurts you to SMS, how can you fight a bloody bull tomorrow, you fool?"

It's day after tomorrow. I have a day to rest. But I have a feeling I'm pushing my luck.

"What do you mean?"

This is the second time I've stumbled during this tour. I have a bad feeling about this. I'm starting to get superstitious. It wasn't so bad last year when I was here. Can't you come?

"To Mexico City?"

Come. I would like to see you. You have the schedule.

Alex looked up from the phone. Beneath her open window, two boys talked about their Economics professor. Next door, someone had tuned the radio to the college radio station. It advertised the availability of tickets for a classical concert at the Long Center and announced another record-breaking weather report for Austin.

Just come to any city on any date you can.

She shook her head silently at the phone.

What do I do with your grandfather's swords? They're with my mother in San Martín. Don't you want them?

Alex?

Alex? You there?

❁

For the rest of the evening Alex lay in the stifling heat of the bedroom, staring as the sky grew red, then black. Nicky came back from class, dressed for a date, tried to talk to her, realized Alex was incommunicado, then went out again in a cloud of her favorite strawberry deodorant.

"Mi Unicornio" played on a loop.

"Hey. I'm back."

"Hey Nick," Alex didn't open her eyes. She knew from the cooler temperature of the room that it was past midnight. "You can turn on the light."

"It's okay. I was just checking if you were still up. I broke up with Andy."

"No way. Oh, Nicky."

"I don't want to talk about it. Still playing that sad song?"

"Yeah."

"What the *hell* is that song?"

Alex opened her eyes and took a deep breath, staring at the pockmarked ceiling. "It's an old Cuban song. About a girl who lost her blue unicorn."

"Like My Little Pony?"

"Yeah. Kinda. Sadder."

The two girls sat side by side on Alex's bed, listening to the piano chords tumbling down an old, worn staircase. Then Alex reached for the remote and turned the music off.

Nicky said, "You wanna talk about it?"

Alex frowned, looking at her shoes. She began to speak, but no words came out. She doubled over in grief. She hardly made a sound. Nicky held her sticky hair back sympathetically and pulled tissues from a box.

"I'm so sorry," said Alex finally. "You were the one who just broke up with your boyfriend."

"No big deal. It wasn't going to go anywhere. I should have known."

Alex squeezed her hand, then crawled back into bed and turned to face the wall. "Let's talk tomorrow."

"Good idea. Good night," said Nicky, turning on the bathroom light and running the tap.

"Night."

❁

That winter, Roberto de la Torre was gored twice, by the same bull, in Lima. The bull had retreated to the same spot in the ring and charged at any man who came near him. A skilled matador would never have allowed that to happen. Roberto blamed the bull; his manager blamed his father for pushing him to sign up for too many fights.

Fortunately Roberto's injuries were light, owing to the fact that he always managed to fall right between the bull's horns when he was lifted—something which fans attributed to his slender frame.

After the Lima incident, in Cali he left the ring in protest after finding fault with a bull. The tabloids were rife with news of Roberto losing his edge.

NEWLY MINTED MATADORS FROM SPAIN COWARDLY IN LATIN AMERICA, proclaimed the headlines of a bullfighting magazine in Colombia. However, in Ecuador Roberto "cut many ears", as the expression goes, and the crowd was delirious with approval. He was photographed with a famous Latin American female pop star and attended a music awards show in Mexico City before flying home to Spain.

He kept messaging Alex after the goring in Lima, but she said she was busy writing her senior honors thesis. They spoke once, briefly, on Skype, but owing to the fact that she shared her dorm suite with another girl, she didn't want to talk much.

By the time the spring festivals came in Spain and the

new bullfighting season started back home, Alex had stopped communicating with him.

After the music awards show, he declined going to the after party and asked to be driven back to the hotel.

He had just stepped out of the elevator when he heard a woman's laughter and his father's voice. Roberto had perfected the art of stealth. He crept softly round the corner and saw his father, his arm around a young blond, trying to open the door of the room.

"It doesn't work," said his father, sliding the key card in and out irritably. The woman began putting her tongue in his ear. "Damn it! I have to go downstairs and get a new key. Shit!"

They began walking towards the elevator. Roberto stole down the corridor and was about to hide himself in the stairwell when he changed his mind. He walked quickly up to them.

His father stared at him in shock. "You're back early!"

Before he could say anything, his father cut him off and said, "Don't tell your mother."

Roberto said nothing, walked slowly and insolently past them, and let himself into his room.

"What do you think of the female novices coming up the ranks?" asked the woman host of the Spanish television show. She wore an extra short skirt that day.

His father had bought him an Italian suit for the interview. Navy blue wool, pinstripe, with a stiff, starchy shirt to match. He had wanted Roberto to resemble one of Spain's current top matadors, someone ten years older than him, who looked more like a Hugo Boss model than a man in the ring. Roberto privately thought the guy a real wanker. So he showed up at the television studio in the worn, grey T-shirt and jeans that he had fallen asleep in the night before. To the disappointment of the fifty-something show host, who was quite old school, he also forgot to shave. Except for the bracelet of patron saint charms on his wrist, he could have been mistaken for a kid working behind a counter in a coffee shop. He imagined his parents watching the television show now, wincing.

"Pilar's good, Carmen's good, and the French girl Magalie is very good also," he said, naming women who were only sixteen, seventeen, and—some of them—barely five feet tall. "Do you follow them?"

"Oh, no, no," laughed the host, hastily. "They are nothing compared to you!"

"You start somewhere. They've had less help." He scratched the side of his nose. The camera, silently transmitting, was hidden somewhere in the darkness. He was usually good at keeping still, but the studio lights burned into his retina.

"Would you consider helping one of them graduate to matador status?"

This was a politically sensitive question. The bullfighting clubs, breeders and bullring managers loathed the idea of women entering the field. Even without the controversy over women, bullfights continued to slide into a culturally ambiguous position in Spain. Practically every week now, as the new season got underway, the French and Spanish animal rights groups would lob a missile to the EU parliament, or to their state or local governments, crying for a ban. The dark, broody, bloody Catholic Spain must be purged, and be replaced by gleaming office towers, fluorescent lights and museums of modern art. Just the other day, someone tied an anti-bullfighting balloon to the windshield wiper of his car (a gaudy yellow balloon with the red motif of a cartoon bull, arms akimbo, admonishing him). Would he help the new generation of women break into professional bullfighting? A reply in the affirmative would mean angering both the old world and the new, and his manager, father and the breeders had told him that the best response, given the circumstances and the dollars and cents involved, would be—

"Yes." Roberto scratched the side of his nose again. His large brown eyes looked briefly into the news camera with a hint of amusement. It was a clip that was instantly uploaded on YouTube, forwarded on emails, and replayed from coast to coast.

"*C'est idiot,*" said the French bullfighting clubs.

"He said it just to get media attention. He can't get news coverage for his acts in the ring because he's not good enough. All the new generation matadors are like that now," said the bullfighting clubs in Madrid. "First he does badly in Latin America, now he says he supports girls! The animal rights people don't even have to lift a finger. We're already dead in the water if people like De la Torre behave like this."

A Parisian writer for the magazine *Marie Claire* decided to write a feature story about girl *novilleros* who were found to be active in the French city of Nîmes. She sent an adoring fax to Roberto's manager asking to interview him. His manager tossed the fax in contempt, both for women and for the French.

A coalition of Spanish anti-bullfighting groups issued press releases saying they had cleared the way for bringing the matter before the next EU parliament. They organized a worldwide anti-bullfighting summit in Barcelona. They published new polls reiterating that over seventy percent of Spanish citizens had no interest in the *corrida*. They expressed great disappointment at the Royal Family for supporting bullfighting. On the subject of Roberto, they were not so kind. Ignoring the fact that he was still a teenager himself, they called him a corruptor of their children, and implored parents to keep their teenage daughters away from him because he might turn them into matadors.

In Madrid, anti-bullfighting protestors rode the subway to Las Ventas, singing at the top of their voices, then streamed into the *plaza* and jumped into the ring waving placards, disrupting a bullfight and causing chaos. In response, a pro-bullfighting coalition of fan clubs and business interests formed and gave angry and articulate press interviews. Words like "history" and "tradition" were invoked at first, but when they ceased to impress, the discourse shifted to "cultural sovereignty" and "fundamental liberty". When that failed, pro-bullfighting Spain turned to its neighbors for support. Suddenly, not only was Spain's cultural heritage under siege, but that of France, Portugal, and Latin America as well.

"Should we hire a bodyguard?" asked his father, pushing him hurriedly into the car when they came out of the arrival hall at the airport. The photographers and the animal rights people were there, waiting for them.

Roberto said he couldn't understand why his father would fear for his personal safety if he didn't mind Roberto going into the bullring night after night facing thousands of pounds of angry animal flesh.

"Not for you," said his father testily, slamming the door shut. "For *me*."

Traditional bullfighting clubs, known as *peñas*, seemed virtually unchanged since the days of Hemingway. Portly, mustached men and their wives still gathered in pubs or club rooms hazy with cigarette smoke. Totems from the bullring hung from whitewashed walls, alongside photographs of people dressed in the fashions from every decade of the twentieth century. Dark, musty stuffed bull heads pouted broodingly from every corner. *Peña* members would gather to watch televised bullfights, discuss live bullfights they had just watched, dish out awards to their favorite bullfighter, hold seminars or charity events, or just muck about in all things taurine. While women often attended *peñas*, the affairs of the *peña* were still mostly led by men.

A small Facebook group started in January in response to Roberto's television interview. Originating in a Parisian high school, it called itself *VirtualPeña* and had eight members. They were teenage girls who were part of the school's women's equestrian club. They suddenly took interest in bullfighting because Roberto de la Torre had endorsed girl bullfighters publicly on national television. The interview clip had been played and replayed on

YouTube and was the subject of endless bulletin board discussions in high schools and universities.

At first, young women with no prior knowledge of or interest in bullfighting were drawn to the clip because they all thought Roberto looked really "cute". Then, when they Googled the girl matadors that Roberto named, they fell in love with the photographs of girls their age dressed up in glittery costumes courting danger, wielding swords and posing with the boy novices. For a generation used to supporting girl tennis players, girl swimmers, and girl fencers in televised sports, the conceptual leap to supporting a girl matador proved to be an easy one. Images of Carmen Sanchez, a sixteen-year-old *novillero* from Sevilla wearing French braids and pearl stud earrings in the ring, became hopelessly modern and irresistibly hip.

Within weeks, *VirtualPeña* spread to many Spanish cities and then to Latin America. *VirtualPeña* was not the first time in Europe that women bullfighting fans tried to start a bullfighting club, but prior attempts had been greeted with contempt and derision by the male clubs. A virtual online club faced no such problem. Your dad, brother, or male classmate couldn't sneer at you because you were quietly doing it on your phone or computer. To the dismay of animal rights groups, the interest in girl matadors — and by the same token, in bullfights in general — began spreading like wildfire on social networking sites. The French *novillero* Magalie Soubeyran was on the cover of *Marie Claire* and compared to Maria Sharapova. Fashion designers took interest.

In response, animal rights groups organized a protest in front of the EU parliament building in Brussels. Twenty beautiful young women in bikinis doused themselves with fake blood, stuck themselves with fake, colorful *banderilla* darts, and lay on the concrete, unmoving, while passersby took photographs in horrified amusement.

In the spring, the managers of bullrings realized that ticket sales for novice fights climbed when the occasional girl novice was thrown in the mix alongside the boys. In bigger cities, groups of high school girls began booking block seats in support of their favorite *torero*. During a fight in Nîmes, Magalie Soubeyran's two male counterparts cancelled suddenly before the show, refusing to share the ring with her. Magalie ended up killing all six bulls herself and drove the crowd wild.

"It's a novelty thing, just like in the old days," the bull-ring management grumbled at a board meeting after the fight. "We're not talking about skill here. We're talking about circus."

The accountant chewed the end of his Biro. "It sells seats in a recession."

❖

It was Fallas in Valencia.

The city's population had swollen to many times its normal size because of the festival. People bussed in from the suburbs to march in the eighteenth century costume parade. Merchants lined the streets with electricity generators and food trucks offering different forms of fried dough. Firecrackers thundered every afternoon, filling the main square with white smoke and the smell of gunpowder. All major streets were cordoned off. The price of a cup of coffee tripled. Cellphones did not work. At every block there were gaudy cardboard effigies that cost hundreds of thousands of dollars. On the last night they would be gleefully burned while the fire department stood by, dutifully wetting the building façades to prevent real fires.

The Valencia bullring was sold out.

"They came for you," said his father in the van as they pulled in the ring. "You're the top biller today."

"That's only because El Rivera's injured," said Roberto crisply, getting out of the van into the mob. The air was ripe with the smell of horse manure.

"Pity. I really wanted you to be in the same fight as him. We would get more coverage that way."

"I could die," said Roberto as he reached into the crowd of fans for the first poster and signed it. "I could die and maybe make the evening news."

"I don't like your new attitude."

They were separated by his manager and smiled for a photojournalist.

Roberto now waited for his turn in the bullring. The *plaza* was a wall of multicolored people. White chimneys of cigarette smoke rose from the crowd. Every now and then, from the streets around the bullring, firecrackers would stutter and pop like solitary gunshots. Disco music thundered from giant speakers on a nearby soundstage. Out there, thought Roberto, they were having a festival. They couldn't care less about what was going on in here. He was just another event in the annual lineup. Towns-people in glittering dresses were parading flowers for Virgin Mary. Tourists were shaking powdered sugar on fried pumpkin puffs. Matadors were risking their life and limb for *aficionados*. Something for everyone, he thought grimly.

As he was the most junior matador that evening, he went last of the three matadors performing. He was assigned the third bull. He took risks to impress the fes-tival crowd. It was a perfect *faena*. The audience had gone wild, but the president had denied him any trophies. The crowd's jeers at the president split the night. *Idiot! Idiot! Idiot!* they chanted in protest at the injustice. Roberto wondered if the president did this because he wanted to see if the junior matadors of his generation had real hunger. Or maybe it was revenge for Roberto's public statement about supporting girl *novilleros*.

He had one more chance to impress the judges sitting up in the box. He still had the sixth and last bull to kill. The second time round, the stakes would be much higher. He had to improve on perfection to get the president to award him an ear. In between, he tried to focus on what was happening in the ring as the other matadors had their turn.

Alex?

Are you coming back to Spain this summer?

Tell me if you do. Strange things have happened.

The day ripened into dusk in the bullring and the stadium lights came on. The gold braids on the matadors' suits began to twinkle. He preferred the amber lights of Madrid's Las Ventas bullring. In Valencia the stadium lights were fluorescent. They caught the white haze of cigarette smoke above the ring and turned the evening into an ugly, ashen grey. He waited for the matador before him to kill a roan-colored monster who refused to topple over. The crowd whistled and screamed at his incompetence. Finally, the matador reached for a different killing sword to dispatch the bull faster.

Alex?

He turned round suddenly.

"What are you doing with that phone!" shouted his father. "Give it to me. It's ridiculous! Pay attention!"

Roberto didn't bother arguing. There was no one else he wanted to talk to anyway. "Take it," he said, glaring. "Take everything."

His manager stepped between them. Under his carefully brillantined and sparsely distributed hair, beads of sweat stood out on his scalp under the lights. "Are you crazy?" he hissed quietly to father and son. "People are watching. And the TV crew is filming."

Roberto subsided. The fifth bull finally keeled over, but it was a bad kill. The crowd was unhappy and restless. The other matadors' bulls had been problematic and had refused to perform. Yet when the matadors tried to kill them quickly, they refused to die. The bull breeder was in the crowd, angry and ashamed by the animals that he had so carefully reared for so many years. Journalists were already formulating short, cynical write-ups for tomorrow's newspaper reviews of the *corrida*. It was past seven o'clock, and the hot and sticky people wanted to go off to eat and see the other Fallas sideshows. He was suddenly dead tired. It was the worst possible way to enter the bullring. People didn't even want to be there anymore, and he knew it. Some people got up and left — the uncomfortable seats, or the sight of the blood, had gotten to them. Most chose to stay to see if he would outdo his earlier performance and cut the first ear of the evening. They fanned themselves busily and bought more beers from the beer boys crawling up and down the aisles. He felt the terrible burden of having to wake up all seventeen thousand of them. He hopped on his feet and adjusted his breeches. He did stretches. *Wake up*, he told himself.

A police helicopter's ominous staccato shattered the night sky above. Outside in the streets, someone had let loose a huge cloud of helium balloons. The crowd murmured, pointing. SpongeBob, Hello Kitty and Dora floated across the sky above the bullring in surreal merriment. People took pictures of the sudden sight. Roberto did not look up. It was the usual Fallas mayhem. He did not want to be distracted. He rested his forehead against the wooden barrier and prayed to every single saint until he ran out of them.

It was his turn.

"Good luck," rasped the matador who had gone before him, pouring a plastic bottle of water over his head. There was blood all over the front of his pants, a frightening image, as if he had just had his balls cut off.

Roberto and his men left the comforting tangle of bodies in the perimeter of the ring and stepped onto the mustard yellow sand. Flashbulbs went off. The press was given special permission to adhere themselves to the wooden barrier around the ring. He was used to them, their telephoto lenses protruding obscenely, the flashes popping in approval as he caped the bull. This time, as he turned to face them, one of them lowered the camera.

Alejandra.

He felt the slightest charge of electricity on the nape of his neck.

She's here?

Did saints answer prayers? But he didn't pray for her, he prayed for a good kill. What the hell was Alejandra doing in the press group?

But there was no time. Trumpets. The red barn door swung open.

Out tumbled the bull.

This was the livelier bull of the two his team had drawn in the lottery that afternoon. The black animal trotted impudently around the ring, massive genitals swaying. It had rammed repeatedly against its pen, for it was kept the longest that evening. Its whole left side was chalky with dust. Roberto's team caped it dutifully.

The first two acts—the act of the spears, and the act of the darts, went according to plan. Determined to get a trophy this time, Roberto dared several dangerous *veronica* passes with the pink cape. The gigantic animal bumped into him several times, smearing him with blood. He did not seem to notice, just as you would politely disregard an impatient child pushing you on a crowded bus. Scattered

86

applause. Then, for those who raised their binoculars, there came a magic moment when the bull rolled himself up into a ball of savage wrath and Roberto's large brown eyes became opaque, his face a complete blank, as if he was in another universe altogether; he approximated the patience of saints in the paintings of Old Masters, facing the onslaught of arrows; the cauldron of boiling oil; the spitting, scaly beast. *Come*, said the glittering figure of the matador mutely, flaring the cape. *Come, please.* The bull whirled in bewilderment, then came galloping back. The man bowed his head and folded the cape around his body humbly, eyes downcast. He seemed to measure his life in millimeters. The world narrowed. The tempo increased.

Yey! Yey! roared the *aficionados. Very good!* The bullring that rose around him was a giant anemone, quivering with people and their tendrils of emotion. Slowly, the wild applause died down; people leaned forward expectantly.

Torero! came a solitary, hoarse cry.

Trumpets again. The glittering *picadores* retrieved their spears and ambled in and out on their horses. The bull charged and rammed against the padded horse. The public began whistling. Roberto jogged over and lifted his hand for the *picador* to stop. The bull trotted off, then charged again, this time lifting the entire horse up in the air for a split second. Would it tip the horse? No. Roberto signaled impatiently for an end to the pics. Enough.

The *picadores* trotted out.

In the last act, there was no one left, except Roberto and the bull—paired from time immemorial in the bullring, he thought, like two dice tossing in a roulette wheel. He stepped onto the sand with the red cape and the sword. Underlying his hot, wet concentration came a deep, cool undercurrent of ennui. *Another day at the office*, he thought ironically, fixing the cloth to the tip of his sword to spread the cape. He was annoyed with not cutting an ear in the earlier *faena*. What was it, his youth? The fact that he wasn't descended from a famous matador father? That he wasn't born in Andalucía? That he hadn't died for them?

What does it take, really?

With a flourish Roberto lifted his hat and tossed it nonchalantly behind him. From the public's applause and shouts, he knew without looking that it had rolled and landed the right side up. That meant good luck. He was the first matador that evening to do that. He had to resort to circus tricks now, he thought. He had to improve on perfection.

The bull stared at him, panting. Blood glittered down the side of its hide, its color hidden by the midnight black of its fur. Its energy was sapped. The great head was hanging low from the pics; the bull drooled a little. Roberto thought about the repertoire of moves and wondered whether there was time to execute them all before he had to decide on the kill. He only had ten minutes. Sometimes it felt like the longest ten minutes of his life; other times it was over in one breath. He watched the animal, calculating furiously. He caped it once, twice, studying its reaction.

Outside, firecrackers continued to boom. They no longer sounded like scattered gunfire. They now sounded like someone was shoving grand pianos out of a top floor window. An ambulance siren tore busily across the night, so loud that it sounded like it was inside the ring. Did a member of the audience have a heart attack?

It was not fair, thought Roberto. Tiger Woods did not have to deal with this shit on the golf course. Golf courses were silent. He tried to focus. Sweat trickled down his back.

They say that when you're in the ring, life's problems melt away, and all you focus on is the bull. The bull looms large. Over one thousand pounds of hot animal flesh, and two crescent horns mounted on a massive head supported by a thick neck, would—as the lore goes—replace everything else in your thoughts.

Maybe.

Roberto drew and caped the bull beautifully; then fixed it in the middle of the ring to the crowd's applause. He tapped it on the nose with his sword, smiling, and lowered his face dangerously close to the animal as tourists' flash-bulbs went off in amusement. He could feel the bull exhaling hot air against his face. It still surprised him sometimes, the amount of air those lungs contained, the clean smell of its breath, in contrast to the smell of sweat and cigarette smoke in the ring. In Roberto's mind, the air inside the bull was still crisp and green—the air from six years of living in moist green hills away from the cities.

This bull, he noticed, favored his right horn. All was going according to plan, and as the bull charged, Roberto was able to spin him around, closer and closer, with the hypnotic grace of a snake charmer. The crowd, mesmerized, dutifully murmured *Olé* each time the bull passed through the cape. The certain, brave rhythm of a good set of passes began.

They say that a good matador winds the bull around him like a belt; that the exotic passes by the matador are akin to foreplay; that the last act—the *suerte de matar*—is like an exquisite act of copulation. They say that matadors in the old days would boast of ejaculating at the climax of the kill.

Roberto knew that he would never be a good matador, because he never knew what they were going on about.

"To me it's like a sport," he had said once to Alex in an email. "It's boxing. To say that I am a matador so that I can have sex with the bull is like saying Muhammad Ali became a boxer so that he could have sex with all the boxers he ever fought with. But don't quote me."

Alex followed the action through the zoom lens of her camera.

They say that the best thing a woman can do for a matador is to be beautiful and watch him from outside the bullring. They say that since time immemorial, matadors —like the knights of old—have performed dangerous stunts to satisfy bewitching women who goad them on from the audience.

Alex thought wryly that if Roberto had seen her—she wasn't sure—she probably wasn't beautiful or bewitching enough, because by her standards there was nothing particularly remarkable about his work that evening. But perhaps the best news in the bullfight was no news.

She couldn't get tickets to the Fallas fight by the time she decided to come see Roberto perform. She had noticed that women photographers were the only females that were allowed to walk about near the ring and mingle freely with the *toreros*. She decided to pose as an American university sports photographer simply by faking an ID, wearing her UT track team uniform with the school logo, and pretending not to speak Spanish. A local press photographer contact, a friend of a friend of a friend of Dr Molina's from San Martín, helped get her in. Nicky had loaned Alex her very expensive Nikon D3 camera with an extremely threatening and oversized zoom lens. The result of two weeks of intensive plotting was a free front-row seat of the action. Up close, the polarities of the bullfight were clear. Roberto was much more handsome. The bull was much uglier. And it was *loud*. She snapped away, half amused, wondering how her amateur pictures would turn out.

"Come on, Rob," muttered Alex, looking at her watch. He was taking too long, trying to impress the audience, trying to get that ear. What was he doing? "Twelve megapixels are waiting for something more than your ass in glittery tights."

She looked up suddenly as the crowd screamed. Roberto was lying face down in the dust. The bull pinned him down firmly with its massive black head, pushing for all it was worth. Its enormous, dark eyes were obstinate and unseeing. The other men in his team hurried over and closed round the bull with their fuchsia capes flapping at it like giant butterflies, hoping to distract it. Roberto lay still as a statue, arms raised to protect his face. Finally, the bull lifted its head away from him and charged at the other men. The *banderilleros* ran behind the protective barrier. His father and manager scurried into the ring to lift Roberto back to safety. The bull's horns, now red with human blood, thudded dully against the wood, over and over again, as it tried to get at the men behind the barrier. The crowd hooted and roared in apprehension with each thud.

"What happened?" cried Alex to the photographer next to her.

"He wanted to try a fancy move and exposed his whole body," he said, still photographing opportunistically, trying to zoom into a shot of the wound. "It looked at him first, before looking at the cape. Even I saw that. He took his chances. Big mistake."

She ran over, beating the other men to reach him.

"Rob!"

His face was pale and his eyes were closed. "Hi Alex. I saw you."

"What's wrong?" She couldn't get close to him, he was surrounded by too many men who looked at her curiously. "Did it get you in the artery?"

"No. But the left leg's bad." He opened his eyes and told the doctor, "Tie it up."

"Am I the doctor or are you?" said the doctor grimly.

"You heard him!" roared Roberto's father. "This is the last bull, let's not waste time! The crowd's getting impatient! You can still save this act!"

Alex got to touch his fingers. They were slippery with blood and felt cold.

"Come on, come on," Roberto said hurriedly, standing up. "Shoes off. Tie it up. Tie it tight." He turned to his manager, "I'm so sorry. I was careless."

His manager checked his wounds. "What should we do?"

"I'm okay," sniffed Roberto, reaching for a cup of water. "I've got him figured out. He's a good bull. It's not his fault. I can finish him off. But after this, Dad, no more."

"What do you mean, *no more*?" cried his father angrily.

"I'm retiring."

"What!"

"I'll do this last one for you, for Mom. Didn't you always tell me to be a man? I'll be a man. I'll go out splendidly, even if it's unfair. I don't owe you anything now."

He reached out to pat Alex on her shoulder, leaving a bloodied handprint. "Good to see you."

"Are you sure?" said Alex.

"Bye."

"Talk to you later," she whispered.

He smiled and walked out slowly into the ring, the red cape folded under his arm, as if he was a man holding a raincoat about to get on the subway after work.

The goring didn't hit an artery, which would have killed him from blood loss, but the wound was deep, in the back of his knee. He tried very hard not to limp, not to show any stiffness. Once, only once, did he flex his leg a bit, but his face was expressionless. His hair was wet and tousled. He had shed his shoes, so his blood soaked directly into the sand.

Alex shivered. There was something pathetic about

watching a bloodied man face death without his hat or his shoes. She suddenly realized how provincial and polite the matador costume was, down to the fake, black necktie that cinched the white ruffles at the neck and the cheery little Christmas tree ornaments that dangled from the shoulders. It was grotesque in its artificial gaiety. If you had to send a man to battle to the death, she thought, at least give him some decent armor. Even a shin guard would have been more appropriate, not these ridiculous party clothes.

Olé. Olé. Olé. Olé!

The crowd was applauding wildly now, thick with admiration for the injured matador. *Torero!* they cried, as he raised his sword for their applause. *Valiente!*

How long could he do this? She hoped that he killed the bull quickly, yet he had a few more beautiful passes left in him. He stood absolutely still as the bull rushed past him. The wind from the bull's charge stirred his hair. Blood continued to soak into his stocking, turning it from fiesta pink to red.

They say that almost all matadors who die in the ring are killed by the bull who had already gored them before in the same fight. Bulls didn't give up once they made impact. Alex was familiar with that kind of tenacity with the animals on the ranch. A genteel cow would explode and charge repeatedly at a wooden fence if you removed her newborn calf. She would go at it until the entire structure was wrecked.

Alex watched the bull's expression carefully. There were details in the bull's head movements, in Roberto's arm movements, that were invisible to the layman. She noted how it charged.

Olé. Olé. Olé. Olé.

The crowd murmured in regular, slow beats, as if in a trance. The band came back on, striking up the merry *paso doble* which was slightly off-kilter with the menace on the sand. Alex bit her lip, at once entranced and sick with fear. How beautiful, the way the bull's tail curled round him. The front of Roberto's uniform was now completely smeared with blood from the dying animal. He twirled and clung on to the bull's back with his left arm. Once, the horns passed so close to his jacket that a golden piece was shorn off, to the delight of the crowd. A standing ovation. *Bravo! Muy bien!* Young men in motorcycle jackets and wraparound sunglasses stood up and clapped, raising their cigars in the air, saluting him furiously. Roberto attracted a younger crowd, now energized and defiant. They were upset with the president of the *plaza* for withholding the trophy. It was an insult to their generation, they thought. *Fuck Valencia!* they texted each other on their cellphones. *They don't know shit!*

Roberto made a particularly elegant pass, ran as the bull charged back at him, then stopped it dead in its tracks with a look. He tapped the bull with his sword, chastising the panting animal. Then he rested his hand on the bull's forehead and stared at it sternly. As the crowd clapped, he came back to the perimeter to exchange his sword for the killing sword. Alex had stopped breathing. It was his last chance to get a trophy if he could kill well. The kill was like the golf put. Everything rode on this one, final, little act, she thought. Everything. If he could put the ball in, he was home free tonight.

He winked at Alex when he drew near, then he was back out again. She noticed that the tourniquet they had tied around his leg had come loose. He bent quickly, removed it and threw it outside the perimeter of the ring in one swift move. Then he drew himself to his full height and aimed with the sword. He gave the cape one final tempting shake.

The bull looked up at him, then, distracted, contemplated the cape.

"No," said Alex, shaking her head. "He's not done yet."

Roberto relaxed himself, tossed his head back once, then stiffened again, looking down the length of the sword, his body straight as an arrow. Then he ran at the bull.

Screams.

He spun and fell down, but rolled, scrambled up quickly and ran as his men and the other matadors closed in on the enraged animal. It pranced about madly; the half-buried sword was flung off and bounced across the sand. There was no way Roberto would be awarded an ear now. The damage was irreparable. Then, worse. The bull charged erratically and brought down another man. With two men down, the bullring was in an uproar. The crowd was suddenly getting its money's worth.

Roberto was suddenly before her in a confusing mess of blood, bull, sweat and sequins.

"Are you okay?" she shouted.

"Kill him," he rasped, and thrust the red cape at her. "I'm done. You wanted it. You do it. *I trust you.*"

Nobody else heard. As he collapsed, his father and manager ran to catch him and the doctor started shouting.

Alex didn't see him fall, for she was already in the ring.

The producer in the Canal+ news trailer parked outside the bullring threw away his cigarette and sat up in his seat.

Everyone in the audience was now standing, hollering and whistling in rage at the intruder in the ring. Some men shook their fists, booing; others waved their seat cushions madly in protest. Camera flashes blinked in the night. Some tourists were appalled; others were hugging themselves with delight. A spectacle would be guaranteed, regardless of the success or failure of this amateur. Outside, the Fallas evening party had already started. Pink and green fireworks whistled like rockets into the night, blooming above the bullring, lighting up the underside of clouds in the night sky. Somewhere, the deep bass of a rock concert began to pound. The modern world declared its wrath on the bullring.

Alex ignored the ruckus. She walked round the ring calmly and picked up Roberto's sword. She kept her eyes on the animal. The beleaguered bull ambled restlessly around the ring, bloodied and dismayed. She had noticed that it favored a spot near the gate where it was first released. She also knew that if it made it back there, it would dig in and be even more dangerous. So she strode calmly across the ring and planted herself firmly between the bull and its safety.

"Who the hell's this chick?" asked the senior matador, impatient to restore order.

Roberto caught his arm. "She's trained. Let her."

"Get him in the infirmary," instructed Roberto's father.

"Don't go in there!" shouted Roberto to the security guards who were preparing to enter and arrest her. "If she fails, then go! Get your hands off me. I'm staying until the bull dies."

"*You'll* die!" hissed his father.

"But you always knew that," said Roberto, holding the wooden barrier desperately for support and blinking away tears of pain.

Alex shouted urgently at the bull. It went for her a bit too quickly and predictably, so she stood absolutely still and let it whirr past. She even got the cape to sweep beautifully over the bull's bucking head. Roberto had taught her how to do that properly, one rainy night under the massive arches of the Puente del Mar in Valencia.

A roar of approval went up in the crowd. All at once they realized that she was a trained bullfighter. A mild scattering of applause. The young punks in their Vespa leathers passed binoculars down their rows and shot videos on their camera phones. The security guards exchanged glances and hesitated.

He's only got one more trick left in him, Alex, thought Roberto, not daring to look. He slid the bracelet of charms off his wrist, clutched it in both hands, and prayed. *Don't push it. Leave while you're winning.*

He heard her shout again, firmly, more girlishly. He looked up. Again the bull charged, passed under her cape, stumbled and skidded forward on its knees. The darts on its back were weakening it. She was smart — she attempted only two passes, both beautiful. Time was running out. Roberto saw her stand tall and assume the killing position. People shushed each other fiercely; the giant sea anemone wavered, stilled and fell silent.

She raised her sword and lowered the cape. His hair stood on end. An audible murmur rippled through the crowd as everyone recognized her pose. She was attempting to kill the bull the old way — the dangerous way. Instead of running at the bull with the sword, she was standing still and urging the bull to charge at her and impale itself on her sword. It was the *recibiendo* — something her grandfather was famous for.

He wanted very much to avert his eyes, but couldn't.

The bull moved forward, she struck and buried the sword. It was over in a trice. Before Roberto blacked out he noted with satisfaction that Alex was still standing. It was the bull that fell. That was all he needed to see.

The entire bullring burst into riotous clamor. Seventeen thousand loud verbal opinions rang out in the night, startling the long line of cab drivers waiting sleepily outside.

"Just my luck to be on duty tonight," said a cab driver to another, thumping the side of the cab and walking back to his. "I'll tune in the radio and see what I missed."

"Catch it on the Internet!" shouted his friend.

"Don't have a computer."

ACT TWO

The Act of the Colorful Darts

SAN FRANCISCO, THOUGHT ROBERTO humorlessly, had sounded warm. After all, it was a Spanish name, the name of a saint from Italy, another warm place he had never been to. There were cities called San Francisco all over the Spanish-speaking world. He chose it because he thought he would feel less homesick that way. He blamed his own provincialism. For some reason, before he arrived, the words "San Francisco" made him think of a Mediterranean city staggering into the ocean, bathed in strong, yellow light—light that was hard, heavy, and warm, light that tumbled down clinking like coins minted from the spoils of the Gold Rush.

If Spain was primary colors, San Francisco was pastels. He had been ripped off. San Francisco, it turned out, was the palest, coldest, and dampest Spanish word he had ever known.

It was three months after the Fallas bullfight in Valencia.

"Sorry I'm late," she laughed, bending to kiss his cheek in greeting. "Couldn't find parking."

"I took the BART."

"What's that?"

"It's the metro. That's what it is called in San Francisco." Roberto rose and offered to buy her an espresso. "What are you having? I'll get it. And don't touch my books."

He returned with her coffee.

"This is so boring," she said, flipping a page. "This is animation? It's all computer stuff."

"I just started. It'll get better."

"Can you read English now?"

"Are you kidding? I just look at the pictures. You don't need English to go to my art school. It's mostly for international students. All you need to show is that you can pay."

"So you can draw?" She reached for another textbook.

"Can't everybody?"

"I can't. Hey where are we? There are a lot of Mexicans around here. Do you live here?"

"No, I live near the school downtown. I just discovered this café. Isn't it cool? Everybody here speaks Spanish. But nobody from Spain, of course."

Alex grinned suddenly and said in English, "How's English classes?"

"Progress is slow," he replied, still in Spanish.

"Say something."

Roberto sighed. "No."

"Come on."

"I'm not ready."

"You'll never learn if you don't say anything."

"Not in front of you." He flushed.

"Oh, come on, Rob, I have seen your ass kicked by a bull in front of thousands of people *and* on television, and you're now suddenly shy about speaking English?"

"Sssh. You'll blow my cover."

"Who are you afraid of? Nobody knows you here."

"I received a letter from PETA. But they seem to leave the girl matadors alone. You confuse them."

He grabbed his books back from her and put them away in his bag. "So why are you in San Francisco, anyway? Don't you have school?"

"I graduated last month! I'm totally done with college."

"Congratulations," he said enviously.

"My bullfighting school's in San Diego. I flew here to see you, then I'm driving down there. You wanna come? I'm terrified of the highways in California, so I've planned a scenic route on the smaller roads. I'm driving along El Camino Real all the way from San Francisco to San Diego. Look." She unfolded a map. "This is the nineteenth century route that connected the original twenty-one Spanish missions in California. I studied it in my architecture class."

"*El Camino Real*?" he repeated the words, tasting them.

"That's right, you guys used to *own* this road, man." She explained its history. He became mildly interested.

"How long would that take?" Roberto studied the state map.

"A few days. Depending on whether I want to stop and sightsee."

"I can't. I have to study."

"Isn't it summer holidays?" She folded the map.

"I'm taking a summer course, too. Otherwise I'll never catch up."

"Suit yourself. How's your mother?"

"Same as always. In and out of hospitals. Now that my dad doesn't have me around, he's stuck with caring for her. Everyone expects him to. It's about time. He was getting too ahead of himself with the lifestyle my career provided him." He looked around him, then dropped his voice in a conspiratorial whisper. "My mom still has your grandfather's swords. When are you going to get them?"

"When I next go to Spain." Alex laughed. "You know, during that Fallas bullfight, I wished I had Pedro's sword in hand when I killed your bull. I always had this fantasy. That I would be in Las Ventas, in Madrid, dressed in Grandpa's suit of lights, wielding his sword. Instead it was in Valencia, using your sword, and just getting two minutes with a bull that you had already pretty much done in."

"Sorry. But it was worth it," Roberto sketched on a napkin absently. "Think of the news coverage. Thousands of teenage girls all over the Spanish-speaking world are watching bullfights and supporting women matadors. There's even talk of American corporate sponsorship."

"Oh yeah? Tell them to send money my way. I need backers." Alex grinned. "You know what really has to happen in order for my career to take off?"

"What?"

"Draw a graphic novel of my life."

"Don't be ridiculous."

"Make the graphic novel, then it'll be turned into a Hollywood movie, then the world will change forever and I'll break in."

"Is that how Americans effect social change?"

"Totally." Alex grabbed the napkin he was sketching on and turned it over. "That's me? You have to make me a blond for the book to sell in Spain."

He smiled and put the pen away. "Do you know I heard the old macho clubs are furious with you? They didn't want bullfighting to be viewed as a kind of a sport, they wanted it to be a male way of life. A sport meant like the Olympics — open to all nationalities and to men and women. But the old way of doing things is dead. You have killed them, you terrible *Americana*."

Alex started giggling helplessly into her cup.

"What?"

"All through senior year, the university really loved that

video clip of me in the bullfight. I was wearing the UT athletic department T-shirt and sweatpants. That logo— of our orange longhorn cow—travelled the world. People thought I came from a special American bullfighting club called 'Ut'."

Roberto, she decided, still maintained a strange, continental politeness with her, so she wasn't going to also mention that Nicky's boyfriend had confirmed, in senior year, that that particular clip was voted favorite jerk-off video by the fraternities on campus. She had to delist herself from Facebook as a result.

Roberto asked, "It wasn't the uniform of your bullfighting school?"

"No!"

"Why were you wearing it?"

"I had to disguise myself as a sports press photographer to get near you. Borrowed my roommate's camera."

"You never explained it properly," Roberto smiled. "I get it now. So, when are you going to do your *alternativa* and graduate to matador?"

"I have a long way to go. Still looking at sponsorship offers, thinking about deferring enrollment to grad school, and dealing with my godparents. No guesses what they would rather see me do. I'm giving myself this summer to make up my mind if I should go on."

Someone asked if the seat beside them was taken. Roberto moved his bag reluctantly and they made room for the newcomers. The café was filling up.

"That's a lot of big life decisions to make."

"Yeah, I'll need a lot of help thinking it over."

"What does your family think?"

"Grandma's washed her hands of this, as you can imagine. Shelly and Tomas said they had only agreed to baby sit me till I turned twenty-one. They're no help." Alex leaned forward as the couple beside them chatted loudly.

"I need to talk it over with someone who is preferably not biased towards the *corrida*."

"Hm."

"Someone who has experience, but the wisdom to assess the *corrida* from a distance."

Roberto kept still under her stare, and then scratched the side of his nose self-consciously.

"Actually," said Alex briskly. "I just need someone to share driving duties with. It's a long drive down to San Diego and it would suck driving it alone."

"All right, all right! I'll come. As long as you don't talk about bullfights all the way."

"You know you want to."

"No, honestly, I don't."

They got up, still arguing, and stepped out onto the busy street in the Mission district of San Francisco. A grubby musician played syncopated rhythms on upturned plastic buckets. The burglar alarm of a shuttered storefront went off deafeningly. They had to shout to be heard.

"I still want to make it to Madrid and fight in that bull-ring!" said Alex, waving him towards her car. "But I can't find a matador to sponsor my graduation fight! Get in!"

"If you're good enough, I might come out of retirement and be your sponsor!" he shouted back above the din. "But don't quote me!"

"It's a deal."

"You have to be *good enough*," he said quietly in the car.

"Define *good enough.*"

"Like, better than El Rivera," said Roberto finally.

"He Man? That wanker? No!"

"Or, whoever is the reigning champion at the time."

"As long as they're not wankers," said Alex, starting the engine.

"You should strive to be better than wankers. In fact, I won't sponsor you unless you promise to defeat one of those guys." Roberto looked out of the window quickly, suppressing a smile. Her car smelled like lemon cake. He realized, all of a sudden, that he had missed her a lot in the past year, even though they talked practically every day on the Internet. He tried to imagine what it would be like to spend a week with her in person.

"Should I change my name?" she asked suddenly.

"What's wrong with Alejandra Herrera? Aren't you doing this for the family name?"

"Screw that. Should I be *El*—something? You know, like Malcolm X. I can be El X." She brightened, slapping the steering wheel. "Hey, if you say it quickly, it sounds like Alex! That's so cool."

"It sounds awful!"

When she dropped him off at his apartment building, he hurried back and leaned into the window. "Alex?"

"What?"

"I just realized, if we're leaving on your trip tomorrow —I never got round to obtaining a driver's permit here. I can't drive," he said desperately. "That's why I take the metro everywhere."

"Roberto de la Torre, if you seriously think I was asking you to come along because I wanted you to *drive my car*, you must be crazy. You're a terrible driver. See you tomorrow morning at eight o'clock sharp."

He squinted against the sunlight. "Really?"

"Yeah. Really."

"Bye."

"Talk to you later."

"So, where are you going?"

It was Tom, one of the few Americans in his drawing class. They were at Starbucks in downtown San Francisco.

Roberto was in a panic, as he usually was when someone addressed him in English. "I am going to San Diego."

It was nearly eight o'clock in the morning. Roberto had a backpack and a duffle bag. He was looking out into the street as the office workers began their daily march out of the BART station.

"Sweet. Who with?"

He tried to unscramble the circuits in his brain. "A friend," he managed to say.

"Girlfriend?"

"She's a girl."

Tom looked at him approvingly. "She pretty?"

"She's okay."

"From Spain?"

"No." He was incapable of conjugating a longer explanation in English.

"From around here?"

"No. Texas."

"I *love* Texas chicks."

Roberto was curious. Texas meant little to him. "Really?"

"So, she your girlfriend?" asked Tom again.

"No."

"But you're on a road trip with her?"

"She asked me."

"Man," chuckled Tom. "You are going to score."

"Pardon?"

"Score, score!" Tom kicked at an imaginary ball.

Why do they always want to talk to him about soccer? He decided not to say anything and took his coffee out onto the street.

He did wonder what Alex had in mind. She was vague about the length of the road trip. It could be anything from two days to two weeks. He had never travelled with a woman before whom he wasn't dating. He always thought of the Herreras as distant relatives. When Alex first contacted him in Spain, he humored her as one would a cousin. He did wonder if they were going to book two separate rooms in every hotel they would be overnight at. It wasn't so much the money he minded, but a kind of glaring awkwardness that gnawed at him. Alex Herrera was family. At least, that was what his mother Cristina thought. Cristina was close to Alex's grandmother, who was well-respected in San Martín. Alex, the curious, sometimes intoxicatingly difficult American distant cousin (even if she wasn't really one), had to be handled carefully.

He spotted her car in the traffic and waved. They had become such good friends over the Internet, had exchanged so many SMSs late into the night, had shown each other the exact and intimate contours of their thoughts in the last year, and yet, at the end of the day, certain barriers can never truly be overcome. In the era of the Internet and jet travel, Roberto thought it strangely exciting that, at least on the subject of checking into hotel rooms with a member of the opposite sex, he felt no more sure of himself than a man would have been a hundred years ago.

"What's that?" asked Alex, as they slowed down and waited to cross Hoover Dam.

He remembered being really bored on road trips when he was a *novillero*. "I'm drawing this. This is beautiful."

His father had a minivan and a driver who drove him and the rest of his bullfighting team around to the bullfights from city to city. Roberto hated those long drives. He used to play handheld video games during the drive. But he hadn't the time to go shop for a handheld videogame for the road trip with Alex. He decided to bring his art books and sketchbooks and pencils. He'd practice drawing in the car.

"I'll drive slowly past the dam so you get the whole thing," said Alex.

"Thanks."

They crawled along the tall edge of the dam while tourists milled and took pictures in the sunshine.

"Isn't this a beautiful country? This is still part of the highway, this is the money shot, look!" She lowered the window. "So many people died in the thirties to build this dam. I've always thought their bodies were in there, in the concrete." She took out her camera phone and snapped some pictures. Then she snapped some pictures of Roberto bent over his sketchbook. "God, if you told me one year ago I would be driving across Hoover Dam with Roberto de la Torre the matador, and he would be sketching it, I would have said you were crazy."

"You are not making my retirement easier by saying things like that constantly," said Roberto, looking out the window.

"You're too young to be a retired matador."

"I am a retired matador."

"If you say it often enough you might persuade someone to believe it."

Alex pulled the car out of the throng of tourists and hit the highway again. For a long time they didn't speak.

Finally she said, "Know what I think?"

"What?"

"I think it would have been fun if I grew up in San Martín. You know, if Sofia hadn't sent my dad away, if I was born in San Martín and went to school there—"

"Believe me," he rolled his eyes, "you do not want to go to the schools in San Martín."

"We could have been great friends. We would have

grown up together. We could have had a lot of fun. I bet your family wouldn't have moved away if I lived next door."

"I don't think I played with any girls when I was a kid."

She darted him a look. "So it was just you and your Atari, huh?"

"Nintendo."

"Oh yeah? What was your favorite game?"

"*Mario Kart*."

"Oh, that was the best." Alex looked impatient as she tailgated a large container truck and tried to pass. "You know, it's cool that we grew up playing the same stuff. You're not some alien after all."

"Is that what you think the Spanish branch of your relatives are? Aliens?"

"I don't know. Every time I go back to San Martín it's like a time warp."

"Time warp!"

"Hey, turn that up, I like this song." She finally passed the truck and accelerated cheerfully.

"I like this song too." He reached for the volume knob.

"You like music?"

"The bullfights are all about the music."

"Yeah, but Roberto de la Torre likes The Bangles?" she howled incredulously.

"Just this song. I was only five. I wasn't very sophisticated."

Alex finished rummaging in her bag with one hand and flung her iPod at him. "I have the whole album in here. Plug it in."

"How?"

"Why are you so hopeless? See that thing on the floor? Put it in the tape deck. Now, connect it to the iPod. Do you know how to use an iPod?"

"I *have* one."

"You do? In Spain?"

"Would you just—"

"Okay, okay!"

Roberto called his mother from the motel room. He didn't mention he was on a road trip with Alex.

"How's the food?" she asked.

"Still bad."

"Do you regret?"

"No."

"How can you move to another country when you don't even speak the language? Nobody believes me when I tell them. I lie awake at night worrying about you. What if you get lost?"

"I have GPS on my phone. Alex taught me how to use it."

"You know what I mean. What if you get mugged?"

"Mom," said Roberto, fighting down a sudden wave of incredulousness. "You let me fight bulls my whole life. This is not half as dangerous."

"But why do you have to go so far away? You could have gone to France."

"Nobody goes to France to study animation."

"Just because you like playing video games doesn't mean you have to make them!"

Roberto looked out the motel room window. There was a small, token "pool" outside with dirty white plastic chairs. A toddler trotted along the edge of it, his fat arms encased in inflatable floats. His overweight mother, her skin lobster pink from the sun, followed him dutifully. "Do you remember the time I was badly gored in Valencia? When I told Alex to go into the ring and kill the bull?"

"Yes, of course."

"It was during Fallas. I was in hospital. They had just

finished operating on me. They had put me to sleep, but despite the medicines I was woken up by fireworks at two in the morning. The sky rocked with the sound of their thunder for hours. It was as if a great hand reached into my soul and wrung it. It was so surreal. It felt tragic and happy at the same time. Although it felt like a warzone, with bombs raining from the sky, I knew it was Fallas, after all. I could hear young people singing in the streets. I couldn't sleep. I tried to think of what I really wanted to do with my life. I realized I wasn't good at anything, that there was nothing that I was really interested in. It was too late for me to try to get into high school. Going to the other side of the world was the only way I could start over. This, this art school, was the only thing I could think of. I want to try to learn something real. I want to be a student, with other people my age, doing something normal, in a place where nobody knows anything about bullfighting, where nobody would even have heard of my name. I worked so hard all my life. Can you just let me try something on my own, just once?"

"Of course, Roberto," said Cristina, moved. She had never heard her son speak this way. It hinted of an interior life that she never knew he had.

They were off the highway in Barstow, California.

Roberto enjoyed the shabby poetry of an American motel room.

"We've been to so many kinds now," he exclaimed, when she opened her door. "They're all the same. They're just different brands. Best Western. Four Points. La Quinta." He was fascinated by the posters of arbitrary art in her room in their plastic golden frames. They were vague prints of fruit, of flowers. He took out his camera phone and snapped at them. "I've never seen art that is so completely uninteresting. It's mind-blowing."

Alex was tired and bored with the road trip. Travelling on El Camino Real, off the highways, was taking longer than she thought. And not all of it was interesting. Brief spurts of discovery punctuated long stretches of languor on the road, during which absolutely nothing happened. Fortunately it was all still new for Roberto. He enjoyed seeing America that way. She said, "Don't you have motels in Spain?"

"Yes, but they're different. I used to stay in them when I first started out, but my father got us better hotels when I became a matador. This trip brings back my *novillero* memories." He went into her bathroom. "Your layout's different. Mine's better. I've got *two* sinks."

"How are Spain motels different?" She went back to watching ESPN.

"We don't usually have these. They fascinate me." He opened up the plastic coffee maker and peered inside, wincing at what he saw. He disassembled the coffee pot. "The coffee's terrible."

"I like the London motels better. They give you biscuits in the room."

"I've never been to London," said Roberto.

"What! It's next door to Spain!"

"I've been to Ecuador, Peru, Mexico, Colombia, and France. And Portugal."

She squealed with laughter.

"What's so funny?"

"All bullfighting countries!"

"I already told you, I don't get to travel for fun. I equate travel with work and misery. And strange and horrible food."

When she next looked up, he had perched in the

antechamber outside her bathroom where the coffee machine was, sketching the things on the sink.

"You should see the world, Rob."

"It's hard enough being in America."

"Why?"

"I'll get over it, I suppose, but it's still a bit of a shock being in California."

Alex flicked the channel again, then said, "Name the three things in California that shock Roberto de la Torre."

"The food. I can't eat a thing. I didn't expect that."

"What's wrong with San Francisco food? They're supposed to be known for their food."

"My stomach ties up in knots when I see American food. I subsist on toast and olive oil."

"Can't you cook?"

"I notice the female foreign students do. I can't. I'd rather just not eat."

"Typical. What else?"

"My name. People can't believe it when I say it."

"Because you're the matador?"

"No, not that. Nobody knows about bullfighting in San Francisco. No, it's the last name. And the first. The whole thing. It's too much for the students and teachers to handle. Something that is so soft in Spain can be so loud here."

"There aren't any Spanish students?"

"A few, but their parents are professor or artist types. I cringe when they ask me what my father does for a living." Before becoming Roberto's handler, Roberto's father was a *banderillero*, a bullfighter who leapt and pierced darts in the bull for a living.

"So, lie."

"I do."

"And what do you say?"

"Depends on who's asking."

"Like, if it's a chick you'd have a different answer?"

Roberto looked up from his sketchpad and grinned. "And the other Spanish-speaking students, their names are just normal. Muñoz, Garçia, Rodriguez. Nothing like De la Torre. You see this sneer on their face when you say it. Someone asked me if I was a model."

"So, say yes," said Alex airily, toggling through the channels listlessly. "Say yes, you're a Calvin Klein model, and they'll let you in the clubs for free."

"Alejandra, don't be ridiculous."

"Robert Tower. That's your name. Just say you are Robert Tower."

"It sounds like I sell insurance." He flipped a page in the sketchbook and began drawing Alex lying on the bed watching a tennis match. "Someone asked if I was a soccer player. Apparently there is a soccer player from Spain with a similar name, so I just said yes."

"Can you play soccer?"

"Yes, but I hate soccer."

"Why?"

"It's not art."

"It's a sport, dude."

"It looks so dull. And I hate the people who go to soccer games."

"And what's a third thing that you can't stand about California?"

"The weather."

"The *weather!*" chortled Alex. "People in America come to California for the weather!"

"Not to San Francisco."

"Why? Too foggy?"

"It's not the fog. It's the clouds. It's not like Spain. San Francisco feels very low, almost sea level, and permanently under a cloudbank. The fog rolls in at night, but even in the day, compared to Spain, the air is heavy and grey, even in the summer. When I was little, I crawled into an old refrigerator. The air was grey and damp and cold. There was a weak yellow light inside. That's exactly what being in San Francisco is like."

"Geez. That sucks, Rob. You should have enrolled in art school in Austin."

"It's hard to pick a school abroad when you don't know anything beforehand. And you did say San Francisco was all right when I applied. You didn't think I would fit in in Austin."

"Are you regretting coming to America?"

"I'll see how long I can stick it out." He sat on the empty twin bed beside hers and turned a page in his sketchbook. "Where are we going tomorrow?"

She began telling him about the various Las Vegas casinos that they should check out.

"Are you going to gamble?" he asked curiously.

"No, are you?"

"Well, it would seem that's the point of being in a casino."

"You gamble, I'll watch."

Rearranging the pillows behind his back in the other bed, he settled down, turned a page and began a new sketch. Alex pretended to watch television but was straining to see what he was drawing.

"I could show it to you," he said, without looking up.

"You seem happy with this new drawing thing."

"I am happy. Especially since we have no video games in the motel and there is nothing to do in the car when you're driving. I have discovered that I am happy when I draw. I have to turn in a final art project before I graduate next year. It could be this road trip."

When he next looked up, Alex was curled up on the floral bedspread, sound asleep. He turned a page, made a study of her sleeping form, then put his pencil behind his ear, closed the sketchbook, turned the television off and let himself quietly out of the room.

❀

AlexH1988: *You awake?*

RobT1988: "Yes."

So, you know how when you come out to the bullring before a fight, all the women fans outside the gate go crazy and they grab you and kiss you?

"It's 3 a.m. Why bring this up now?" He almost wanted to add how utterly ridiculous it was for them to be having an SMS conversation when she was just next door in the motel. He wondered if he should just go to her room to talk. Or telephone.

Do you kiss them back?

"No."

Just curious. Why not?

"Because I'm about to go into the bullring, and I'm nervous, and I'm not in the mood."

Oh. So, when I become a matador, when I show up at the bullring, are the men gonna grab me and kiss me the same way?

"That is a very good question for which I don't have an answer."

I think it would be cool. I mean, it might be kinda gross, you know, because of H1N1. But if I get mobbed in the same way, and all these cute guys scream and hug and kiss me, I could get used to it.

"If you are famous enough, they might even faint for you."

Faint???

"I had women fainting for me. At least, that's what the press said. I never saw any fainting."

I want to be famous so that cute guys are fainting at the sight of me. That would really be the apogee of woman matador achievement.

"So work hard."

I want to email one of the girl novilleros and ask them if guys kiss them.

"I'm sure that can be arranged. How else may I help you tonight?"

That's all. Thanks. Goodnight.

"Goodnight."

The coins toppling out of the slot machines made a deafening noise. It went on for so long that Alex finally came over for a look.

"Good going, Rob," she said, as a waitress came over with a bag for Roberto to fill up. "There's my matador training fund, right there."

He was listening to The Human League on her iPod. He removed the earphones. "How much do you think this is?"

"A few hundred dollars. Let's go change it. God, it's heavy."

"All I did was put in one quarter." He bent and picked up the stray coins on the floor.

"What else do you play? Can you play blackjack?"

"Yes."

They stood in line at the cashier while Alex plotted Rob's gambling future.

"There have been matadors who retired to become artists," said Roberto over dinner. They couldn't decide where to eat, and ended up in a Polynesian Chinese restaurant for tourists. It was full of kitschy lanterns and silk paintings of carp.

"Yeah?"

He named a few. "So how much did we make tonight?"

"Almost nine thousand dollars."

He calculated that in Euros. "That's pretty good."

"Let's go to the bank tomorrow and put that in your bank account. I don't want to be robbed on the road."

"I'll split it with you."

"Really?"

"It's your matador training fund."

"That's very generous of you, Rob."

"I still haven't figured out American money, so it's no skin off my back. Just help me out when I become a starving artist."

The food arrived. Roberto wouldn't eat.

"Try it," said Alex.

"But what *is* that?"

"It's either this or Denny's next door."

Reluctantly, he put down his pencil and picked up his fork.

Alex looked over at his sketch. "You're pretty good at drawing."

"Thanks."

"Are you learning that in art class?"

"Yes."

"Do you get to draw nudes?"

"Sometimes."

"Cool. Men or women?"

"Always women, for some reason."

"So unfair."

"Not to me."

A huge punch bowl arrived. Alex had ordered it. It had five paper umbrellas stuck on top.

"Hey, honey, can you take the umbrellas out for me?" said the waitress to Rob, winking. Alex thought she had a thing going for him ever since they came into the restaurant. He pulled them out of the drink, fascinated.

"Stand back," said the waitress, holding out a plastic lighter.

She flambéed the drink dramatically.

"God," said Roberto, wincing and reaching for water. "It tastes like gasoline. To think when you came to Spain last year, I took care to show you the good stuff."

"This is the good stuff. Don't you want to fit in as an American college student? Every student needs to be familiar with the Scorpion Bowl. So, what are you going to do when you finish your art degree?"

"I don't know. It seems a long way away. What about you? You've graduated."

"I don't know. I have to start business school next August. Between now and then, I'll train for as long as I can afford in San Diego, then get a job back in Austin. I'll live with Tomas and Shelly to save money, then go to Spain again. With my matador training fund."

"When are you thinking of going to Spain?"

"Spring, maybe. You coming?"

"Alex, I'm enrolled at school. I can't keep taking time off to be with you."

"You're coming," she said.

"No, I'm not."

"You're going to be my manager."

"No, I'm not."

"I need a manager."

"You can hire one."

"Who would work with me?"

"I'll recommend someone."

Alex said resolutely, "But I want you."

"No. I'm done with bullfighting."

"I'm not asking you to fight, I'm asking you to help me fight."

"I have school."

"You're so lame!"

"Was that the whole point of this road trip?" he asked suddenly. "Suck me into your matador plans?"

"Yes. Of course! That's why you came!"

He said nothing for a long time. He looked at the young couple chatting at the next table. "Why can't we be normal."

"Because we're not."

"Look, I just want to have a normal life."

"What, like have an office job? Rob, so many people can't do what you do. I can't do what you do. Do you know what I do every night on this road trip when I go to my room? I watch video clips of your past *faenas*. I've analyzed them to bits. You're really, really good. Nobody comes close."

"Then why was I performing so badly last year?"

"Because your heart wasn't in it. Because you were mad at your dad. But if you truly believed in it, Rob, you would be truly great. Everybody knows it except you."

"You're my manager now?"

She folded her arms, perplexed. "You can't run away from a gift."

"It's not a gift. It's just something I was made to do, because I was too young to know better. I did it, it's done. It's over. I don't ever want to go near another bull for the rest of my life. Whenever I hear any news or get any emails from people in that world, it sounds completely alien to me now. It just kills me that you're getting into something just as I am getting out of it. I can't bear to watch you go through all this, because I know exactly how it must feel. They'll rip you to shreds, Alex, sponsor or no sponsor.

You'll last one or two fights, as a novelty, before they take you down."

"One fight. In Madrid. That's all I want."

"But why?"

"For Grandpa. For Dad. For Mom. For myself, then I'm done. Then I'll go to business school. I'll interview, get a job on Wall Street, get married, quit my job, have kids, push a stroller around Whole Foods. Happy?" There were tears in her eyes.

The waitress, of course, had to interrupt. "Now," she said brassily, "who's ready for dessert?"

Alex tossed around in bed. She touched her phone and the dark room lit up with its soft, blue moonglow.

AlexH1988: "Hi." She waited, smiling a little. Maybe he had fallen asleep.

RobT1988: *Hi.*

"You still awake?"

I'm listening to your iPod.

"So that's where it is! Don't you have one?"

I do, but I can't listen to it anymore.

"Why not?"

All my playlists consist of music I used to listen to before bull-fights. To calm me down. I can't listen to that music again, I associate it with that time. My adrenalin level would go up for no reason.

"That sucks. You need to build a completely new library."

I will.

Roberto later said that it was on that road trip that Alex

first began sowing the seeds. "She was relentless," he said. "It was something she wanted ever since she was a kid. She wasn't going to stop."

"I just thought if I bugged him and bugged him, he would agree," said Alex, smirking. "I mean, who else was I going to bug? He was the only professional matador I knew."

"I had to defer spring semester and go back to Spain with her," added Roberto. "I never finished art school in San Francisco—

"—but you never liked it anyway, it was *cold*—"

"There's no question about it. She ruined my life."

Those who knew Roberto and Alex knew better. They said if you had a racehorse who had potential, but who refused to race, there was only one cure. You put it on a racetrack with another racehorse. If you race them side by side, the stubborn one would pick up speed, and might even win.

Alex needed Roberto. She was always brutally honest about it. But it was only later that Roberto realized he needed Alex.

Silvio slid a bolt of crimson silk back into its place on the shelf.

"Shall I cash-out the register?" asked his assistant.

"No, I'll do it tonight. Why don't you go ahead."

"You sure?"

"But don't shut up the storefront. I've got a special guest coming in tonight for a fitting."

"You don't need me around?" His assistant was surprised.

"No, you go. Go on. *Go.*"

The young man wiped the glass counter clean and put

away the chalks and receipts. It began to drizzle. As he stood outside the store squinting in the rain, a taxi pulled up and a couple got out. The young man lit a damp cigarette and began walking down the street, then stopped and looked back suddenly in surprise.

But the couple had disappeared into Silvio's tailor shop.

❀

"I knew it!" cried Silvio. "I knew you'd come back! Are you opening in Valencia? At last! At last!" He glanced admiringly at the young woman in the back of the shop and gave an approving thumbs-up to the man before disappearing quickly into a doorway behind the counter.

Roberto leaned back, smiling, his elbows against a glass counter. "What are you doing?"

"I've got your measurements all ready! Come on in!"

"Silvio?" called Roberto.

The old tailor hummed happily. "Julio thought you'd use him! He thought if you ever came out of retirement, you'd try him for your *traje*. I said, forget it, old boy! He's from San Martín, there is only one tailor for *toreros* in San Martín, that's me. He's never going to get his suits from Madrid! He's a loyal boy!"

"Silvio," drawled Roberto, smiling to himself, beckoning to the woman.

"What?" The tailor's head popped out of the doorway, his measuring tape already slung around his neck, like a doctor's stethoscope. He loved doing what he did for a living; he looked professional and ready.

"I'll like you to meet Alejandra Herrera, granddaughter of Pedro Javier Herrera."

Silence. The tailor's glasses twinkled in the bright lights of the store. Alejandra noticed his hairy knuckles twitching with uncertainty as his hand came to rest against the

123

welt pocket of his grey flannel vest. He looked at Roberto expectantly, his brow wrinkling with curiosity and dismay.

"I'm not coming back to the *corrida*, Silvio," said Roberto. "We're here for a suit of lights, but it's going to be for her. She's the matador."

Early mornings in Cadiz province were damp with rain and mist.

"Coffee?"

"Black," said Alex, pulling on her boots.

"*Café con leche*. Same for me," said Roberto to the housekeeper.

"I said black! And not a thimbleful, either! I want a big cup of black coffee! I am an American!"

"Yes. Whenever it's convenient for you, I notice."

The coffee came. He held out his cup as the housekeeper poured frothing milk from a stainless steel pitcher. Then the housekeeper gave Alex an espresso, and poured hot water in it, giving her a dirty look. They went out into the yard. Roberto held his hand out and felt the wind. "It'll dry off by the time we walk over to Fuentes'."

"Walk? Where's your car?"

"There's a path round the storage sheds. Don't worry, we'll be far from the animals."

"Afraid the bulls will attack your precious car?"

"No. It's muddy."

"Exactly. I don't want to walk."

"I don't want to have to wash the car. There's no car wash for miles."

"You're illogical, Rob." She pulled up the hood of her parka and stared at the parting grey clouds. "I can't believe I'm up at six in the morning. It's criminal."

Roberto put a couple of apples in his jacket pocket and

put away the coffee. "Come on, Alex. You want to see the bulls, don't you?"

They squidged and squelched up the muddy cattle trail. The air smelled richly of manure. Alex asked, "So, does this house belong to your dad?"

"Not exactly. He invested in real estate, vacation rentals. That's what he did with my money. He rents this out. Not many renters, really, these days. Recession."

They stood back as the foreman's white jeep came roaring down the path, scattering gobs of mud. They tried to get out of the way. Too late.

"Brilliant idea, Rob," said Alex, removing cold mud from her eyelashes. "Are we still meeting your manager for lunch?"

"He called late last night. It's a no go, Alex. He manages El Rivera now. He won't have anything to do with us. We're entirely on our own."

They rounded the corner, treading carefully among the deep puddles.

"Can't you be my real manager?"

"You'd want a professional."

"Fuck that."

"Look, we'll go visit Fuentes, see what he says."

"So, what's the big deal with this guy?"

"He's got the best bulls I've ever worked with. And he's Magalie Soubeyran's patron, so he might be sympathetic to you. Try and be nice. It's going to be like a job interview. You need to convince him to take you on."

"How did *you* get started? Did it cost a lot?"

"It was tough. We had to raise a lot of money. My grandmother wasn't as savvy as yours about managing Grandpa's bullfighting money, or what was left of it. At one point we had to choose between treatment for my mother and money for bullfighting. But she wanted me to be a matador. The whole family's like that. My uncles and

125

cousins wouldn't stand for any other outcome. Neither would my dad. God, when I think of the money we spent all those years. So many people, so many salaries. Travel expenses, equipment, clothes. What was it for?"

They came to a metal fence. It was one of the larger bull ranches. The bulls were far away, huddled under some trees. In the morning, they looked Neanderthal, like a painting on the side of an old cave. "Nice," said Alex. "Three years old?"

"Three, maybe four."

"Check out the size of that one. The one with the star on its forehead."

"That's the stud bull. I tested it when I was sixteen, right on this ranch."

"Oh yeah?"

"He was a mean old bastard. All of the bulls you see here are descended from him."

The rain, as Roberto had predicted, stopped and bits of sunlight filtered down into the plain. He threw her a green apple. They munched in silence.

"Why the hell did we get up so early?" demanded Alex.

"Fuentes is going to show you his training ring in about twenty minutes. We're meeting there—just down this hill."

Alex threw her apple core across the fence as hard as she could. It shot out angrily into the distance and disappeared into the mist. "Let's get the hell out of here."

"What! Why?"

"I don't feel like begging."

"I wouldn't blow off Fuentes if I were you. He's pretty powerful." Even as he said it he instantly regretted. He was beginning to learn that nothing made Alex more determined to do something than when one told her that it couldn't be done. He wondered how she got to be that way.

"I don't want to go begging around for some rich guy to adopt me. I want to do it my way."

He hurried after her angrily. "Where are you going?"

"Let's take your car to Cadiz and go watch a movie."

"What?" He pulled out his cellphone, wondering if she was serious about cancelling the meeting.

"Come on. Let's take a day off." She strode resolutely down the cattle trail back towards the village. "I want to watch a movie, have a beer and eat some fries. Tomorrow we'll come up with a better plan."

❂

Roberto nearly jumped out of his skin.

Somewhere, miniature trumpets were blaring the declamatory opening of a bullfight. *Paaahhh! Paah-da, pah-dum, paaaaaaaahhhh!*

"Your phone's ringing," said Alex.

He dug it out of his pocket. "You changed the ring-tone!"

"Isn't it cute? I downloaded it."

He glared at her and answered it. It was Shelly calling for Alex. He handed the phone to her, "It's not funny. My adrenalin level's way up."

"Calm down. Have some Coke."

They were in a café behind a cinema in downtown Cadiz, waiting for the show to start.

"Hi, Shelly!" said Alex, dabbing a cold, damp fry into a mound of ketchup. "No, I'm being cheap, I don't turn on my phone, the roaming is crazy expensive. So yeah, continue calling Roberto if you need me —" she broke off and asked, "You're still on a flat rate plan with Telefonica, right?"

Roberto looked up from his sketch pad and shrugged.

"We're in Cadiz. Cadiz. You know, the town that's

spelled *Cadeez*? It's pretty far south. It's on this little spit of land that if I sneeze it will break off and float to Africa any moment. Nope, the downtown is cute and tiny. It's like visiting, you know, Fredericksburg. You're not missing anything. Feel better? A package for me? Open it. I don't know what it is. Not a bomb. Who is it—oh, *them*. Yeah, okay. Read it."

Roberto put away his pencils and sketchpad and pointed at his watch.

"Hey, I gotta go. We're watching a movie and it's about to start. Can I Skype you later? What about tomorrow? I know it's his birthday, I sent him something already, it'll come a bit late. What are you guys doing for his birthday? Not that place again! They still do the chicken tikka masala? I know, I miss it. Love you too."

They went to the dim foyer of the cinema. A nervous, pimpled boy tore their tickets and let them in.

"So, Shelly said I finally received a sponsorship offer from that sportswear company I told you about," said Alex. "In writing."

"Really? Are you going to take it?" Roberto fiddled with his phone, erasing the ringtone called *Torero*.

"Dunno. She's reviewing the terms. She's got a cousin in New York—an entertainment lawyer type—who can interpret the fine print for her. Watch me sign away my soul to Mr. Big Corporation."

"Sounds exciting," said Roberto, a little reluctantly.

"Yeah." Alex wondered if he was jealous, or just afraid of what might happen if she went full steam ahead with American sponsorship. She wondered if he was hurt because she walked out of the meeting with Fuentes that morning. Despite having spent last summer with him on the road for two weeks, she felt like they had set the clock back again to day one this time in Cadiz, and he was being all continental-polite and continental-inscrutable again.

Perhaps it was her command of Spanish. Foreign languages had such a strange way of creating ambiguity. She was always second-guessing his emotions in person in a way that she never did when they were instant messaging, talking on the phone, or emailing. She wondered if she made him uncomfortable in person because he didn't like being seen in Spain, in public, with her. He had been— probably still was—a celebrity. The public had a short memory, and in the interim many new matadors had taken his place. People accepted the reasons he gave for his retirement. Once they heard he was leaving for America, they promptly looked elsewhere for entertainment and he dropped off the tabloids entirely.

They walked past big cardboard cutouts of the latest Hollywood films. Roberto had wanted to watch the latest sequel in a Hollywood action series, but Alex wanted to watch a Spanish film. Alex won in the end because she claimed if Roberto didn't humor her, he was being rude to a guest and to a woman, which—according to her— he was genetically not allowed to be.

"Fine," he said. "I'll get back at you later at *Halo*."

"I don't care. I hate *Halo*."

"You just say that because you're not good at it. You hate everything you're not good at."

"Better than being you. You hate things you're good at."

He looked a little upset at her remark. "Popcorn?" she offered in a reconciliatory manner.

"No. I don't like junk food. I don't know how you can eat all this stuff and not get fat."

"I don't do milk in my coffee."

Roberto said if she would stop eating junk food and behave like an adult, he would take her to a really good restaurant in town afterwards.

"What, like one of those with legs of ham hanging from the ceiling?"

"There is no ham. Why do you hate ham so much?"

"Grew up on a ranch. Sick of meat."

"There will be no ham."

They walked down the aisle. Everyone had gone to see the action film next door. This auditorium was deserted. It was like a private screening. They sat down. Roberto dug out his sketchbook from his backpack.

"What are you drawing?" she asked. "You're drawing nonstop now."

"I'm trying to keep up with my classes for the fall."

Alex said suddenly, "I am really grateful you took a semester off for me, Rob. What can I do for you in exchange?"

"Watch *Transformers: Revenge of the Fallen*."

"I can't watch that crap. The women have shit roles."

"There is a reason why this cinema is deserted, Alex."

"I'm in Spain, I wanna see a Spanish film."

He groaned and went back to his sketchbook. Before the lights dimmed, an elderly couple walked up to them. They were the only other people in the room.

"Excuse me," said the man pleasantly. "Roberto de la Torre?"

"*Si*," said Roberto automatically, rising to his feet and shaking hands. He signed an autograph with his drawing pencil and exchanged a few pleasantries. The old lady told Roberto that he had been very brave in such-and-such a fight during the April fair in Sevilla, and that she hoped to see him back in the ring someday. Roberto murmured various polite forms of expression.

The house lights dimmed.

"Fans?" hissed Alex.

"If we were watching *Transformers* next door, no one would have recognized me," he said. "Nobody my age

cares about matadors. I hope you enjoy your fuddy duddy
film. What's it about, again?"

"The life of a sixteenth century Moorish mathemati-
cian. Don't you know? They invented math."

Roberto made a face in the dark. "Remind me to never
go on a date with women like you."

"What is this then?" she whispered.

"This is not a date," he whispered back.

"All right, it's not."

"This isn't a date."

"Did I say it was?"

"You said—"

"I didn't say it was a date."

"All right, you didn't."

Then he had to shut up because the film was starting.

"Hi! How are you liking Spain?" asked Nicky, trying out
her high-school Spanish on the phone.

"Um, I'm *from* here?" said Roberto, a little incredulous.

"Oh, yeah! So, what do you do?"

"I'm a university student," he replied. Alex said Nicky
didn't know he had been a matador. She thought he was
in a boy band. He thought being a student sounded much
better. Anyway it was true. He was paying a lot for tuition.

"What are you studying? Music?"

"Animation."

"Oh? In Spain?"

"No. In San Francisco."

"Oh, I love San Francisco! Have you been to Macy's in
Union Square?"

Rob darted a look at Alex, who was grinning, a guidebook open on her lap. "Would you like to talk to Alex?
She's right here."

"Oh, okay. Talk to you later, Rob."

He handed her the cellphone and got out of the car, stretching.

"Nicky? You know he just parallel parked the car—with one hand on the wheel—while he was talking to you? It's amazing. Yeah, what do you want?"

Roberto walked up the street, then waved at Alex in the car. He pointed at the building and she nodded for him to go ahead.

The San Martín museum of bullfighting was founded in 1924 and looked like it was frozen in time. In the early eighties, with funds raised from local restaurants and hotels, they installed new glass cases for the exhibits. But even those new cases looked dated and decrepit today.

The elderly guard at the door was reading a newspaper and didn't look up. He murmured, "Good afternoon. Admission is free. Please fill out the guest book."

Smiling, Roberto reached for the ledger and signed his name. He stepped softly through the doorway into the musty darkness, up the creaky old stairs with a worn red carpet held in place by small brass rails. The walls were crammed with old photos of merchants, supporters, *peña* club members, many with the stiff moustaches of the early twentieth century.

The townhouse was taller than it was wide. The exhibit began on the second floor.

The first thing to greet him was a stuffed black Miura bull. Even though it was dead, the sight of the animal looming in the ill-lit room caused his heart to constrict a little. That old sinking feeling came back—apprehension, ennui, an embarrassed kind of defiance. It had been nearly twelve months since his last bullfight during Fallas in Valencia—it felt like twelve years.

Roberto remembered the first time he saw the stuffed Miura in the museum—he was so small that he couldn't even see the white-grey horns high above its head. His father had to carry him. "*Toro!*" he had cried. It was one of the first words he learned.

One of the glass eyes was now falling out. Roberto pushed it back in, but it fell out even more, dangling desolately by a thread.

"My God! It's you!" came a voice up the stairs. The guard climbed up hurriedly.

"Hi, Hector."

"You're back! Oh, my knees! I can't do these stairs these days."

Roberto helped him into a chair. Hector didn't really need help, but he liked to play up his frailty before young people, and Roberto went along with the pantomime, as he always did. Hector complained about the weather for a bit, then he looked Roberto up and down. "Think you can still get into your *traje*, my boy? American food can be fattening."

Roberto said there was no danger of weight gain. "I can't eat their food."

"My sympathies. Take care of yourself, my boy. Keep exercising, stay fit, eh? Don't wait too long to come back, don't wait until you're too old, otherwise you'll miss the window. How old are you now?"

"I'll be twenty-one this October."

"You'll still have time. Why, El Cordobés was old when he started. It's good you started young. Plenty more years ahead. But what's this nonsense I hear about you hanging out with girl matadors? You just have to walk around San Martín and all the beautiful women will fall all over you, and you have to go hang out with *those* tomboys."

"I'm not hanging out with girl matadors, Hector," said Roberto, walking down the corridor, surveying the exhibit coolly. "Who told you?"

"Silvio the tailor. Your father. The tabloids. The talk

shows. The whole world knows." Hector opened a drawer in a bureau carefully and pulled out a stack of shiny photographs. "Hey, while you're here, sign these for me, would you? I sell them for twenty Euros apiece. Raises money for the museum."

"I thought they were ten Euros." Roberto pointed at the price sticker at the back.

"Price has gone up since you retired."

"Wouldn't the price go down?"

Hector peeled the stickers off busily. "Nope. I'm selling them for more. People are mad for them now that you've left. Francisco says he had to get his grandson to buy them on eBay, where they're going for *fifty* Euros."

Francisco was the local impresario who staged and managed the bullfights for the San Martín bullring. He was also Hector's brother-in-law.

"Look at you! Look at you! Isn't that a beautiful picture?" said Hector, fanning out the photographs on the table. "The great Vicente Morales took that one, he's always so fantastic with his camera. Where was that, Ronda?"

"No, a special *corrida* in Madrid," said Roberto soberly. "It was a beautiful day. Feels like a lifetime ago now." He left the photographs and walked around the exhibit, noting old and familiar objects, as Hector continued chatting.

"Don't talk like that, boy! You make old men like me feel young again. Can't wait to see you return. Start it off in San Martín, yes? We haven't had a great bullfight in the San Martín ring since you left. Nobody important wants to come here, we can't afford to pay them. The *novilleros* are god-awful. I honestly do not know where they get them from these days — random villagers, rubbish people. A real hodge podge . . . Hello there, miss! I'll be down in a minute. Admission is free. Let yourself in. Sign the guestbook please. Exhibit starts on the second floor. Where are you from?"

"United States," came Alex's voice up the stairwell. "I've been here before."

"Oh, have you?"

Alex came up the stairs and found Roberto. "Hey."

"Hey."

"Nicky's getting married, I told you, right?"

"Yes," said Roberto, absently, looking at the exhibits.

"She's asked me to be her maid-of-honor, but I can't afford to fly there and back again just for her wedding."

They stood silently before one of the glass cases. Inside, there were two mannequins. One of the mannequins wore an old, blue suit of lights; the other wore red. Hector walked up to them, humming contentedly.

"Ah, together again," said the old man, darting a mischievous look at Alex.

"Hello, I am Alejandra Herrera." She offered her hand.

He shook it slyly. "I guessed. Silvio is doing a *traje* for you."

"This is one of the tomboys I'm hanging out with," said Roberto. He looked at Alex. "His words, not mine."

"News travel fast in this small town," said Alex, grinning.

"Yes, we get our news at the pub, it's faster than email," said Hector, looking her up and down. "The *peñas* are ready to kill you, Herrera."

"That doesn't sound very friendly," she replied, still smiling.

"Yes, but you know what I say? I say, we must have a big bullfight in San Martín, with Herrera and De la Torre! Who cares if Herrera is a girl this time? They didn't produce a grandson, so let's take whatever we have! It's the two greats, together again!"

"How can I be in the same fight as Roberto?" asked Alex. "I'm just a novice. I thought we could never be featured together?"

Hector said gleefully, "Yes, yes, we can have you perform together if it's a charity bullfight! We'll say it's to raise money!"

"Raise money for what?" asked Roberto.

"The museum, of course! Can't you see it's falling to pieces?"

Roberto had done charity fights for Down's Syndrome, the Red Cross, earthquake victims, a convent, even a child with cancer, but raising money for a bullfighting museum seemed a bit suspect. "I don't know if the public would buy that as a good cause."

"Oh, come on, of course it is!" cried Hector. "I'm desperate enough these days with the rubbishy matches to see something good like that. And even if she's really bad at it, your name alone might sell tickets."

"She's not half bad," said Roberto.

"How do we know? All we have are the two minutes in Valencia to go on. Yes, yes, the famous, classic, Herrera *recibiendo*, I saw it on the telly. We've recorded it too, and played it over and over in the *peña*. People argued about it."

"Oh yeah? What do they say?" asked Alex warily.

"They said women usually fail at killing, because, you know, you have—" he swept his hands across his chest, "— which you must protect."

"You guys have ideas about women's bodies that women don't seem to have. At least not where I'm from."

"But it's natural for a woman to be more protective of the front of her body, no? When you pass your chest over the horns for the kill?"

"Maybe if I had boobs like Salma Hayek, but I don't," Alex glanced at Roberto, who was pretending to be very interested in an old painting on the wall.

"Maybe, maybe. I must admit, you impressed some people. It was an excellent kill, you've got balls. But it could have been beginner's luck. It's hard to say with kills. It's like a golf swing, you know. Practice all you want, but a lot of it is circumstantial. At least that's what the *peñas* in San Martín think."

"Circumstantial!" cried Alex. "But I'm not really a beginner. I've been training since I was ten. That's as long as Roberto's been training."

"Look, you don't have to convince me, I'm already sold! I told the *peñas*, just thinking of the poster with both your last names on it gives me chills!" Hector pointed at the glass case where old posters from the 1950s were pinned up, showing the last names of the grandfathers of the woman and the man who now stood before it. "So, when can you do it?"

"When?" asked Alex, suddenly alarmed.

"Yes, pick a date. You have a date, don't you? Why else would you both be here?"

"Actually," said Roberto slowly, "we just arrived and were thinking about going to see Francisco tomorrow."

Hector rubbed his hands in glee. "*I'll* talk to Francisco. Leave it to me! What time are you going to see him tomorrow? I'll see him in the pub tonight and say you are both in town. But it's gotta be a bullfight with you both. With luck we might get a few others, maybe a *rejoneador*. I'll make some calls. Who wouldn't want to help raise money for a bullfighting museum!"

"But I don't want to be in it!" said Roberto, appalled. "I'll never fight again. I'm out. For good."

"Hey, don't do this to me. You broke San Martín's heart when you quit. You, our young hero, the first San Martín matador we have performing in first-class bullrings in five *decades*, and you walked out on us because you saw no future in it. We're still reeling from it. Can't you do a small little charity *corrida*? It's for San Martín, it's just going to be us San Martín folks watching. We're not inviting

Madrid or national press. They don't care what goes on here! We have been so low on the totem pole after your grandfathers died. The Andalucians laugh at us. The critics have long stopped covering our bullfights. Still, it's a good bullring. A beautiful piece of architecture, eh?" He rapped on the glass exhibit that showed the nineteenth century diagrams of the octagonal San Martín ring. "Come on. Next month?"

Even Alex was shocked. "I'm not ready."

Hector said sternly, "Didn't you say you have been training since you were ten? Don't you have a *traje* made? Come on! We need this! I need a new stuffed bull, this one's been pulled apart by kids."

He stood there, impatiently, eyes shining. Alex looked at Roberto, who put his hands in his pockets solemnly and said he would not fight. "I'm done with the *corrida*, Hector."

"Fine, fine, I'll see what Francisco says. You young people are so difficult, you know that? One doesn't want to do something he was born to do; the other one wants to do something nobody would let her. To hell with you both. I'm glad you're not my children. I'll go insane. Hey, Roberto, sign the photos, don't forget. Sit, sit down for me and sign the photos." He pulled out a rickety wooden chair. "Alejandra, come with me. I've got some of your grandpa's newspaper clippings in the store room upstairs, want to see? They're the scandalous ones, the ones your grandma didn't want us to put up. They're great, you have to check them out. Come on."

Roberto was left alone on the second floor, a black marker in one hand and the sheaf of photographs in the other. He looked at the pictures. Was that really him? Usually the photos were of him turning the red cape, the *muleta*, as the bull charged. But on that day in Madrid, a particularly artistic photographer had chosen to capture a quiet moment in the fight. He was wearing a special costume, the *goyesca*, that day. It was not adorned with the usual gaudy twinkly golden braid. It was a solemn costume of black ink, nubby with black embroidery, in the style designed by Goya. The only color he wore was the obligatory pink stockings. He liked that one, because it was the only one that didn't make him feel like a Christmas tree. He wondered where that costume was now. Did his father sell everything when he retired?

In the photograph, the sun came down at an angle and threw the semicircular shadow of the bullring across the mustard yellow sand. His country was a large, dry mountain, thrust up heavenward. The Spanish sun was very close. It was a brutal, dusty, declamatory sun, not like the soft golden champagne light of Northern California, not the same sun that gently ripened green-grey grapes in Napa Valley. It threw harsh shadows and only recognized primary colors. He was in black, the bull was black, and the only other colors in the photograph came from the yellow sand, the pink stocking, and the blood-red cape. His back was to the photographer, his face in half-profile, the *muleta* stretched towards the left, and the bull just sauntering past. Sauntering, naturally, not charging. A solemn boy and his cow, on a walk in the country. There was complete harmony in the picture. It wasn't a very large bull, and he was only eighteen, and his hair kept long. Looking at the picture made him feel at ease. It was beautiful, the *corrida*. At least when shot at high shutter speed. This photograph froze a moment that didn't even exist for him. It made it almost worthwhile, made him forget how awful it was. It was good to look back from a distance, put on the mindset of a visitor, an aesthete. All that killing, all that tension, was Alex's burden to bear now. She wanted it.

He signed the photograph soberly.

Upstairs, Hector chuckled and Alex went, "Aw . . ." She

came tumbling down the stairs excitedly, waving a clipping glued to a piece of cardboard. "Look! It's my grandpa kissing a famous opera singer! Sofia would be so jealous if I told her I saw this picture! Look how handsome he was in a tux!"

Her smile faded when she saw his expression.

Later on, at dinner, she asked him why he cried at the museum.

He shrugged, staring out the window. They were sitting in a tapas bar in a corner of a small, dusty alley. It had no name, bare walls, fluorescent lighting and a menu that consisted of only six items, scrawled on a chalkboard. Roberto said it was his favorite place to eat out in San Martín. It had the world's best roast potatoes, and nobody would harass them there.

She turned to the young waiter and ordered.

"Anything else? Ham?" pleaded the waiter.

"No," said Alex firmly.

Roberto said to the waiter, "She's a vegetarian matador."

"Clearly," said the waiter drily, and disappeared.

Alex looked around. "Have you ever noticed that in these places the waiters are always young and skinny while the bartender is always old and fat?"

"Did Hector see me? Cry, I mean."

"No. You looked fine by the time he came down."

"Good. It's embarrassing. Don't you *dare* tell anyone."

"Who'd I tell?"

Roberto looked out the window at a girl walking her dog. Behind them, an old man put a coin in a jackpot machine that spun and emitted merry little electronic gurgles.

Alex wriggled. "Why were you sad?" she asked, finally.

"The photograph Hector made me sign."

"I like that one. It's a gorgeous photo, Rob."

"Yes, but it is so unreal. That was not how I felt that day."

"These kinds of photos aren't for you, Rob. They're for your fans."

Roberto turned the candle votive on the table round and round in his hands, avoiding her gaze.

Alex hailed the waiter. "My friend here, he needs the hard stuff."

"A bad day at work?" said the waiter, unloading dishes at the table.

"He hates his job."

"Don't we all," said the waiter.

"You've got some brandy?" asked Alex. "Two, please."

"I don't drink brandy," said Roberto.

"I don't either. It'll be a first. Come on! This whole bullfighting business is getting too heavy."

"I don't want a brandy," said Roberto, as the waiter brought two brandies.

"It's still early. Let's go to a pub after this. No, let's go to a club."

"There aren't any clubs in San Martín. At least, not for young people."

"Oh yeah? Not according to this guidebook!" Alex dug into her backpack and showed him a page she had marked.

"*That?* That's not really a club. It's terrible. They play Abba." He downed the brandy.

"Hey, we're sitting here listening to Rihanna." Alex darted a glance inside the restaurant, shaking her head. "How much worse can the music get? Anyway, I'm curious to finally meet the young people of San Martín."

"They're all going to be the horrible Swedish and English exchange students from the local language center. Nobody from San Martín goes there."

"All the better!" laughed Alex. "They won't recognize

you. Nobody will know who we are. Come on, Rob. Somehow I feel that we won't have many evenings left in Spain to be silly."

Roberto asked for another brandy.

❁

They were in Valencia to meet more bullfighting people.

"So, he was serious?" asked Roberto.

"It's all set up, dude. You're going to walk out on me now?"

"Walk out? I never signed up for this!"

"You signed up for this the moment you agreed to go on the road trip with me to San Diego." Alex walked so quickly that he couldn't catch up with her amid the crowds of shoppers on Calle de Colón. It was a public holiday in Valencia; he wore a hat and sunglasses to avoid being recognized. She ducked into a bookstore.

"What are you doing in here?" he whispered.

"I need a Spanish dictionary."

He followed her into the basement of the store. "I can't possibly be in your bullfight."

"So, you're serious about *never*. Just checking."

"Yes, I am serious. I'll never put on that damned suit again. I'll never kill a —" he shut up abruptly when some children came near them. When they ambled off he said in a low voice, "Look, I thought you always understood. I never signed up to be in a fight with you."

"Francisco says this charity bullfight ain't happening without you. He needs your buy-in, one hundred percent."

"I'll talk to him again. What about Diego Alvarez? Did you call him? I gave you his number."

Alex flipped through a dictionary. "He told me to fuck off. He won't be in the same fight as a woman."

"Did you say I sent you?"

"Yes. He said why don't you be in it. If you are, he might reconsider. No one wants to go first with a woman on the *cartel.* '*It's not because I think you are no good. It's just that I would hate to see you get hurt,*' he said." She made a disdainful noise.

"What about Luis Brava?"

"Says he's had a bad season and that going up with me would only injure his reputation."

"And Joselito Rodriguez?"

Alex picked a book and went to the cashier. "El Pepito? He's in hospital. Didn't you know?"

"No, did he get gored?"

"He tried to kill himself. Said he wasn't good enough anymore, that he let the public down."

"Is he okay?" said Roberto in alarm.

"Cut his wrists. He'll live. He talked on the phone with me from the hospital. Sweet kid. Said he wished he could help, but he's at the end of his tether. His fans criticized him incessantly. He now thinks he sucks as a matador. Said next time he'll use a gun."

"Oh, God. He's only sixteen." Roberto sat on the steps of the bookstore, took his sunglasses off, and buried his face in his hands. "Welcome to the profession."

"The *traje* is a very special thing, Alejandra," said Silvio solemnly, walking her to the back of the shop into his fitting room. Her new suit was on a tailor's dummy. It was black and gold. "When you put it on, you are declaring to the world that you are ready to fight."

"It's amazing." She walked round it. "Is it ready for me to try on?"

"Yes. I'll leave you in here. I don't have any women

assistants in the store. Would you be able to figure it out yourself?"

"No problem. I've tried on Grandpa's a thousand times."

Silvio shut the door firmly behind him and went out to the shop where Francisco, the bullring manager, Hector, and Roberto had gathered. Silvio flipped the sign on the door to CLOSED.

"Well, gentlemen," said Francisco, "we have a suit of lights, a *novillero*, a matador. Do we have a *cuadrilla*? Do we have a show?"

"We don't even have a manager, let alone a team," said Roberto quietly.

"You're her manager."

"I'm not."

"What have you been doing this past year? Weren't you in America with her?" said Francisco abruptly.

"No, we were in different cities."

"Are you sleeping with her?"

"No," said Roberto, annoyed. "She's like a relative."

"So she's not your protégée, she's not your girlfriend, she's like a relative," said Francisco slowly, going through mental calculations. He was thinking of how to spin this to the tabloids. He was a consummate marketer.

"That's right."

Francisco lit a cigar. He offered Roberto one but was declined. "There is only one thing that's going to get this show off the ground. The fact that she's related to you and Pedro Javier Herrera."

"She's not related to me, she's *like* a relative on the account of our grandfathers. Our families lived next door to each other in those days."

"I'll call that 'related'," nodded Francisco to the others. "That's what's going to sell. Pedro and Javier. It's a good story—their grandchildren stepping up to the plate. That's what's going to save her. Ever since Cristina Sanchez, I've lost count of how many aspiring girls come to me and say they want to be matadors. They train for two, four, six years as *novilleros*, waste all this money, postpone school, then cry and drop out. They all have talent, don't get me wrong. But not enough money, not enough ambition. I say to them, my dear ladies, you've got to want it. You've got to want it so badly, like El Rivera, that you would sell blood to raise money to fight. You've got to be so desperate, that even if you were starving, abandoned, a beggar in the streets, you would still be trying to fight a dog with a rag."

"Oh, come now, Francisco, it's not so bad in modern times," said Silvio. "You exaggerate."

"You know what I'm talking about! That's what I'm looking for—the hunger. But even if they had the hunger, they fail because they don't have enough connections. They're not plugged into the bullfighting world. No family name. I always tell them, my dear ladies, you may be talented, but you don't come from a taurine dynasty. You don't have the name, you don't have the men to back you, to bring you in. But this one's solid gold. She's royalty. She's a Herrera."

"That's what I said!" said Hector excitedly. "Even if she's rubbish, she's got the name. We can have her fight once."

"And more importantly, she's got Roberto on her side. Your name is still decent currency, my boy. Alone, it's valuable. Together with Herrera, it's priceless."

"Good to know," said Roberto. "It's not happening."

"Remember Cristina Sanchez and El Cordobés Junior? It's going to be a beautiful pairing. The tabloids will go for it."

"That's what I said! You heard it here first!" said Hector, thumping the table. "The tickets will sell themselves."

"Question is, is this a one-time thing?" said Francisco. "Because if it's not, she better have a manager."

"I'm trying to find her one."

"Can't you be her temporary manager?" asked Silvio curiously.

"On one condition," said Roberto. "I don't fight."

"Your father said you had developed some kind of phobia," said Francisco, looking for an ashtray. The tailor rushed to get him something before the ashes fell on the scrupulously clean carpet. "I was there when he said so. Your manager tried to get you to see a doctor. But your dad said you're better off just being locked up in a pen with a bull. He said that'll cure you."

"He said that?" said Roberto sharply.

"He could have been a matador, if not for that streak in him."

"You mean hunger? I thought you liked it."

"Nah," said Francisco, grinning, his cigar in his teeth. "He doesn't have hunger. He just has spite. Spite and cruelty. It's not the same thing."

"You've seen him lately?" asked Roberto.

"He's in Madrid now with your mom. She's seeing a specialist. Did you know?"

"Yes. I call her every week. She never wants to talk about her illness."

"Come to the *peña* tonight," said Francisco crisply. "Without Alejandra. If you bring her it'll provoke them. I'll call a meeting with your uncles, your guys from your old *cuadrilla*, your old manager."

Roberto said he already talked to his old manager when he was in Cadiz, without success. "He's afraid of pissing off Dad."

"He'll come if I call. We'll talk to them about the girl. We'll sell them the story."

Hector said anxiously, "Does she want to do this for real? Does she have any patrons?"

"She has some American corporate sponsor, but she

146

needs a professional manager to deal with them and the money and the bookings," said Roberto. "They've only sponsored athletes before, they think it's the same model, but it's not. She needs a whole lot more management, money, support before she can graduate."

"Did you tell her?"

"She won't listen to me. That's why I can't be her manager."

"Americans," said Francisco. Then he added, "My wife and daughters are dying to meet her, by the way."

They heard Alex's apologetic voice, "Rob?"

He went to the back of the shop.

"Sorry to ask you to do this—"

"I knew you couldn't tie it up yourself. I never could." He went into the fitting room with her.

Outside, Francisco nodded at Silvio. "Cute. Says he's not her manager. Can't imagine the better man for the job —who else would take her on? Plus I'm sure he would do it for free."

Silvio said, "Says he's studying art in San Francisco these days."

Francisco made an impatient noise at the back of his throat.

Hector asked, "Do you think he's sleeping with her?"

"Probably. Why else would he care so much about her?"

"It's not good to have sex mixed up in this."

"Are you kidding? I *love* it. It sells seats. Can't get people to shell out for bullfighting tickets these days, but if it's a love story, the women will come. Oh God, I can see the headlines now. We'll get them to pose together every time."

"No, I'm serious. If they were to have a lover's quarrel, we won't have a show. They won't fight together. See how perilous it is? Think of the show," said Hector.

"Hector, old man, you worry too much," said Silvio. "Just leave them alone. She's a nice kid. Very respectful."

Hector said, "I'm just dying to announce it to the *peña*. Do you think the *peñas* would come?"

"They'll rally round," said the tailor. "After all, it's for the museum."

"It's more than that. I need people to come, to feel proud of their *plaza de toros,* and renew their annual subscriptions," said Francisco, removing a shred of tobacco from his lips and flicking it off. "The city's received an offer to buy the land the bullring's on."

"What?" said Hector, anguished.

"I got the call yesterday. It's prime land, right downtown. You know it was bound to happen sooner or later. If we don't do well this year, the city would have to sell, and our *plaza de toros* might be torn down and turned into a giant shopping mall. That's right. Zara and DFS."

"You wouldn't dare!"

"Look, my family used to run half a dozen bullrings; they've all closed down. I've been holding on to the one in my hometown for as long as I could. But the city's run out of money to subsidize bullfights. If this recession continues, it'll all fall apart." Francisco got up and patted his pockets. "I'm off to talk to the *aficionados* at the pub."

Silvio asked, "And this news about the offer? Is it confidential?"

"Oh, no," said Francisco, taking out his car keys. "Beat the drums. Tell everyone you can. Scare them into buying tickets for *De la Torre y Herrera*. Make them believe this is the last bullfight San Martín will ever witness if they don't renew their subscriptions."

"But when is the girl going to be ready to fight?"

"Don't worry. Create the demand first. I'll think of the rest."

Silvio took a special pride in his fitting room. It was as large as the tailor shop itself and filled with several full-length mirrors set in carved frames. It had special spotlights that made the suit of lights sparkle.

Alex had already struggled into her shirt and trousers. "Can you believe this shop? A real time capsule."

"It's been in Silvio's family for a long time."

"When is it from? 1920s? 1880s? I feel like I should be ordering a flouncy lace dress with a big bustle, maybe a parasol to go with it. Check this out," she pointed to the portable heating lamp in the back amid cardboard cartons of sewing paraphernalia. "This is totally a fire hazard. Didn't this town have a great fire in the last century? No wonder. Should I tell him?"

"Mind your own business. You call that dressed?" He pointed.

"Okay, what am I not doing right?"

"The pants aren't pulled up all the way."

"That's as far as they can go, bro."

"You'd be surprised. Put your hands on my shoulders. Both hands. All right, I'm going to yank it up. I want you to jump up on the count of three. One — two — three!"

"Aw! Jesus Christ!"

"Imagine how bad it is for *me*."

She whispered suddenly, "So do you really tape your balls to one side? How do you pee, then? What if you had to go between acts?"

"Is there a question that you do not ask about bullfighting?"

"You know who else wears tightly laced clothes and tapes their balls?"

"I don't want to know."

"Drag queens."

"Right."

"Isn't this proof that *toreros* should most naturally be women? Aw!"

"Hold still." He pulled the thin laces tight behind her back.

"This is totally S&M."

"All right, stop admiring yourself in the mirror. Hold out your arms." He fitted the jacket over her. As he tugged and pulled to get it into shape around her shoulders, she chatted brightly, "—what this reminds me of? I saw this movie about the guys who defuse bombs in Iraq, they put on these bomb-proof suits, and their team suits them up, just like this. The bomb suit's so heavy you can't do it up yourself, see. You stand there with your arms sticking out while people zip you up."

He said nothing, unfastening the black silk belt around the front of her waist, which she had knotted wrong. He retied it.

Alex beamed down at him. "I feel like the bomb squad guy—"

"Not a drag queen?"

"—I'm going into the bullring to defuse the bomb. If I fuck up, I get blown up. Right?"

"There," said Rob, adjusting the knot. Alex had a strange feeling that he hadn't heard a word she said.

They turned and looked in the mirrors quietly.

"Now for the pants. Where's the hook thing?" Roberto looked around the fitting room and found a long metal fastener. Alex put her left foot up on a chair as he prodded her trouser cuffs with the device and hooked the metal buttons tightly through each buttonhole.

"Right leg," he said solemnly. She raised her other trouser leg.

"You're so serious," she chided. She seemed completely at ease.

150

"It is a serious moment. I remember the first time I tried on my suit." He clapped her leg and stood up. "Stand tall. Let's have a look."

"Oh honey, it's beautiful."

Nicky sucked in her stomach and stood on her tiptoes to look taller. "I don't like the train. Can we cut the train off?"

Nicky and her mother and three sisters were at Neiman Marcus in Dallas, in the bridal department.

"Keep the train," said her sister, busily tying the millions of ribbons that cascaded down the back. "It makes you look taller."

"I think she should ditch the train."

"I disagree. The train's the best part."

"It does make you look short."

"Mom!"

"What are you gonna do for shoes?"

"Try the veil. Try the long one first."

The shop assistant smoothed the veil fussily and fitted it over Nicky's beaming face.

"Awwwww." A camera phone went *click*.

"My beautiful, beautiful little girl."

In a nineteenth century tailor shop in a narrow alley in Spain, a few thousand miles away, Alex posed in the mirror, arms at her hip. "I can't breathe, but I look cool."

The *traje de luces* had a way of making one puff one's chest out and hold one's stomach in. There was no other way to wear it. It very naturally made one look proud and belligerent. "The jacket's so stiff," she added, moving her arms about.

"That's because it's new. You're used to playing with your Grandpa's old things."

"What's in the pants? Lycra? Does it stretch much?" She stretched and made a pass, bending her knees. They were encased in silk and thickly encrusted with gold sequins and thread. "It's *really* prickly and hot. I'm sweating already."

"You'll get used to it. Wait, don't move." He hunted round for a pair of scissors and knelt on the floor behind her.

"What are you doing?"

"There are stray threads. I'm cutting them. You don't want those."

"Why?"

"Bad luck."

"I've got to do something to my hair, it looks wrong. Should I cut it off?"

"No. Don't cut it off, they'll say you're pretending to be a man." He watched as she tied it up. "They have some way of braiding it. Just look at pictures of the other girl matadors. Copy them."

"There aren't that many, really."

"Well, make something up. You're in charge now."

Alex looked into the mirror, then noticed his expression. "What?"

Roberto looked thoughtful. "The costume is important, but a true *torero* is one even in ordinary clothes."

"Yeah, yeah, yeah, that's what they always say."

"It is true, you know," he hesitated, searching for the right expression. "It's almost like a calling. Once you have it in you, you carry it wherever you go, no matter what you are wearing. It's a character, a personality. Not just a costume. Not just a performance."

"You don't think I have that character?"

"I didn't say that."

"I know what you're saying," said Alex, looking at her reflection. "I've heard it all before. That's why I think it's bullshit that they say a true *torero* cannot be a woman. A true *torero* is a human being, is the quintessence of a human being, someone who is fallible, someone who stakes everything for nothing, in the hope of that one great moment that flashes once, then is no more. Someone with that nature can come in whatever shape or form. God made Adam, then Eve. If God only made Adam, the Bible wouldn't be half as interesting. I'll show them. I'll be a *torero*. Hell, I'll *out-torero* them all. Here, take a picture of me with my phone. Wait, let me put on the hat first."

He took a picture of her. She smiled into the camera. His hand shook a little as he tried to snap her picture. Roberto hoped she didn't notice. The peculiar mix of feelings that went through him when he saw Alex in her first suit of lights, passionately declaring herself to be a *torero*, was more than his nerves could stand.

Nicky ransacked her refrigerator and found a bar of non-fat ice cream. "So, explain to me again why you cannot come to my wedding so I don't hate you forever?"

"Look, I've already said sorry," said Alex.

"Yeah, I like the wine fridge you got me from the registry, but it still *sucks*."

"You know how much that cost? It's from my matador training fund, too."

"All right, all right. Thanks."

"I've finally persuaded Rob—after *months* of bugging—to take a semester off his art school to come to Spain with me. It's the start of the bullfighting season, and we're looking into how I can become a matador. I can't fly back for your wedding and come here again, it'll be too expensive and I might lose the momentum and the interest of the folks here. Anyway, you hardly gave any notice for your wedding."

"Hey, dude, when Andy proposed, I totally said yes. He wanted to get married before moving to DC. Anyway, when people propose, you can't say *no*. You can't put them on a wait list. I don't want to miss the boat."

"Why are you always afraid that no guy would like you? You're getting married at twenty-one!"

"Yeah, and by the time you finish business school, Andy and I will have two kids. We win."

"If I go to business school."

"What? You've already deferred once."

"I read their guidelines — you can defer up to twice."

"Um, can we just say, *Alex Herrera ain't interested in business school*?"

"I don't want to go to Boston. The only thing useful about being in Boston is that it'll be a bit closer to Spain in terms of flight time."

"If you don't go to grad school, what can you see yourself doing then?"

Alex looked out the window into the night. It was raining in San Martín. To the right of the deserted street rose the gold-lit spires of the cathedral. The town was wet, drab, and lovely. "I don't know. I don't want to go back to school. And I don't want to interview for a job. I can't see myself working in a real job, commuting to work, having only two or three weeks vacation a year. I'd suffocate."

"Hey, I hear you, pal. You could run the ranch."

"It's boring. Anyway Tomas and Shelly already run it, they don't need a third person. It's just a hobby ranch."

Nicky clicked busily away at her keyboard at the other end. "Are you on email?"

"Yes."

"I just sent you a photo of me in my wedding dress."

"It's gorgeous, Nicky!"

"Um-hum, and you won't be there!"

"Hang on a minute. I tried on my matador suit last week, let me find the photo. I'm sending it now."

"You're really serious about this matador thing, aren't you? Geez. Opening it now . . . *woah!*"

"Nice, huh."

"Screw you, Alex. You totally *kick ass*! Man, this is so impressive, it is *sick*. So what does Rob think of this matador bullshit?"

"Rob is a matador."

"What!"

"He is. Was. Well, is. He's a famous matador in Spain. I'm sorry I never told you."

"Get outta here! He's not in a band? He said he was a student!"

"Well, he's trying to get some education."

"I thought matadors were all macho, greasy guys? He just looks like a skinny kid!"

"They start young. I watched his fights my whole life."

"I thought you did it because of your grandparents?"

"If it weren't for Roberto, I wouldn't have stayed interested in bullfighting. When I was in high school, he began climbing the ranks, and you could see his performances televised on the Web. I always wanted to do it, but it was Roberto who showed me that it was really possible."

"Oh my God. He's the reason why you are insane."

"I have to try, don't you see?" Alex said helplessly. "I have to try to make it. I don't have anything else in my life that I want but this." There was another call coming in. "Hey, I gotta go."

"Bye, faithless chick."

"Love you Nicky."

"Hello?" said Alex, answering the incoming call. It was

a woman's voice. She switched to Spanish, said she was answering Roberto's phone, and asked politely who was calling. The woman hung up right away.

Alex looked at the phone. It was an unidentified number. On a whim, she scrolled through Rob's contacts. They were all names that she didn't recognize except for her own. She then went to the call log and scrolled down the archives. Only one woman's name occurred several times.

Delfina.

The men were huddled around a marble-topped table outside a bullfighting bar, lighting cigarettes.

"This is the way to do it," said Antonio.

Roberto took the papers out of the manila envelope and looked at them briefly. "That's a good price. Thanks for getting them to agree to perform."

Hector said anxiously, "Antonio, what about also letting her do the *alternativa* this upcoming season? I can't wait a year."

Antonio had driven overnight from Madrid to San Martín for the special meeting. "What's the hurry? You want her killed?"

"Okay, then what about just some *novilladas* this year, after the charity fight? She could substitute for someone last minute," said Hector.

Roberto said Alex had said the same thing, because she was impatient and she wanted a certain number of novice fights before September of the following year.

"Why, what's happening then?" asked Hector.

"She has to start business school," said Roberto, not looking up from his papers.

"Is this girl for real?" howled Hector.

Antonio suggested that Alex spend the current year training. "No graduations this year. Anyway which matador will graduate her and give her his bull? She's an unknown."

Hector pointed his cigarette at Roberto.

"Seriously?" asked Antonio sharply. "You're coming out of retirement?"

"No," said Roberto hastily.

Francisco, the bullring manager, bought another round of beer. "Now that I have calmed down a bit, I think that Antonio's right. We've only seen her in the ring once. We have to do everything by the book. We don't want her to be trading on the family name, graduating too early and lacking the staying power."

"Who said anything about staying power?" said Roberto. "I don't think Alex intends for this to be a career."

"Look, you know, and I know, that it is probably going to be a one-time thing, but does everybody have to know? We haven't had a star matador from San Martín since you left. You think people are going to be happy if we said: 'hello, here's a freak show from America, a girl, a cultural tourist, she's just going to do this once for fun, come buy tickets,' that people will come?" said Francisco. "I'm a businessman. I have to sell seats. I've got my reputation to think of. I have a call to Fuentes in Cadiz to donate his bulls—the same breed of bulls that your grandfathers used to fight in that same ring. Let's do it properly. For my sake. For the town's sake. And mind you, everybody outside San Martín will hate us for being involved as it is, since she's a girl. It would look better if we took time and train her."

"We?" asked Antonio.

"Are you in or not?" asked Francisco.

"I'm managing El Rivera at the moment. I can't just join this madness."

Hector hissed and Silvio chuckled. "El Rivera!" said Silvio. "El Rivera's a wanker! All testosterone and muscles and no grace!"

"He's coming up the ranks," said Antonio, defensively.

"They think by hiring you they can clone Roberto's style! Dream on!"

"His father's got money and manners. That's enough for me."

A debate ensued about the pros and cons of El Rivera. More people crowded into the pub.

"Oh," drawled a bullfighting fan, looking at the table of men approvingly, "this is a good sign. Roberto de la Torre with his old manager. A very good sign!"

Another *aficionado* leaned forward, clasping Roberto on his shoulder. He was the head of the local *peña*. He was slightly drunk. "A man should step up to the plate, honor his grandfather. You broke our hearts. Because why? Because we are mourning still for Juan Carlos de la Torre and Pedro Javier Herrera. The Herreras produced no matadors. The De la Torres? We held our breath for your dad, for your uncles, when they first entered the ring. We were lost children, we looked at them for signs of life. Silence. Silence. No matadors. Just *banderilleros*. Handfuls of dust. Then you came along, and we were found. We were no longer mourning children. You fulfilled our hopes, you reminded us that a man may be immortal, that he may return in the guise of his children and grandchildren. Roberto. I followed your fights since you were this tall. There is a spirit shimmering there. It reminded us so much of him. The day you quit, so suddenly, I cried. My whole family cried."

Roberto lowered his eyes, nodding humbly.

"Roberto de la Torre! Good to see you! Dare I hope?" said an elderly gentleman, on his way to the bar. "If you are planning to fight again, *maestro*, do it in the next six months. The doctor says I don't have much longer. Do shake my hand, thank you. God bless. Where do you live now?"

"California," said Roberto.

"Ah, California! I went there once. Twenty years ago. Where's my son? He's here. You must meet my son."

More bullfighting fans crowded into the pub. They had just come from a *novillada*. Roberto got up to leave, taking the papers with him. He knew if he stayed any longer, conversation would be impossible.

Antonio said, "I don't want to be involved, but if you're her manager I'll pick up the phone for you if you need guidance. Strictly off the record, of course."

"I can't be her manager, but I'll temp until we find her one." He slipped away and left by the back door of the pub.

"It pains me to see him like this," grunted Antonio. "Twenty-one. At the prime of his youth. After all my efforts. His proper place is in the bullring."

"We'll get him back from California, by hook or by crook," said Hector feelingly. "Even if we need to use the girl as bait."

"Ah, love," said Silvio. "Love can make you do such strange things. They remind me of Romeo and Juliet."

"Don't say that, that's bad luck. These kids drive me nuts, but I don't want them to end up dead." Antonio turned to Francisco. "Now, is the bullring really going to be turned into a shopping mall? My wife said it's about time this town has a Carrefour."

"What's this?" Alex took the package warily. They were sitting in a café in the Plaza de la Virgen in Valencia. The city was busily constructing a massive Virgin in the center of the square for the annual Fallas festival. It consisted of a solemn painted head mounted on a body that was just an empty pyramid of wooden slats. During Fallas, costumed women of all ages would pass by the monument. The job of these *falleras* was to wear heavy, princessy costumes and weep through their thick makeup. They would each offer the Virgin a few stalks of flowers. Men would climb up the pyramid like little bees, filling the slats with the white and red blooms. Slowly, after many hours of non-stop processions, the Virgin's body would fill up like honey in a honeycomb. It was during Fallas, a year ago, that Roberto was gored by a bull in the *plaza de toros* and Alex jumped into the ring to kill the bull as the news cameras rolled.

"You're going to one of the best matador schools in Sevilla. I know the artistic director. He's willing to give you a try. You can join the current semester."

"Right away?"

"Don't worry, I talked to Tomas. He sent over the contract from your American sponsor, and I've had a lawyer look it over. The lawyers on both sides have talked. It's all in the revised contract, read it. Your sponsor's going to pay the school. Assuming, of course, that you agree to go ahead with it."

They watched the construction of the Virgin in silence.

Rob asked, "Have you seen the *falleras*?"

"Yeah. When I was little."

"Ever thought of taking part and being one?"

"Are you kidding me?"

"It's part of our culture too, you know."

She didn't smile. "If I have to wear an eighteen century costume and look like a Christmas tree, I prefer one that came with a sword."

"Makes sense to me."

"So, when are you leaving for San Francisco?"

"Saturday morning."

"So, this is it, huh."

"It's what you wanted," said Roberto. "Isn't it? This is a really good school. You're really lucky that our town got behind you. I couldn't have asked for a better outcome. Once you're in, you'll find that we really take care of our own."

"Thanks, Rob. For everything."

"You're welcome." He thought she looked unhappy. He wondered why.

Alex flipped through the papers. "Can I have my iPod back?"

He hesitated, then pulled it out of his pocket.

"Unless you want it?"

"No, that's fine, it's yours, you should take it back."

She took his cellphone out of her bag. "Here's your phone back. I'd rather you have it. I would like to be able to call you from matador school."

"Thanks."

"And oh, Delfina's called many times."

He flushed. "She's probably heard from my mom that I was back in Spain."

"She's your girlfriend?"

"An old girlfriend."

Alex looked up at the elderly waiter. "Agua de Valencia."

Rob ordered a beer. He kept his hat and sunglasses on so that people wouldn't come up to him and ask for kisses or autographs. He also discovered that if he dressed in clothes he bought in California and kept his hair short, nobody recognized him, which was a relief.

They watched as a little girl emerged from a group of tourists. She was wearing a cheap, acrylic *flamenco* dress and whirled clumsily across the square, practicing some steps. There was no music except what she heard in her head.

It was a royal blue twilight and the cathedral was gnarled and old in the light of the orange streetlamps.

Their drinks came.

Rob said, "You used to say only tourists drink that drink."

"I *am* a tourist," said Alex evenly, still looking at the little girl.

❁

AlexH1988: *I'm fine. The hospital's world class.*

RobH1988: "What happened? I thought you weren't doing live animals yet."

We're not. I was gored by the mechanical bull.

"What!"

Can we talk about something else?

"How did that happen?"

I was tired. During practice, I tripped and fell on it. It isn't deep. It's so LAME.

"Why won't you pick up the phone?"

I'm fine, Rob. Don't call, please. We can't pick up the phone during training. Anyway, I hate to think you're hovering. I'm in good hands. Everyone's friendly. I don't think they dare to shortchange me.

"They tend to give opportunities to the men and not the women."

Don't worry. There are other girls here — two in fact. We watch each other's backs. How's YOUR school?

"It's a public holiday weekend. July 4th."

I forgot. You should have come back.

"It's too short of a holiday to fly back. I finally got my driver's license. I got a speeding ticket the very next day."

LOL.

"Not used to driving on the highway. Do Americans all drive at the same speed? I hate the California highway patrol. Yesterday I nearly hit a car in a bank of fog. Saw my life flash before my eyes."

What!!! Where were you?

"Outer Sunset. I was trying to look for this jazz café."

Roberto hanging out in jazz cafes in San Francisco? Dare I believe my ears?

"Very funny. I even got used to the "coffee"."

Jazz???

"I'm trying to rebuild my music library."

What's summer like over there? It's hot as hell here.

"It's freezing here. Some summer."

Are you speaking English yet?

"Yes. I am going to class. American girls find my accent very alluring."

What about that chick, Delfina? You still going out with her?

Roberto lay in the darkness of his room. The only light came from the phone which he held in his hands. His apartment was thirty-five floors above a now-silent downtown. He had never lived in a high rise before. In the distance, he could see tiny yellow taxis lining up outside hotels in Union Square. A solitary American flag, mounted on a flagpole on top of a skyscraper, stretched taut in the brisk night wind coming in from the west. Beside him, a young woman lay fast asleep, a velvet eyemask over her face. Her name was Megan, she was a student at his university. She was from Berkeley. They met at a cafe; she was blond and spoke fluent Spanish.

He typed back: "I am not going out with Delfina."

You know what's weird? We're totally reversed. Now you're there, and I'm here. Now you're the student, and I'm the torero. Isn't life strange? Sometimes I miss you.

Roberto looked at the yellow smiley face that signed the end of the sentence. He tried to remember what Alex looked like, but the only image he could recall was the afternoon she put on her *traje de luces* at the back of Silvio's store.

He had to let go. So, instead of saying he missed her too, he said that he was looking forward to the weekend, because he was going camping in the East Bay.

I'm going for breakfast now. Enjoy camping! Take photos.

"Okay. TTYL."

TTYL.

❂

She taught him how to make S'mores over the campfire. Theirs was the only tent at the campsite.

"What's the matter?" asked Megan, when he grew still in the middle of their lovemaking.

"Too many noises outside," said Roberto, pulling on his clothes. "It's disturbing."

"Where are you going?"

"To the bathroom. Will be right back."

He took the flashlight, unzipped the tent, and crept away quietly. He found the portable toilet. When he came back out, he went and sat on the hood of his car and turned off the flashlight. It was pitch black at the campsite. Yet there was so much light pollution from the cities in the heavily populated East Bay that he couldn't see the stars.

The night was alive with wilderness. An unidentifiable bird chirped loudly and boldly on the branches above him. Small, invisible animals moved constantly in the undergrowth. He heard a crackling sound, trained his flashlight behind the car, and saw a large raccoon pulling a candy bar wrapper out of the trash and turning it over and over in its nimble black hands. It glared at him, unmoving, before he turned the light off.

He felt a little less desolate.

In the distance loomed the coal-gray shape of a mountain with a shimmering red-gold streak in it. He had mistaken the glowing color for the electric lights of civilization, but Megan had said earlier in the day that there were no houses on that mountain. The lights were actually forest fires that the Bay Area fire department had been unable to put out for three whole days. If they turned on the radio, she said, they would be able to hear the status reports.

"Isn't it dangerous?" he asked, surprised at her indifference.

"No. We get forest fires all the time."

"Then why don't they know how to put it out?"

"Maybe they've stopped trying. Maybe it's cheaper to let it burn itself out. Nobody lives there. There's no real danger."

He stared intently at the reddish-gold gnash in the heart of the mountain. If that light was from forest fires, he wondered why it didn't flicker. Instead, it burned steadily and confidently like the light of a distant star. He was too far away to smell any smoke in the air. It was astonishing and beautiful. For all he knew, there were trees toppling, there were animals dashing for safety, there was chaos and calamity, but he couldn't hear a thing from here.

He wished he had that kind of quiet incandescence. There was an unsteady fear in him that gnawed at him during his waking hours. He slept poorly. He was restless, despite the possibilities of companionship offered by Megan. He tried so hard, he was liking California, he convinced himself that it had always been his dream to be here. And yet he found no peace. He slept the troubled sleep of a traitor, but he wondered who or what he had betrayed.

He had tried talking to his relatives and matador friends about this. None of them were any good on the phone, and the emails they sent were blundering and unsympathetic. Only one of them had ever been to America, and only to Disney World. The ones who were retired were too old to understand him. The young ones were impatient that he come back to the bullring and join them. They spoke of political tensions in Spain, about separatists politicizing the *corrida*, about animal rights groups crowing in triumph about his change of career, about Internet chatrooms that speculated that the younger generation of matadors were "waking up to the cold hard reality that there was no future in the art", as symbolized by his premature retreat and his enrollment in a college.

"You think you can run off to America, but we're getting the flak for your actions," complained Joselito Rodriguez, a junior matador, in an email. Joselito was famous for starting young. The public had suggested that he quit bullfighting and get some schooling, like Roberto. "You should come back and share the pain."

He stopped reading those emails.

Was twenty-one too late to start over?

Megan thought he was simply homesick. She suggested he see a psychotherapist. She did not know anything about his past career. She spoke Spanish because she had a Mexican nanny growing up. To her, the Spanish-speaking world was Costa Rica, Puerto Rico, Mexico. She had even gone backpacking in the Yucatan. But she had never been to Spain. Her father was an economist and the regent of a famous local university. Her mother was a chemistry professor. Her family had been in Berkeley for generations, were well-connected. She liked him because he was exotic, and because her parents didn't. Through her he began to see how he could live in America.

And yet the fever would not abate. Roberto wondered if he always had this fever, and that it was bullfighting that kept it tamped down, but now that he had no outlet, it raged up and down within him, burning him up. He found no solace in music of any kind. Drawing calmed him down, but Megan laughingly forbade him to bring his pencils and sketchbooks. They had to hike ten miles to the campsite; they had to travel light.

Was it simply one fever, or were there several? Roberto wondered, lying down on the damp hood of the car, one arm resting on his forehead. He felt the cold dew seep through his sweatshirt. What was it that Alex had said in her SMS? He groped for his phone and turned it on to see her last words. He never erased her chats.

Sometimes I miss you.

Why *sometimes*?

There were several fevers, Roberto decided, and they had all rolled into one. There was the *corrida*, and there was her, and now they were one and the same. Which did he desire more? Why did Alex go back to Spain? Was he infected by her, or just by her desire to fight? Did she make bullfighting interesting again, just as he left?

Or was it simply that she reminded him of himself when he was younger?

Did they really take away his ability to grow up? He had to try. Something must replace those lost years. When he spoke English, he was a different man. A new person-ality expressed itself through this language. Most of the time he liked it. He didn't think he would. He had been so impressed by his own independence, until now. Who was he trying to impress? It was much simpler when he was just a bullfighter. Everything was arranged for him. He knew exactly what he had to do. Everything had its order and its prescribed parameters. If he had a different father, he might never have left.

"Roberto, are you coming back?" called Megan, making him jump. "What are you doing?"

"Just looking at the forest fire."

"It's *still* going on?"

Yes, he thought soberly. It was still going on—raging, smokeless, consuming a barren hilltop. In the distance, a helicopter, bearing water, perhaps. But it was too far to make out.

He looked at his phone absently. It was seven in the morning in Sevilla, a city he associated with an ancient, lemon-yellow *plaza de toros* on the shore of a broad, brown river. The cathedral bells would just have tolled. Alex might already be up. He itched to call her, but Megan would wonder who he was talking to. He put the phone away before he was tempted to send her an instant message.

One day he would learn not to live on Spanish time in California, not to wonder every night before he fell asleep what kind of day Alex was waking up to in Europe, not to be jealous of the people she would see every day, when he was not there.

She said she missed him sometimes. But they were just four words in an instant message, sent in a micro-second, of no import at all.

Megan's father asked Roberto if he wanted an extra blanket. It was the tail end of summer, and the entire family invited him to a Shakespeare production. It was held outdoors in an amphitheater in Orinda, in the East Bay. Everyone in the audience was rolled up in blankets, sleeping bags and hooded sweatshirts. On stage, three witches were talking to a pompous guy who was tall and slightly balding.

"What's going on?" he whispered to Megan in Spanish.

"They're delivering prophecies."

"Oh, really?"

"They're saying that Macbeth cannot be slain by a man of woman born."

"So he can only be killed by a man who is given birth to by a man? How modern."

She shook her head impatiently. "Just watch, it'll become clear later."

Roberto looked at his watch. "How long more?"

"It just started, sweetie."

Roberto found it hard to follow most of the lines in the play. He could tell that the acting wasn't very good and the action failed to sustain his interest. He shivered inside the extra blanket.

"Aw, come here," whispered Megan, wrapping her arms around him and putting her head on his shoulder. "Sorry. Family summer tradition. But it's always too cold, that's why we always come prepared."

He could not imagine his friends watching a bullfight sitting partially zipped in sleeping bags. Masochists. There was too much talking for the rest of the play. He understood individual words sometimes, but couldn't string them together for meaning. Roberto took out his pencils and pad and began to draw even though it was getting dark. Megan's father eyed him doubtfully.

"Here comes his nemesis, Macduff," said Megan, nudging him an eternity later. "That's his killer. He fulfills the prophecy because he says he was not of woman born — he was from his mother's womb untimely ripped."

Roberto looked indifferent.

Megan's father whispered something urgently to her, and she translated. "Dad says that this is Shakespeare's genius, you have to appreciate it. Macduff is the destroyer of Macbeth's hubris. Macduff is the outlier, the exception, the black swan. Dad's really fond of black swan theory. It's a popular new theory in a book he's teaching. Have you heard of it?"

He shook his head. Shakespeare, now this.

"Black swan theory is about how historically Europeans believed all swans were white because they'd only seen white swans in their own country. But there are black swans in Australia."

Megan's father whispered to her again. He was an academic. The instinct to lecture apparently did not stop even during a play. She nodded and said to Roberto, "And when you finally see a black swan—how do you say this in Spanish—it has an unpredictable effect on your assumptions. Your beliefs would be destroyed. Your reality would be re-adjusted. The world would be changed forever."

Megan's father leaned over, "*Entiendes?*"

Roberto began to smile, "Yes, I understand," he said in confident English. "I know a black swan."

❁

In December, the Catalonia government finalized and announced a proposed ban on bullfights. The Anglo-American press ran eloquent elegies, announcing the twilight of the gods.

❁

He found he could lie without guilt in English. English was so polite, most of the time it was full of white lies, anyway.

"Are you kidding me? Do you know how difficult it is to get a table at Chez Panisse the week before Christmas?"

"I'm so sorry," said Roberto, as the maitre d' handed him his winter coat. "Can you please explain to your parents when they get here?"

"Explain what?" cried Megan, ignoring the bemused

looks of the other guests waiting in the narrow hall of the restaurant. She followed him out into the street. "What could possibly be so important?"

"Look, there's been an accident," said Roberto, pulling his phone out of his pocket and checking to make sure the ringing volume was set on high. "They're going to call me right back. I have to get to a land line."

"Who's in an accident?"

"It's my mom. I told you, she's ill." He suddenly became aware that he was making no sense at all, even in his lies.

Megan's face softened. "Is she all right?"

"Yes, she'll be fine, I'm so sorry. Can you please apologize to your parents for me?" He got into the car. "Can they drive you home?"

"I suppose. And you won't be coming to the play after dinner?"

"I don't know. I'll call you, okay?"

"Call me," said Meg, as he pulled out of the parking lot. "I wanna know what happened. Okay?"

It was Saturday night. Roberto found himself at the end of a very long line of cars waiting to get on the Bay Bridge back to downtown San Francisco. He took a deep breath, then dialed a number. "Hi, it's me. I'm stuck in traffic. Please tell me what happened."

The reception was awful, which further increased his anxiety as he could only hear every other word.

It was Antonio, his old manager. Alex had been gored and was now undergoing surgery in the multiple trauma unit of the local hospital.

"It was during a *capea*, put on by the school, in a portable bullring in a small town just outside Sevilla," said Antonio. It wasn't bullfighting season. He had been invited by the artistic director of the school, an old matador friend of his, and had gone to watch her out of curiosity. "An accident. It's not her fault. It had gored one of the young *banderilleros* in her team, she was trying to save him when it attacked her. It was a riot. God, these kids. Four total, in hospital. She's got it the worst. The rest were outpatient. It's one of the best hospitals in Spain, no doubt, but it's touch and go for now. Too bad you're not here. Unfortunately she's got your same blood type. You remember how hard it was to get it in hospitals."

"I'll get on the first plane."

"They'll find a donor by the time you come."

"Where did it get her?"

"Right leg, back of thigh. At first they said she might lose her leg, but the latest word is that it's not that serious. But she's got one wound right under her rib, that's the one to watch. When she went down, it went for her again, she had a concussion. She remembered to protect her face, good girl."

He suddenly had a glimpse of the bull's face and felt the moment of impact. His hands rested on the wheel; he felt blood drain from his fingertips. The picture was all too clear. It was the old nightmare. It had never left him, after all.

"How long was she out?"

"Very briefly. She woke up once in the ambulance."

"Are you in the hospital?"

"Yes, I'm the only person here who knows her. The school's contacted Sofia Herrera, but she's too old to take a plane here, although I think she's going to try. Does Alex have anyone else in Spain?"

Roberto inched his car forward helplessly as the traffic crawled towards the bridge. Something at the toll plaza must have broken down again. "No. I can call her god-parents in Texas. Do you think it's necessary?"

"Hang on. It's the doctor. He wants to know if she's Catholic?"

"Why?" snapped Roberto.

"In case — you know, something happens. They have a priest here."

He was suddenly furious with the Bay Bridge, the traffic, and the entire highway system. "I don't know. Look, I'll call you later. Let me talk to her folks in Texas. And thanks for being there. I am grateful."

"The kid's got talent. I just happened to be in Sevilla to see my mother and got the invite. I had to see for myself. She's brave. I hope she makes it. I'm glad I'm here. If there is anything else I can do."

"Just stay there, I'll call you right back."

Roberto dialed another number. He came up to the tollbooth and handed the toll operator the first bill that came out of his wallet. He didn't even wait for the change before accelerating past the tollgate.

There was a single, narrow bed installed in the back of the van. It resembled a hospital stretcher. That was how they travelled. Roberto's uncle had it specially designed for him. A cousin wanted to silkscreen the family name on both sides of the black van, in white and gold curlicues, with a baroque crest that an artist friend had designed. The team decided against it when they heard that the animal rights people were going around puncturing car tires whenever *toreros* arrived in cities. "It's okay. We'll use it on your website," said his cousin proudly, showing Roberto the printout of the crest.

"Grandpa didn't have a crest," said Roberto quietly. The team was watching the televised reruns of that evening's performance on the news.

"It's part of your PR collateral, it's important," said his father.

He learned to sleep on the road. He was always

exhausted. The motion of the van made him sleep, despite the murmuring talk that always went on in the background among the rest of his team riding with him. They often clambered on board after hours at the pub, and brought the smell of the crowd with them in the confined vehicle. The team always had *flamenco* music on the radio. Roberto slept with his earphones fixed firmly in his ears, listening to pop music instead.

Over the years, he lost count of the hotels that they had checked in upon arrival. He had so many keycards in his bag, which he had forgotten to return, that sometimes, late at night, he could be found standing blearily outside a door with a number on it, a stack of keycards in his hand, trying each of them because he could not remember the name of the hotel.

"That's why matadors keep a different woman in every city, they help take care of things like that," joked one of his uncles. They hired an assistant for him and he retreated even further into his solitude.

He would get offers of sex from women of all ages, every night. He took advantage of them when he was younger. When he was sixteen, he fell in love with a petite blond half-Italian girl called Delfina from Sevilla, and they dated seriously for two years before it fell apart. She went off to university in London and became embarrassed she was dating a bullfighter. Her brother was also a bullfighter. She decided she was done with the bulls. London changed her. She grew ashamed of her family. She broke up with him with an email that began: *It is not easy for me to write this, but* . . .

After that, his love life consisted of hurried snatches of deeply thrilling lovemaking with different women whenever the need arose, or of horribly sterile, proper dates with upper class girls so that he didn't have to go to society events alone or be labeled homosexual.

The truth was, there was nothing he could carry in his head in those days. Two things always loomed large: the bull, and his own impending, premature death. On his eighteenth birthday, he woke up and was surprised that he was still alive, that he hadn't been seriously gored or maimed. A few days later, while being trucked to perform in Bilbao, he heard on the radio that Manuel Martinez, his friend who had been gored the day before, did not survive the night.

"What's wrong with the doctor!" shouted the men in his van, appalled.

"They should open an investigation."

"Nobody dies from such a small wound these days!"

"An infection; it was an infection. Sssh, listen, they're interviewing the doctor."

By the time his team arrived in Bilbao, Roberto de la Torre had decided that he wanted to live, and be normal. Although he would never admit it to anyone except himself, he was also a little wrecked by Delfina's betrayal. And thus began the quiet tide of revolt.

"Why are you saying this? After all our sacrifices? Especially now, when we must hold out against the political groups?" asked his father.

"I just want to get out before I get too old to do anything else with my life," said Roberto.

"What else are you going to do with your life?"

"Go to university."

"Which university would take you now? You didn't even do high school!"

"I'll go to a vocational college. I'll learn a trade."

"What, be a mechanic?"

He faltered.

"Listen, Roberto," said his father, stopping his pacing about the hotel suite. He drew up a chair, "ours is a bull-fighting family. You're Juan Carlos' grandson. Your grandmother had six sons, and none of us made it. None of your cousins can do it. But you! You're climbing the ranks. I got you the best trainer and the best manager money can buy. After all those years in training, after all the investment, this is the easy part. And besides," he lowered his voice in hushed indignation, "who else is going to pay you this kind of money for only a couple of hours of work a day? Who?"

❁

He stayed up all night making travel arrangements and calling various people in Spain. Megan hadn't called him.

"I just sent you my itinerary."

"I'll pick you up and bring you right to the hospital," said Antonio.

"Don't bother, I'll take a taxi."

"I'll pick you up. For God's sake."

"How is she?"

"She's out of the operating room. Hang on. You want to speak to her?"

He was relieved that she could talk. The concussion must not have been that bad. "You bet I do."

"One moment. Let me get to her."

Roberto looked out of the window. In the distance he could see the light turning shell-pink over the sea. He had lived with his parents his entire life, when he was not travelling in hotels. This was his first apartment. It was near the school, in a tall building. He chose an apartment on a high floor of the tallest building he could afford, because he wanted to get above the fog line, to be nearer to the sun. But it was a small apartment — six hundred square feet of isolation, encased in hospital-white walls. He had a view of the Bay. He could see the crowded communities of Sausalito and Tiburon, spilling down the slope into the great Pacific ocean. Megan's parents took Megan and him in their yacht, across the Bay, to one of those towns. They had burgers in a yacht club overlooking the water. The family talked about college football scores the whole time. He learned all about the "Pac-10", the colleges in Western United States whose games they cared about the most. Megan's father tried explaining the rules of football, which he had warned Roberto in advance was a sport so subtle that foreigners would find it very difficult to understand. "But if you want to live in America," said Megan's father, "you have to understand American football."

A familiar voice came on the phone, "Hi, Rob."

He had run away to the very edge of the Western world. There was nowhere else to run. Reluctantly, he turned his feet homeward.

He said, almost with relief, "Hi, Alex."

Unexpectedly, she began to cry.

"What's wrong?"

"It hurts." Her voice petered out weakly.

"Of course it does."

"It wasn't even a very big bull. It sucks."

He agreed it sucked.

"I'm not going to be able to fight for *months*. The doctor said. *Weak*."

"I called Shelly and Tomas."

Alex groaned. "They're going to kill me."

"They got an earlier flight from Texas. You'll see them before me."

"Oh, God they are going to *kill* me."

"Alex, they love you. They're worried about you. They want to see you."

"This *sucks!*"

"And your grandmother, she wants to fly to Sevilla, too, but she hasn't been on a plane for decades. I told her to reconsider on account of her health."

Alex groaned again. "I'm causing so much trouble for everyone."

Roberto was about to say something when he noticed an incoming call. Megan. He began to smile in spite of himself. "You are getting a lot of people into trouble, Alejandra Herrera."

"Goddamn it, I *know*."

"Look, if you want to be a professional bullfighter, you have to be ready to be gored, to be in and out of hospitals. You're going to get hurt, and you will hurt everyone you love. Over and over again. Remember? That's what I said. So get used to it. Stop being a baby."

Antonio took over the phone. "Hey, the nurses have come. They don't want her to be on the phone for long. They've asked me to leave the room. I'm going to get some sleep, I've been here overnight—"

"Hey," interrupted Roberto, "thanks."

"You're welcome. She's got no one. Never been through the Spanish hospital system before. I filled out her forms and insisted for the doctor that you had before— remember that guy? He's fantastic. And more sympathetic to bullfighters. She looks like she's in better shape that I originally thought. She's in a lot of pain. Lucky she's young."

Roberto watched as morning filled the streets of downtown San Francisco. People accreted at the traffic junction. When the light changed, they flowed ceaselessly into their office buildings. He opened one of the windows and the cold winter air roared into the apartment. "If she is able to swear on the phone, she'll live."

"I'm starting to get very interested in this *novillero*. Let me see what I can do for her. Say she's out for a month or two. In three months it would just be the start of the new season."

"Don't let her hear you, or the hospital might have a hard time restraining her."

"Don't worry. I won't say anything until you get here. You're her manager. Well, I mean, her *temporary* manager."

Roberto shut the window and opened the closet, looking for his suitcase. "I must go. I have to pack and make it to the airport. Thanks, Antonio. I'm sorry I bailed out of bullfighting. I caused you a lot of grief. Thanks for still looking out for me."

"Well, I was a matador, too. We stick with our own."

"Alejandra used to say that matadors aren't good outside the ring."

"Oh, did she? And what the hell did she mean by that?"

"Said some famous American writer—"

"Hemingway, the son of a bitch?"

"No, John something. He wrote that we're not really brave outside the ring. That in real life we don't really have any courage, or honor, or loyalty."

"Oh, yeah? How did he know? Was he a bullfighter?"

"No."

"Well, screw him!"

The breeder Luis Ricardo Fuentes was in the ground floor lobby of the hospital in Sevilla.

"Good evening, *maestro,*" he said, as Roberto walked in. "When did you come back to Spain?"

"I just got off the plane," said Roberto. "I'm back briefly to see a friend who's in hospital. I'm not staying."

They exchanged pleasantries, during which he learned that the breeder had just been to see Alex. When Fuentes realized that the matador had flown from San Francisco to Sevilla just to see Alex, he was impressed.

"You can't really manage a *novillero* properly long

distance," said Fuentes, following him down the crowded corridor. Roberto explained that he wasn't Alex Herrera's manager. Fuentes said it was too late, the bullfighting tabloids already said he was, and that he should just roll with the punches.

"To be sure, they hadn't really paid her very much attention until now. Four men down! Well, three men and a woman. I've never seen such courage, such cowardice, such glory and wretchedness on display all at once. It was rejuvenating. It was spellbinding. Did you see the clip on the Web? Someone posted it."

"No, I don't want to, I get the idea."

"So, do you miss the action?"

"Not really," said Roberto. Retirement gave him the courage to be blunt with people like Fuentes. "Look, why are you here?"

They waited for the elevator in a throng of people. "This is my business, I'm a patron. I look at the new kids, and I see who I want to support. I'm supporting one of the girls, Magalie Soubeyran, she's doing really well in Nîmes, don't you know? It was on your account, actually, that she came to my attention. You talked about her on TV. It makes a good story, now that you're back in the scene with Herrera. A much better story, too, because of your grandparents. The newspapers are going crazy with this story. San Martín's in the news again. Amazing turn-around. Some of the younger reporters couldn't even find San Martín on a map."

Roberto was glad he had never made it a habit to read the tabloids. They always had a cheap, surreal quality to them. The Spain of the tabloids seemed only to exist on certain television channels. That was the Spain he had tried to run away from. Except that the damp, rolling clouds of San Francisco had somewhat defeated his resolve.

"You take her back to Cadiz and we'll talk," said Fuentes. "I could put her in the same fight as Magalie."

"She didn't want to talk to you the last time."

"That's because she hadn't met me. She has now. She's changed her mind."

"She already has a patron. An American corporation."

"Yes, but they wouldn't mind a local partner. I know this game. I'm donating the bulls for the charity bullfight, but you can't have her fighting in charity bullfights forever. You can't do this on a shoestring budget. Her *novillero* career will take time and money. And you should get a salary as her manager."

"I'm not her manager. I don't have the time."

"It's good to have you back, *matador de toros*," said Fuentes cheerfully, his hand raised in a wave, as the elevators door closed.

It had been a long time since anyone called him that, thought Roberto in the elevator. *Matador de toros*—killer of bulls. The word *matar* simply meant to kill. Ever since bullfighting was banned from national television in Spain, the only time one heard that word on television was in association with murder trials. Crimes of passion, drug crimes. *I did not kill her*, a man would say squarely to the press outside the courtroom.

There was a time when *matar* was associated with kingly men of slight build in glittering clothing who were revered by entire cities. Famous writers and war reporters followed them around. Newsreels were made of their movements, as if they were generals of armies. But now *matar* was associated with crime, with courtrooms, thought Roberto. He didn't want anyone calling him that again in public. He had been to America. All that had been expunged. It was no longer a cross he had to bear.

❧

"If you hadn't deferred grad school, we would not be spending Christmas in a hospital in Seville," said Shelly, after she finished crying.

"Ah!" cried Tomas suddenly, as if he had been struck. "Roberto de la Torre!"

Handshakes, embraces, questions, hugs. A nurse came in and told them to quiet down on account of the elderly patient who was the only other occupant in the room. The son who was visiting that patient took out his camera phone and quietly snapped pictures of Roberto. It was hard to recognize them when they were not in costume, thought the son excitedly.

"Hey," said Roberto to Alex. He leaned over and hugged her tightly. She smelled of starched bandages and antiseptic. He remembered a time when she smelled of lemon cake.

"Hey, you."

"Still alive?"

"Barely."

"I saw Fuentes downstairs."

"He's okay. He invited me to recuperate on his ranch. Free."

"Did he? Let's talk about that later."

Alex had a bandage on her head, midriff and right leg. "Doesn't this just scream *amateur?* Some matador. You should have heard the nurse. I got an earful."

Shelly sniffed and leaned over, combing Alex's hair with her fingers. "I can't deal with this. Look at your face."

"Hey, have you ever seen matadors who got gored in the eye? I'm totally lucky. It's just a scratch. At least they

182

didn't shave all my hair off to fix that. They shaved one spot, though. I have a bald patch right here, under the bandage." She pointed while her godmother fussed. "It'll look crazy when I get out of hospital, I'll have to wear a hat. Or maybe a wide hair band."

Shelly whimpered.

Tomas looked at Roberto approvingly. It was the first time he had ever seen him in person. "You know, I'm a believer in destiny. Deep down in my bones, I always knew someday we will all meet, in circumstances like this. We're in historic Sevilla, in Spain, in a hospital, and here I am, with an injured *novillero* and a famous matador. It's full circle. It really is. Back when Alex was little, chasing the goats around the ranch, I had a premonition of this moment."

"Grandma would say it's the old nonsense starting all over again," said Alex.

"I got a call from her. She's really coming. She's taking the train, though. She'll be here tomorrow," said Tomas.

"It's so good to see you all," said Alex suddenly. "It's almost worth getting gored. I'd been so lonely in matador school. I can't believe you guys are all in the same room. They say funerals bring people together. So many people came to Dad and Mom's funeral, remember?"

"Not funny, Alex," said Shelly.

"Sorry."

"You have no idea how much last-minute air tickets from Austin to Sevilla cost."

"You guys should move here."

"I have a ranch to run," said Shelly. "Last time I checked, it belonged to your dad, and I was running it for you."

Antonio appeared at the doorway and gestured urgently for Roberto, who excused himself. The two men disappeared down the hallway.

"He's a shy kid, isn't he?" said Shelly.

"He's not shy!" said Tomas. "Shelly has never seen Roberto in a bullring! She thinks he's a shy foreign student. That's just because he can't speak much English, I tell you. He comes across differently in his own language. He's a *matador de toros*, for God's sake."

Shelly shuddered. "I don't want to see either of you in a bullring. Is that okay with you, if I am just spared that? Tomas is obsessing over your video clips, but I won't watch a thing. I won't. Now, is there anything you need? Do you have toiletries, clothing? Can I go to the store and buy something for you?"

Alex had shut her eyes momentarily at a wave of pain. She opened her eyes and forced a smile. "If you can go to my apartment and pick up my stuff and bring it here, that would be great."

Tomas said suddenly, "Do you want me to get Roberto? I don't know where he's gone."

"It's okay. I'm sure he'll be back."

Tomas exchanged glances with Shelly, then said, "I don't like how we are over there in the States while you're all alone here. You don't even have a manager. The only relative you have here is Sofia, and she's not even close, and she's what, eighty? If anything like that happens again, we'll go berserk. You should have seen Shelly on the plane. I'd never seen her pray."

"I wasn't praying."

"Yeah you were."

"I was asking whoever was up there to take care of Alex."

"That's praying, you stubborn, proud woman," said Tomas fondly.

"I can take care of myself," said Alex.

"You can't even go to the bathroom yourself," said Shelly.

"I've got nurses!"

"Alex, if you want to be a real matador, you need a manager," said Tomas. "You need a team."

"My matador school provides the team for now. Don't worry."

Tomas looked at Shelly, who told him not to look at her, because she didn't know the first thing about bull-fighting.

"Can we offer to pay Roberto to be your manager? I know you said he won't fight again, but we're just asking him to manage you," said Tomas.

"You mean babysit me? Look, you guys, I know you're worried, but you can't just be my godparents till I'm twenty-one, then fob me off to another babysitter after that. I've got to do this on my own. Anyway, he won't be my manager, he's already said so. He's got a degree to finish. He's already pushed back one semester this spring because of me. I can't ask him to defer."

"Why not? You're the queen of deferring school," said Shelly.

"It's not right," said Tomas, pulling at his lower lip thoughtfully. "It's just not right."

They needn't have worried. Things were already in motion.

❁

Roberto was on the phone in the hospital cafeteria. From the corner of his eye he could see a young woman creep up and snap pictures of him with her camera phone. He nodded at her tolerantly.

"No, he doesn't know what he's doing," he said in a low voice on the phone.

Antonio brought their coffees and sat down across from him.

"Not him either," he said again.

Antonio gestured but Roberto turned away, intent on the phone.

"No. He's a fool, look what he did to R. I'm in public, I'm not naming names. You know who I mean . . . Yes . . . Of course it was all the manager's fault, everybody knows this and nobody wants to admit it. Don't quote me . . . No. Not him . . . No, too old . . . No, too expensive, and never really earned his keep, from what I have heard . . . No, he's good but I happen to know that he's busy with Brava . . . No, too inexperienced . . . Who? Him? Have you met Alejandra? She'll *never* get along with that guy . . . Hold on, there's another incoming call." Roberto looked at Antonio, sipped the coffee, and rolled his eyes. "Hello? This is Antonio's phone . . . Well, I happen to be Roberto de la Torre . . . No, I'm not kidding. What do you want, who is this?"

A smile began curving on Antonio's lips. This was not the Roberto he remembered. Where did he learn this new manner?

"Fine. Fax it to Antonio. Or email, whatever. We'll take a look . . . I'm sorry, no comment . . . No, you can't talk to her, she's too sick. Try again next week . . . No comment. Sorry, I have a caller waiting on the other line . . . Hello? . . . Yes, who else do you have?"

Finally, Roberto clapped the phone shut, exhausted, and handed it back to his old manager.

"Well?"

"The only person I trust is you. You should be her manager."

"I wish I could, but my plate's full with El Rivera, and I manage a couple of good-for-nothing *novilleros* on the side as well," said Antonio. "Had to keep busy after you retired."

Roberto looked at his old manager sullenly and help-lessly.

Antonio grinned. "By the way, has anyone told you that you have an American accent now when you speak Spanish?"

"You are saying this just to irritate me, aren't you?"

His old manager surveyed him squarely. "You know, she's rubbed off on you."

"Who?"

"Alejandra Herrera. You remind me of her. Alejandra y Roberto. I think the act will sell."

In San Martín, a bunch of elderly men trickled desulto-rily into a bar.

"Problem number one, she is a girl," said the president of the local *peña*. "It's impossible."

"In times of war, you have to use the womenfolk."

"Problem number two, she is American."

"That is harder to fix."

"Problem number three — she has had patchy train-ing."

"I read about the Sevilla accident. She impressed some people at the school. Brave."

"But green. Very green. Having the balls to do a *reci-biendo* is great, but the rest is quite dismal."

"Problem number four — she is a *novillero*, she is not a full matador yet. Will she ever get anywhere? Or is she just wasting everyone's time?"

A general murmur of disenchantment.

"Problem number five — De la Torre has retired."

"*That* is the biggest problem."

"Sofia Herrera should never have sent her son to America."

"Agree."

"We only have two bullfighting families to choose from, and neither one is working properly. It's sickening."

"The mayor said he's trying to attract more immigrants to move here, have you heard?"

"I never listen to what he says. Why?"

"Shrinking population."

"Can he try to attract bullfighters? Maybe we'll have another César Rincón."

"What are the chances De la Torre will fight?"

"Zero. He is Californian now."

"I have half a mind to move back to Sevilla."

"Why don't you?"

"Don't want to be near the in-laws."

"Rob? You still here?"

She reached for the night light. It illuminated the ward. The patient in the other bed had departed that morning, so she had the room to herself. The armchair by the side of her bed folded out into a small bed. Roberto was huddled in it. White earphones trailed from his ears into his pocket.

"Pssst," said Alex. He was really asleep.

It was four a.m. She crawled out of the bed, grabbed the drip stand, and hobbled to the bathroom, trying not to make too much noise. After a week, she was finally able to go to the bathroom unaided, but it still took her a long time. After much difficulty, she crawled back in bed again. She couldn't sleep. She worried about him. He was spending too much time here in the hospital. The nurses were sweet on him because he was Roberto de la Torre and they remembered him from before, when he had been a patient here with his own wounds from the *corrida*. He had brought his clothes and toiletries. He showered and shaved there and often slept there, in the folded-out armchair, which was too short for him. At first Alex worried about visiting hours, but in that hospital it seemed *de rigueur* for relatives to sleep by one's bedside twenty-four hours a day, doubling as nurses. That was what the convertible armchair was for.

That night she had told Roberto he had to go back to his hotel. But he was unusually talkative. She had a third operation scheduled for the following morning for the abdominal wound, and he thought he'd stick around that evening for moral support. He told her about his classes. He mentioned his girlfriend, Megan. Some California chick. Studying oil painting at his school. They met in a café; started talking. One half of Alex was listening to the stories of Megan sympathetically, asking polite questions. The other half of Alex—the subterranean half—raged silently in utter darkness, ramming occasionally and blindly at the small enclosure that it found itself in, maddened by an incessant, pricking pain.

And now he had fallen asleep, even though he said he was going back to the hotel. He must be having jet lag. He wouldn't say when he was going back to San Francisco. She wondered about his class schedule. She hoped he hadn't abandoned school. He sounded pretty serious about getting that degree.

She sat up and gently removed his iPod from his pocket and pulled the earphones away from him, fixed them in her ears, and turned it on. She looked at his playlists. They were all new. Some of the bands she had never heard of. Must be a Northern California thing. He had new friends, went to new concerts, listened to new radio channels now. He played this music in a new car, with somebody else in the passenger seat.

Their positions were completely reversed. He was

rushing headlong into an American future while she crept slowly back into the catacombs of the past. She knew exactly what she was chasing. Did he?

Alex closed her eyes and tried to imagine his American existence.

When the bull charged, she found herself lifted and tossed into the sky. The sun felt very close.

The first few stunning seconds were always admirable, when the flesh just showed knuckle-white dents, like the bark of a tree, like the side of a wooden fence. She thought that would be all, that she had got off easy. Then the flesh remembered what it was made of and the blood began to flow.

She was thirsty in the ambulance, but she couldn't drink anything because there was sand in her mouth, between her teeth. She tried to hold her breath, not to breathe too hard. She had a vision that if she sneezed, that she might accidentally lose her insides. She could feel her blood leaving her body. *Stay inside,* she prayed. *Come back.* She could feel herself blacking out again, her forehead growing cold. Her eyes were wide open, but she could not see. She blinked.

"I can't see," she said to the medic. The ringing in her ears was so loud that she couldn't hear her own voice. She was horribly embarrassed; there was something embarrassing about being so weak, about losing grip, about sliding away like that. Right before she fainted, she apologized to everyone in the ambulance.

"Grandma!"

"Your face!"

"Don't worry, it's not permanent." Alex held her face up as her grandmother inspected her bandages. "Came pretty close to my right eye, didn't it? Imagine, I would have had to wear an eye patch."

"Don't even joke about this kind of thing," said Sofia sternly.

"Don't worry about my face, if anything's going to kill me, it's this." Alex pointed at her midriff. "This is the unkindest cut. This is the one that is going to keep me from training for weeks. I've had three operations already."

Sofia remembered the old dangers. She looked beseechingly at Roberto. The relatives of matadors had a unique understanding of medicine.

"They're trying to ward off infection, I think it'll be fine, if it hasn't happened by now," he said. "They bombarded her with antibiotics early. This hospital is used to goring wounds." At the sight of Sofia's expression, he added, "Can I get you some coffee?"

Sofia got up, embraced him and kissed both sides of his cheek. "How are you liking America?"

"I'm adjusting."

"Then stay there. Don't come back. *Never* come back. Don't be like Alejandra."

"Yes, ma'am."

Sofia chatted with Alex for a while, then rose slowly and took Roberto's arm. "What's that about a coffee? Is there a coffee shop in this hospital? I would like to speak to you."

Roberto darted a look at Alex. "It's on the second floor."

"Let's go. We won't be long, Alejandra." Sofia walked determinedly to the door.

Roberto followed. Alex opened her mouth, then shut it.

The young nurse came in with her lunch and changed the TV channel briskly. "Watch this," she told Roberto and Alex.

It was a famous journalist on a talk show. He was denouncing bullfighting.

"Eh?" said the nurse to Alex, expectantly.

"He says teenager matadors are uneducated," said Alex calmly, peeling open a carton of orange juice. "I've got my BA. And I'm going to business school."

The nurse rolled her eyes and left the room.

"She's sweet on you, but she hates me," said Alex. "Says that young people shouldn't be matadors. I said you were younger than me, and she said: *but he's a boy, and he's a professional.* Can you believe it?"

"Yes."

They watched the show as opinions rang out loudly among the talking heads, including a politician and an animal rights activist. Roberto changed the channel in disgust.

Alex said, "I can't really worry about the bulls. I am in such a personal hell of my own making, in my head, that I have no energy to worry about the bulls. I'm relieved to be in hospital. It's a relief to look at physical wounds."

"I never knew you were that mentally tormented," said Roberto.

"I'm a basket case. I'm trying to grow up, find my culture, defer business school, break into bullfighting as a novice, be a feminist, keep my family happy, and be myself, all at once. Add to that the hopeless vanity of an athlete, the ego of an artist, and lots of other things, and it's no wonder I fail in the bullring. Oh, and you should have seen my inbox: I've got 288 emails in the last 2 weeks. Some joker figured out my Hotmail account and posted it on some animal rights website after they televised the Sevilla goring. I've got a million death threats from vegetarians. They don't even know me, and they hate me. I'm just waiting for the guy from the US Embassy to show up and deport me."

Roberto said nothing for a long time. He stuck his hands in the pocket of his jacket, jiggled his car keys, looked out the window. He knew exactly what she was going through. Finally, he said, "You've got too many distractions. You need to go someplace quiet and just train. You need to surround yourself with the right people who just care about the quality of your art. Forget about everything else."

"It's easy for you to say, you're out of it, living in San Francisco."

"You just need to be one thing. A good matador. Forget about the crowds. Don't watch any television, don't listen to the *aficionados*, don't read what people say in the press. You've got to tune them all out and focus on your art. Find out your expectations of yourself, then live up to them. Then, when you are ready, let the people back in again. You'll be better equipped to face them then."

"You really think so?"

"I've been down this road before."

Alex stared at him thoughtfully for a long time, until he grew embarrassed. He pointed at her lunch tray. "You eating that orange?"

A few days later, when she was better, Alex's matador school friends came to see her in the hospital, including the two other girl matadors, Isabella and Luisa, who were a lot younger than her. The school only took students aged fourteen to twenty; Alex barely made the cut-off age. She was the oldest, tallest, and the only foreigner. It was nearly Christmas. They didn't know what she liked, so they brought her nougat.

There was a bit of a commotion when they realized Roberto de la Torre was around.

"José," said Alex, pointing, chewing nougat. Roberto nodded encouragingly.

"I messed up; she tried to save me," said the teenager shyly.

"That's Ignacio, Rodrigo — all four of us got fucked up," said Alex. "You guys got discharged already?"

"Yeah, you got it the worst."

Alex grinned. "Yeah, I'm the biggest, I've got more surface area to get hit."

"That's okay," said Roberto, signing autographs on whatever scraps of paper the teenagers could find. "You gave her a chance to be a hero. She likes that."

"Do not!"

"Should have heard her on the phone to me when she was first admitted," said Roberto to the students. "Cried like a girl."

Giggles. Roberto said he had to go run an errand and left.

"He's not as built as I thought," said Ignacio, flexing and looking at his biceps self-consciously. The students often talked endlessly about exercise and competed on stamina.

Alex said from the bed, "God, Ig, if you work out any more, you're going to look like a psycho."

"Roberto's cute when he doesn't shave," said Isabella. "He looks American." Luisa said he looked better clean-shaven, with longer hair. A solemn dispute began in which Alex was asked to take sides, and refused. The boys lounged in the back of the room, texting their friends on their cellphones about Roberto, half-sniggering, half-jealous.

194

"He kissed my cheek," said Isabella. "I shall not wash my face for a week."

"Is he coming back?" asked Luisa.

"No, not with you guys here," said Alex. "You asked him for autographs. I told you not to."

"Sorry!"

"Can't help it!"

"He's *still* big."

"You don't have it," said Ignacio smugly. He was looking at her cellphone.

"Have what?"

The boys looked over his shoulder as he stabbed some buttons. They whispered and snickered among themselves.

"I just downloaded it for you, trial version of *E-Faena*."

"What the hell is it?" asked Alex, examining her phone.

"It's a new bullfighting game. Get good at it, I'll take you on in the two player version."

Alex screamed in triumph. "I love it! Why didn't you tell me when I first checked into the hospital! I was getting sick of talk shows!"

❁

It was one a.m. in the hospital. The night nurse stuck her head into Alex's ward. She told Roberto, "If you guys scream or shout one more time, I'm kicking you out."

He was perched at the end of her bed, furiously playing *E-Faena* with Alex. They had their earphones on. They both looked up, momentarily disoriented.

"What?" asked Roberto politely, pulling an earphone out of his ear.

The nurse repeated what she said, scribbled on Alex's clipboard, and left in a huff.

"When can you get out?" asked Roberto, pausing the game. "We need to play this on a big screen."

"No shit. We need the full version of this; play it on the console. We need to get serious."

"We need to get very serious."

"Let me talk to the doctor tomorrow. I don't see why I can't be released. I mean, I can *almost* pee on my own."

"What's your apartment situation here?"

"I rent a dumpy studio in the old part of town. Shelly and Tomas were staying there before they flew back to Austin. Said they threw out my old furniture and redecorated it. Aren't they the best?"

"Got a TV?"

"No."

"Give me the keys. I'll put a TV in it."

"Cool." She reached in her drawer and tossed them to him.

He swung his long legs over the side of the bed. "I'll go before the nurse comes back. I can't wait for you to get out. Antonio's been busy talking to your school. He's friends with the artistic director. He's going to have a meeting with the school when you're out. And you've got to get back into shape."

"You going back to SF?" asked Alex casually.

He had been in Sevilla for two weeks. He spent Christmas at the hospital. ("Who am I going to see? I don't want to see anyone else in Sevilla.") Often he got phone calls from California at odd hours of the night and she pretended to sleep while he crept outside and took them.

Roberto yawned, wound his earphones around his phone and put on his jacket. "I blew past my return date on that ticket; I've got to find a ticket now to go back in the New Year. I'll see you tomorrow."

"Ciao."

AlexH1988: *They've just released E-Faena 2.*

Roberto was in his hotel when his phone chirped. He opened one eye and reached under his pillow. It was seven in the morning. Did she ever sleep?

RobT1988: "No way."

Way. They've improved on perfection.

"How do you know?"

Someone posted about it on VirtualPeña.

"What's that?"

Facebook group for girls into bullfighting. You should check it out, you're out of touch.

"I remember now. It's for girls."

That's why you should look. It's got all kinds of old photos of you and comments. Listen to this: Te quiero mucho Roberto . . . Qué GUAPO! xxx *from* Carmen. Roberto = el mejor!!! x Maria. Roberto. . .sin duda el numero uno! *It goes on and on and on for dozens of posts. What does this mean:* Roberto de la Torre es un tremendo bizcocho! *You are a tremendous cake? Isn't* bizcocho *cake? Or is it biscuit?*

"This gets very old. You'll see."

I have a fan page. I only have 20 fans.

"20 fans is a start."

They're all the students at the school. You have 2,789 fans.

"So work harder."

Nobody says I'm a big biscuit.

"Sign in under a different name and post that about yourself."

Can't you post something encouraging?

"What about: 'Because of you I have seen the perfection of God.'"

Yes! Yes!

"I just posted it as RobT1988."

Thank you!!!

"You're very welcome."

You should read VirtualPeña, *it's better than the bullfight-*

*ing news in print. These days they've fixated on El Rivera
though. They say he's got real abs unlike you.*

"Quite the clown, aren't you?"

Must be my meds.

Alex was in the hospital for fourteen days.

"My plants all died," she reported from her postage-
stamp-sized balcony. The apartment smelled musty. She
pulled back the shutters and opened the single window. It
was raining heavily.

Roberto set her bags down. He laid out the bottles of
medication and their instructions on the kitchen table.
"See this? You have to take this. If you skip it, like I did
once, you'll regret it."

"I'm not a pill person."

"Neither am I, but it's not something you can skip if
you want to recover quickly. Trust me."

"Where are you going?"

He put his hands in the pockets of his wet coat. "Back
to my hotel. My bags are there."

"Is it nearby?"

"Right round the corner. It's a pension. Here's my
room number and my address. Shelly's paid your phone
bill when she was here; the phone works. So does the
Internet."

"You're really staying then?" asked Alex tiredly.

"Who else is going drive you to the hospital three times
a week for your rehab?"

"Shit, that is a lot of trouble for you. I'm so sorry."

"I've had to move things around, but that's all done
now. I've got a phone, a rental car, Wi-Fi, a bed. I brought
my things from San Francisco."

Alex slumped in her bed and winced.

"After that, we go to Cadiz to Fuentes' to train. You need to train with more live animals. In order to do that, you have to get out of the city."

"Who's paying for all this?" she asked suddenly.

"Read the amended contract, it says there."

"Thanks for negotiating it."

"I learned a lot from Antonio on the phone. He helped. I'm starting to realize all the shit he's had to deal with on my behalf for years."

"How do you like being my manager?"

"Temporary manager. We're still looking for a real one for you, but let's make the best use of the time."

"I'm sorry you had to quit school."

"Temporarily."

She wanted to say something about his girlfriend in California, but decided it would be presumptuous. It would come out wrong, no matter how she said it.

"What time would you like to eat? I'll come get you for dinner."

"You don't have to eat with me. Don't you have friends in Sevilla?"

"I don't want to see them," said Roberto, looking at an old magazine. "All they'll want to talk about is bullfighting."

"*We* talk about bullfighting."

"No, we won't. We'll talk about *Mario Kart*."

It wasn't until about half an hour later, when Roberto was back in his hotel room, when a message popped up on his phone:

BTW thanks for the TV. It's bigger than the bed.

They developed a routine. On the days she had rehabilitation appointments, he came to pick her up. He would sit outside the clinic and draw while she worked on her exercises. Roberto could see her through the plate glass window and began drawing her every time she worked on a new routine. He wore a baseball hat and mirrored aviator glasses so that nobody recognized him.

On the days she did not need to go to the clinic, they ran. Her apartment was near the Guadalquivir River that bisected Sevilla from the gypsy neighborhood of Triana. She chose the apartment precisely because the riverbank provided a reliable and continuous path for runners. She loved its expansive views; it allowed her to believe in possibilities.

They ran in the morning and at night; they ran even when it rained heavily. They ran the length of the river on both banks. These were long runs during which they hardly spoke.

It was an athlete's life; a monastic existence. She went to the gym and kept a food diary; he drew. The only amusement they allowed themselves was playing *E-Faena*. Sometimes, in the late afternoons, his cellphone rang, he would step out of her apartment into the narrow balcony and shut the sliding door. She could hear him speaking English; she heard a woman's name.

No one talked about bullfighting.

In the third week, she ducked into an alleyway in Triana.

"Where are you going?" he panted.

She disappeared into a bakery and came out with a sugar-encrusted Frisbee studded with aniseed. "I just had a sudden craving for these *tortas*."

"They're all fat and sugar! And there you were, keeping a food diary, you fraud!"

"I'll work it off. So, will you show me your drawings?" she asked, munching.

"Nothing to show."

"You're drawing me. Are you finally making a graphic novel of my life?"

"I'm linking the panels up into some kind of story. I'm not sure what yet. I've got speech and thought balloons, but they're empty."

"Well, am I in it?" she said, dusting sugar from her hands.

"Yes."

She looked thoughtful.

A local taurine tabloid ran a photo of them running in the city, and for a while one or two photographers were always lounging in the tiny plaza outside her five-storey apartment building, waiting for them to emerge.

"Just smile. Look right into the camera and smile," Roberto whispered, taking her hat off. "They're just doing their job — do yours."

She took the cues from him and did what he did.

A runner, thought Alex, sees the city differently from normal pedestrians. You develop a special acquaintance with lone alleyways, shortcuts, sleeping tramps, the pale, unseen undersides of bridges. You learn to avoid the older parts of the city, full of winding streets that dead-end into nondescript plazas. You follow tram tracks and broad avenues. You speed past dog walkers, street sweepers, construction workers, lovers, touts; you are completely oblivious to their duties, their trials, their sorrows. When it rains, you realize that Sevilla's cobblestones are not your friend. When it is dry, your mouth turns bitter from the stiff wind and the dust of the road. Above all, you only have ears for one master.

I, demands the pavement. *I, I, I.*

Roberto ran beside or behind her most of the time. They did not speak when running. But they each had silent conversations with themselves. Sometimes their thoughts would bubble forth when they slowed down to cross at a busy intersection.

"Have they found other matadors for my bullfight?"

"Not yet."

"I can take on six bulls by myself."

"It's a charity bullfight, Alex. You're not supposed to commit suicide at such an event. There will be kids in the audience."

"You can be in it with me. Three bulls each. *De la Torre y Herrera, mano a mano.*"

"No."

"One day, Roberto de la Torre, you will graduate me in Las Ventas in my *alternativa*. You will hand me your bull and I will become a full-fledged matador."

"That sounds nice. Unfortunately, only a fantasy because I'm out of it now."

"For now. Hey! Where are you going?" She stopped short as he ran past the Triana bridge.

"I don't like running across this bridge."

"You always say that. But I want to get across. I want to go to my *torta* place."

It began to drizzle. He reluctantly ran back to where she stood, at the start of the wrought iron bridge.

"You see these padlocks?" He pointed to a cluster of steel and brass padlocks fastened on the low black railings.

"Yeah? Bicycle locks?"

"No, they're not. They're put here by couples. They split the keys, and years later come back and unfasten them. Kind of a pledge. Love pledge."

"Really?" It was raining heavily now. She stooped and peered at the locks, which were mostly stainless steel and brass, of all shapes and sizes. "They've got names written on them with black marker. Aw. How cute."

He walked further along the bridge, searching in the rain. "Delfina put one here. I forgot where."

The rain now came down in torrents. They jogged hurriedly across the bridge and ducked into the Triana central market at the other end to stay dry. The stores were mostly closed. Shopkeepers were cleaning up. It smelled of dried fish.

"God, it's really pissing down," said Alex, staring at the grey clouds. But Roberto had disappeared into a store in the market. He emerged with an enormous red and black pair of bolt cutters he had borrowed from a shopkeeper. He went back out in the rain and looked at every single padlock carefully. She called, "What are you doing!"

"Cutting!"

She began to laugh. "Give it up, Rob! Maybe it's not there anymore!"

In the distance she saw him bend down and cut something, struggle a bit, then rip a lock free. He tossed it into the river. But he wasn't finished. He walked up and down the length of the bridge with that bolt cutter, a determined look on his face.

"There's *more?*" howled Alex gleefully.

"Be quiet!"

"Did each woman know that you already had a lock on the bridge?"

"Wasn't my idea!" He bent and cut another lock.

Alex ran back out in the rain, watching him. "Hey! Don't cut the *wrong* one! You'd break someone's heart."

"I know. I'm not stupid."

She was amused by the tiny spark of subversiveness in Roberto. It would flare out once in a while, out of nowhere, then disappear as mysteriously as it came. He flung a total of four locks vehemently into the swollen river. He went back into the market and gave the bolt cutter to the shopkeeper, looking very pleased with himself.

"I can't believe you just di—" began Alex.

"Shut up. I don't want to hear it. Run."

❁

"I didn't mean to involve so many people."

Alex had reached new depths of self-pity after four beers.

"I didn't think it would cost so much money."

It was Sunday and raining again. It had rained for a whole week. The streets in the old center of Sevilla had turned into a minefield of treacherous, water-filled cracks and potholes. They gave up running that day as every single pair of running shoes they owned were damp.

She stared at the ceiling. The only source of light came from a desk lamp near Roberto. Through the thin pane of glass in the balcony windows she could hear a pony trap clop-clopping down the street. The sharp, bright clatter bounced madly around the narrow canyon separating Alex's building from the one across the street.

"I hate those pony rides for tourists," she said from the depths of her armchair. "Why do they have them every-where?"

"God, that is so loud. Sounds like it's heading right into the apartment."

"There goes another one. There are always two or three in a row."

They listened. If she shut her eyes, thought Alex, she could be in the last century.

"How much are you paying for this place? No one

rents in this part of town except retirees and foreigners," said Roberto, looking out the window.

"My choices were: the seventies, the fifties, or the eighteenth century. Guess which one I picked."

"I don't like driving in the old city center. I scraped the side mirrors of the rental car getting to this street. Look at how narrow it is. And there is no parking."

"I'm sorry." She finished her can of beer. "I didn't think you would have to come here and drive me to rehab, train with me, live out of a suitcase in a hotel for me."

"Funny what managers would do for matadors that they wouldn't even do for their own girlfriends."

The rain blew against the windows. "Is Megan upset you are in Spain?"

"I think she's hooked up with some musician from El Salvador."

"What!"

"Plays the guitar. She keeps talking about him. Met him in some World Music concert."

"That's crap," she said sympathetically. "I'm sorry."

He was drawing. He erased a tiny corner of the page, brushing away the eraser bits absently. Finally, he said, "Antonio said retired matadors become managers. It's just something that one is expected to do. That's what he did."

"You didn't pull out of bullfighting just to be the manager of a second-rate bullfighter wannabe."

"I didn't know I was one. Are you second-rate?"

"Didn't you hear the doctor in the hospital? Professionals don't get gored."

He looked up sharply. "We all get gored. Everyone. I haven't seen you in the ring since Fallas two years ago, Alex. In fact, I've never seen you in front of the bull except for that one time. But I know what I'm seeing. You're almost there. One day, you'll wake up, and you'll know.

Deep inside you, you will have this ridiculous feeling that you will never be gored again. You will just know."

"Really?"

"Really. It may not be true, but the day will come when you get that feeling. You just have to hit that zone."

"What if I never get there?"

"It's too late to ask that question."

She slid further in the armchair. "I'm fine risking my own life and postponing grad school and pissing off Shelly and Tomas. What really scares me is that I have somehow dragged you into the thick of it, just when you were getting out."

"Did you think about that when you first made that phone call to me in Madrid nearly three years ago?"

"I didn't know you were getting out. If I had known you were quitting . . . Anyway, *you* called *me*."

"I did?" He was surprised.

"Yeah! I was at my grandma's. I will always remember that call. You called me."

"How did I get your number?"

She searched her memory, then smothered a smile. "I threw you a paper airplane during a bullfight in Valencia."

He continued drawing. "Precisely. You started it all. Are you regretting now?"

"I didn't think you were going to quit. I didn't think you would go to America, enroll in art school, find a girlfriend there, get all nicely settled, and then have to come back and drive me to rehab. I feel so guilty. I really do. I hate it. I want you to go back to San Francisco and just finish whatever you were doing."

He erased something on the page again, then put the paper away in his portfolio, tied up the black tape around it, and went over to the kitchen counter. "Want some water?"

"I want another beer."

"I'm coming with you to Cadiz, Alex, whether you like it or not. You can't back out now. There's too much riding on it. You got me out of retirement. You started it, you finish it."

She moaned at the ceiling. "God, I've been drowning in so much guilt ever since I was in hospital. I might fail to become a matador and accidentally end up a real Catholic."

Robert was silent. Then, "Anyway, maybe this is my way of finding out if I really mean to leave Spain."

"What do you mean?"

"This is a test." Roberto tossed her the last can of beer in the fridge. "Knock yourself out. I'm off. See you tomorrow morning. Is that the last clinic appointment?"

"Second last." She pulled the tab, thought about the calories, and set it aside.

"Good. The end is near."

After the door closed behind him, she realized he had left behind his portfolio. She sprang out of bed and opened it curiously.

"You know what your problem is?" said Antonio.

Roberto came back in from the tiny roof terrace of his hotel room. It was past midnight. "What?"

"You're the same age. The manager of a matador is supposed to be an older, wiser, more experienced matador. You have to be her manager, her trainer, her butler, her shrink, her confidante. But you can't possibly. Why? Because you're her age. You can't possibly see far enough to advise her. You're still in the woods yourself."

"She's older than me," said Roberto, smiling suddenly, turning on the television and putting it on mute. "By two weeks. She never fails to remind me."

"You were born two weeks apart? What are you, twins?" His old manager was in a bar in Madrid, calling him after a bullfight.

"That might explain why I have put up with more of her shit than I have ever put up with any woman."

"Yeah, didn't you can Delfina when she acted up?"

"Delfina canned me, actually."

"Rubbish."

"She was ashamed of dating a matador once she went to university." He winced when he remembered her words: *embarrassing, outdated, like dating a pro-wrestler, a circus performer.*

"Really? Was that how it went? Well, I told the press you fired her because she was getting temperamental and affecting your performance."

"No wonder she hated me. She's tried calling me this year, I wonder what for."

"I'm glad I never remarried. They're just trouble. And the ones who want to do a man's job are the most trouble of all."

"I thought you liked Alex."

"I do. But that's not going to change the fact that what she's doing, as a foreigner and a woman, is impossible. Oh, a British reporter in Madrid just interviewed me about you. You refused to talk to him. He had to cast a wider net."

"I'm sorry."

"He asked if you're crazy to be her manager."

"What did you say?"

"I say, sure, you're crazy, but why should they care, according to them bullfighting's on its way out anyway. Why should they care so much about our outmoded, tribal customs, about having our matador ranks invaded by beautiful, hot-headed American women who are scions of long-lost taurine dynasties, by temperamental French teenage girls backed by wealthy Spanish ranchers? Didn't they always say that we were a bunch of old, leathery, retired has-beens? So leave us alone to our strange, feudal, laughable practices."

"You say all that?"

"Let me tell you how it works with the foreign press. They need an interesting headline on a slow news day. Another Andalucian matador with a long, mournful face gets gored? Not interesting. But an English-speaking American college girl gets gored? They'll eat it up. Alex getting injured in Sevilla was a nothing story that got syndicated around the world."

"Yesterday some journalist stopped us in a bar and asked her *why do you want to be a female matador?*"

"She must have perfected her answer by now."

"She said it's because she didn't get enough love in her childhood."

"Ha! I approve!"

Roberto shook his head absently, changing channels. "I've been struggling so much with Alex that I forgot to pay attention to that other aspect of bullfighting. The publicity."

"You sure got your work cut out for you. I'm not convinced that it's your destiny to be her manager—temporary or not—but it sure isn't mine."

"You're right. I can't see far enough. I don't enjoy it, but now I believe that this is something I'm meant to do. It validates something. Gives a meaning to all the work I've done."

"I know what you mean. That's how I felt when I first worked with you."

"You were a good teacher."

"I tried. But look at how your career turned out."

"I'm sorry."

"Don't apologize. I'm not saying this to blame you. It's

just that we're all a bit worried about you and where you are heading."

"I'll be fine."

"I have to go. El Rivera texted me, complaining about something or other. He's on a diet. You know, fuck all these amateurs. Fuck them. You were the real thing. You have to come back in the ring. And you have to come back by your own will. Not your dad's."

"It's not going to happen. If I'm sure of anything, I'm sure of this."

"You know, I was just thinking the other day. It's good that you went to America to study and came back. You seem to be a bit smarter now."

Roberto smiled, watching animal rights protestors on the television waving placards mutely in Barcelona. "Talk to you later."

In the morning, he let himself in her apartment. She was in the shower.

The television was on the morning news. Another news feature about the proposed Catalonia ban on bull-fights. He found his portfolio by her bedside table.

She had filled in all of the empty speech balloons in his panels.

He looked up. Alex strode out quickly in her bath towel, grabbed her clothes, and went back into the bath-room and shut the door. "I'm be ready in one minute!"

He heard the hairdryer go on.

Suddenly, he realized why she always wore long trousers and sleeves. There were old goring scars on her legs and arms. She had mentioned them before. He simply forgot.

"It's one minute," he called.

"Very funny."

The news sent a little tingle of betrayal, of disappointment, in Alex. She caught herself in surprise. Why did she feel that? Where did it come from? She said cheerfully, "Congrats Nicky! That was quick."

"Yes. Don't do the math, you'll realize it doesn't add up."

Alex laughed. "I can't do math anyway. It's good to hear your voice."

"I'm nervous about giving birth. But after hearing about your wounds in your email, I think I'm going to have it easy. A dirty bull's horn in your gut is pretty gross."

"Childbirth is pretty gross to me."

"Where are you, anyway?"

"At a gas station. We're driving back to Cadiz. I'm going to spend the next three months in a bull breeding ranch, apparently."

"Huh? Why?"

"This bull breeder Roberto knows, he allows matadors to stay and train on his ranch. We get to live there. The guest house doesn't even have a phone. I insisted that they get me Internet access or I won't go. If I can't email Shelly and Tomas they'll go nuts. It's going to be a real pain. It's out in the country. There's nothing for miles, no cinema, nothing. Roberto thinks it's necessary to take me out of matador school at this point and train me himself. He said the school could only take me this far."

"Are you sure you still want to do this?"

"Too late to back out now." Alex had wandered off into the field behind the gas station, loving the anonymity of the highway. If she closed her eyes and listened to the sound of the cars zipping past, she could almost believe she was in Texas. She was suddenly, immensely, homesick.

ACT THREE

The Act of the Kill

It WAS FEBRUARY.
"Get up!" He shouted from across the barrier in the training ring. "Alex!"

She scrambled up and decided to run for it. She vaulted across the barrier into the narrow walkway between the two ring fences while the cow gave chase. Then, in a beautiful smooth leap, without breaking stride, the cow vaulted easily over the barrier. Both Alex and Roberto leapt back into the ring in alarm. The cow then thundered merrily around the ring on the other side of the barrier. Fuentes' men finally succeeded in corralling it after it went round the outside of the ring three times.

Alex and Roberto stood sheepishly in the middle of the ring.

"I've caught it all on my phone, on video!" said Fuentes cheerfully. "I've never seen anything like this! Two matadors inside the ring while the cow's on the outside! It's brilliant!"

Alex opened her mouth. Roberto said, "Don't say it. Don't say anything."

She looked up at him. Her eyes were full of laughter.

"Do women matadors have female assistants to help them dress?" she asked, as he held up the jacket of her new suit of lights.

"No idea." He tugged her suit down, causing her to bounce a little. They looked in the mirror. The parcel had arrived that morning. It came from Silvio, with a note:

Sofia Herrera had me cut up one of Pedro's old suits and make you a second suit. She paid for it, it's a gift from her. We thought for a long time about what color it should be, since you already have one in black. Sofia chose this red color: sangre de toros. She said since Pedro wore blue, and Juan Carlos wore red, we should reverse the colors this time to ward off bad luck. Personally I think the color suits you. I hope you like it. Warmest wishes, Silvio.

"How do they clean this?" She peered at the embroidery worriedly. "Drycleaner's?"

"No. You soak it in a tub. Or you have an assistant do it for you after each fight." When she looked at him, he added hastily, "*Not* me."

"It's not machine washable?"

"No. Why do you look so worried?"

"Because I don't want to ruin it. It's probably more expensive than Nicky's wedding dress!"

"If I were you I would worry about getting gored, not my costume."

Alex didn't hear him. She was looking at the fabric thoughtfully. "Wish he would make it out of plastic. We can just hose off the blood."

Roberto buttoned her up busily, adjusting her in the mirror. "Planning on shedding a lot of blood, matador?"

"It'll be the bull's blood, matador," she said airily.

He had driven to downtown Cadiz to buy more pen and paper for drawing. On the way back, he passed by a truck carrying some bulls on the highway.

"Where are you taking them? The season hasn't started yet," he said over lunch. Fuentes was reading the newspaper. He lived with his boyfriend in a modern mansion in a nearby town; when he was overnighting at the ranch, he treated it as vacation and never got up before noon.

"Slaughterhouse."

"What's wrong with them?"

"Nothing. I have too much inventory. You know that. The bullfighting season's getting shorter every year. There are fewer and fewer bullfights." Fuentes turned a page. "It kills me. It's not the money, you understand: I need matadors; matadors need me."

Roberto shook his head as the staff offered him wine. "Alex and I have been practicing with mechanical bulls. If you are killing them, you might as well let us use them."

Fuentes made a vague noise at the back of his throat.

"Is that a yes or a no?"

Fuentes shrugged, buried in an article about a gay sex scandal at the Vatican. "Arrange it with the foreman. I have more than enough. Just don't get her killed before the big fight. I have the best seats for the San Martín fight. I literally do not have any other matadors to watch in the upcoming season, because everybody is refusing to talk to me now that they know I am hosting and supporting Herrera in Spain and Soubeyran in France. And oh, try to keep Herrera alive, please? I don't have doctors living near this ranch and I don't want to get bad press if somebody dies here." He looked over the paper as Roberto rose to go. "Your parents sent a box of stuff for you today. Three of your *trajes*, and your swords."

Roberto was startled. "I'm not going to fight."

"I had them all sent to the guest house. Try them on. For fun. See if they still fit." Fuentes wasn't sure if Roberto heard, for he had already left the sunny patio.

❁

When Alex was training, Roberto was on the phone with the rest of the bullfighting world, carefully renewing his contacts. Journalists and the chairmen of various bull-fighting industry associations were used to hearing from his manager Antonio. Roberto was relieved when they picked up the phone for him.

"Are you back in action?" was always their first question.

Their second — "A *woman*? Not *another one*? Why do they even bother? *She's not even Spanish?*"

Their third — "Would you like to be a spokesperson against the ban on bullfighting?"

He was asked the third question enough times that he began to wonder if there was anything in it. Finally, he mentioned to the bullfighting critic of a major newspaper that he was working on a graphic novel. The bull-fighting critic was busily blogging and promoting a half-hearted and poorly-made historical documentary about the *corrida*. It was part of the bullfighting lobby's massive campaign to gain some ground after the Catalonia government's proposed ban on bullfighting. He asked if Roberto could send him some sample pages for his bull-fighting blog.

❁

The first day they arrived at Fuentes' ranch, Roberto told her that there was no time to waste. The goal of the training was to get her to practice with as many live animals as possible. She had to make up for lost time.

"We'll try to do in a few months what should have been done in a few years," said Roberto.

"Fine by me," said Alex. "I get better under pressure."

"Yeah, right. I've seen your tantrums."

"Hey, hey, let's keep up the illusion that I'm a whiz at this."

They started with calves.

"You have to be prepared to fight in whatever outdoor conditions that God sends your way," said Roberto.

It was raining heavily that day. Alex's hand was cramped from holding on to the sodden red cape, which was much heavier than it looked. Her body was coated with sand from the training ring, because she had slipped and fallen. Her shoes had come off. She urged the calf to charge and managed to go for a series of intricate passes.

Roberto kept a small notebook and jotted down notes as he watched her. He kept track of her consistent flaws. He did not allow her to forget them. Sometimes she did a string of classical passes, passes that her grandfather was famous for. When she was bad, she was dismal. But when she was good, she was very, very good. At times he was mesmerized, he felt his soul being threaded through a needle, he was afraid to breathe. Was this what it was like, he thought, when someone watched him? Not everyone. It had to be someone who had skin in the game. Someone who was more than a spectator.

"He-llooooo? Anybody home?" She was asking him a question from the ring. "*Señor Maestro?*"

"Your hand should be here for this move," said Roberto, springing forward and correcting her posture. "It's an old habit of yours. Try again."

Sometimes the foreman and his family came to watch. They lived on the ranch. She got to know their names.

They told her about the history of each calf. They compared notes about ranching in Texas and in Cadiz.

"You okay?" shouted Roberto.

"This cow is evil." She picked herself up and dusted sand off. "Hold it, hold it! Time-out!"

She left the ring and walked up to Roberto, panting and reaching for her gym bag. She pulled out a bright pink tube of lip balm and applied it. They observed the recalcitrant cow warily as it ran around the ring.

"Be careful," said Roberto. "If you get gored there is no hospital for miles."

"Do you think she smells strawberry lip balm and would charge at me because of it?"

"*I've* never had that problem."

Her cape work did improve as the days passed.

"No, no, no. Stop," Roberto put down his notes and went into the ring. "You always do this. When you do this," he imitated her, "you are doing it for yourself. But if you do this," he showed her the correct pose, "you are doing it for the public. For *them*. Not for yourself. *That* is the right way."

Roberto made her fight in light rain, in heavy rain, in high winds that whipped sand into their eyes and stung their lips.

"Make up your mind what you want her to do!" he shouted furiously above the wind. "You can't hesitate! Remember, you're in control, not her!"

Alex had the calf cornered against the barrier.

"You've got no choice! You have to take her there! She's meek, she's not moving! You're taking too long!"

She managed to cape the animal again and again, squeezing herself against the barrier. If it was a full-grown bull, she ran the risk of being impaled against the wood. That was a common fatality for matadors, when there was no possibility of retreat. The space narrowed, she continued caping the animal, the cape flapping treacherously in the wind.

"Hold it!" he jogged forward and dampened the edge of the cape with a pitcher of water to keep it weighed down. "Now, continue!"

"I'm tired."

"No, keep at it!"

He made her lift weights until her arms ached, so that she could hold the cape and never falter.

To his relief, he found that Alex had a far better vocabulary of reading the animals than he had suspected. She attributed it to growing up on a ranch with longhorn bulls, which she claimed were smarter than the Spanish fighting bull. She was often just a beat behind him in figuring out the animal. It was a gap that she would close swiftly the moment she began working the *novillada* circuit. If anybody would let her.

Fuentes occasionally allowed them to use one of the less perfect bulls, and a group of house guests would gather round to watch.

"What's wrong with this one?" whispered Roberto.

"Rejected by the ring at Cáceres. They said he was odd," said the foreman. "I think he's perfectly fine. The vet found nothing wrong with it."

They watched as Alex caped it. She came back, a worried look on her face. "How old is he? Four?"

The foreman nodded.

"This bull has a secret," she said.

Roberto called a time-out. "I'm not happy with this, it's too dangerous. I don't trust the look of that animal."

"We'll be fine," said Alex confidently, reaching for her sword and *muleta*. "I'll find out what his secret is."

Roberto was suddenly glad that he had brought his old sports car to the ranch. As Alex went back into the training ring, he whispered to the foreman, "Jorge? Take my keys. Bring my car up to the front, stay inside and keep the engine running. If something happens to her, I can get her to the hospital in fifteen minutes in that car."

The foreman hurried off.

The men around the ring murmured *olé* approvingly, rhythmically. The silence was punctuated occasionally with the sudden gallop of hooves. The bull bellowed in despair. Roberto watched silently, parting his mouth when he realized he was clenching his jaw. It was much worse to watch her fight than to fight himself, he decided.

Fifteen tense minutes later, Alex killed the bull. The audience was pretty worked up. They whistled and screamed, *Yey, torero!*

Roberto walked into the ring. "Was it his right eye?"

She nodded. "Yes, he was just the tiniest bit short-sighted. I took a risk."

"That was brilliant for a novice."

"Thanks."

"Go talk to Fuentes and his guests. They're quite impressed. Remember, be humble. Let them think they discovered you."

She grinned and ran off.

One evening they caped young cows until it was so dark they couldn't see the animals.

Roberto called out, "Let's call it a day."

"I'm not done," said Alex, striding purposefully to the center of the ring. "I want to try your favorite fancy move."

He hesitated and stopped to watch.

She folded her arm behind her, putting her body between the cow and the cape. She slid her foot forward on the sand. She was tired. Her voice was hoarse. *"Toro! Toro!"*

The cow scrambled towards her eagerly. At the very last moment before it hit her body she yanked the cape heavenward; with a whoosh it swept past her with scarcely an inch to spare between them.

"Ha!" she shouted, triumphant. "Good *toro*! So, how did it look?"

He smiled. "It's different when the guy's over a ton."

"You've got to start somewhere. When can I try it on a big guy?"

"Tomorrow."

"I heard from Francisco," said Roberto. "He hasn't found any matadors who want to appear with a woman matador for the San Martín bullfight. He's fixed the date, though. Easter week."

Business discussions with Fuentes were held in front of his big screen television in the den of the main house. The television was permanently turned on to bullfighting, Formula One Grand Prix, boxing, or gourmet cooking shows. It could be very distracting.

Fuentes was calmly eating fruit before the television. His boyfriend was peeling the fruit and cutting it in neat slices. The boyfriend, whose name was Rojo, was a celebrity chef. "I have the same problem with Magalie Soubeyran," said Fuentes, eyes glued to the television. "She's been ready to graduate since last year. We kept cancelling because we couldn't get anyone to be on the same *cartel* with her. We'll figure something out. She might have to do it in France or Portugal. Is Alex willing to do it in Portugal?"

"She wanted Madrid. A charity fight in San Martín is already a concession."

"You don't like Francisco's dream team idea?"

"And what's that?"

"*Roberto de la Torre, Magalie Soubeyran, Alejandra Herrera. All our problems solved.*"

Roberto said hotly, "I may be retired, but I don't have to go down in flames!"

Rojo snickered. "I've figured you out. It's not because you're an artist now, a university student, a retired matador. You just don't want to do it because you don't want to show up badly against the girls."

Fuentes said, his mouth full of fruit, "Mmm — mm — one matador, two girls. It really takes someone with balls."

"Ridiculous."

"Think of the news coverage."

"It'll be a bloodbath one way or the other. Either figuratively or literally."

"On the other hand," said the older man thoughtfully, delicately chewing on a slice of kiwi, "it could have a great psychological effect on you. Because not only do you have to worry about the crowd, your reputation, the bull — perhaps in that order — you have to worry about losing to the girls. A man could really crack under that pressure. It's a peculiar kind of hell. Francisco, Antonio and I talked about it. Antonio said it was a good news angle for the taurine press. Francisco said he could write a whole novel about the psychology of such a fight."

"What is he, a novelist now?"

"You think you have a monopoly on writing, with your graphic novel? Bullring managers see a lot. I would love to buy a novel by Francisco. It would have so much dirt in it. Aw! Look, did you see that?" He pointed at the television screen excitedly. "That is pure art! Bravo!"

Roberto left Fuentes to his boxing match.

. . . Mrs Mackey said scornfully that it's tough for a woman to

go to business school because (she heard) there is still a lot of sexism at famous schools and aren't you afraid of the beating you will get from the men in class. I laughed so hard I almost peed in my pants!

Love, Shelly.

❂

"What the hell." Alex looked out of the window. The guest house was on a slope overlooking the training ring. She could hear occasional shouts and the telltale, rushing gallop of hooves. "He's not *retired*. The fraud."

There was a cow in the training ring with Roberto, who was in full grey and white training regalia. She had no idea where he got those clothes from. Fuentes was testing the cow for fierceness to decide whether or not to breed it. The foreman and *picador* were out in full force with their horses. Fuentes and his boyfriend Rojo were in the stands. Rojo had a video camera.

"Hey! Hey!" shouted the *picador*, shaking the pic at the brown cow. It looked at him with doe-like eyes, confused. He thumped the stick on the ground. Without warning, the cow dashed at the padded horse and rammed for all it was worth, pushing earnestly. Robert came up behind the cow with the pink cape, spreading it and waiting patiently. Suddenly - *"Toro!"* he shouted. He whirled elegantly as the cow took the bait and charged at his cape. It wheeled around and was eager to charge again. Roberto jogged back quickly to change capes and retrieve his sword.

"*Toro! Toro!*" cried Roberto urgently, this time shaking the *muleta*. It charged again and again. Fuentes began nodding approvingly. At one point, the cow became so mesmerized by the cape that Roberto was able to pull it around him for four or five non-stop passes. He was in complete command. He hadn't practiced for a long time, yet everything came together fluidly. He looked happy; he made faces at the animal; he commanded; he taunted; he ran and spun and tapped it with his sword. One could be forgiven for thinking that one was looking at a man and his trained pet. At one point Roberto laughed, which was very uncharacteristic of him. From the ring came inter-mittent bursts of applause and satisfied drawls of *ay, to-re-ro!* They were having fun. Everyone seemed to forget the danger.

And there was no place for a woman in that happy scene at all. None.

How are you, Alejandra? I hope your training is going well in Cadiz. I cannot speak English, so I write in French and trans-late this online using automatic translator software, I excuse myself my mistakes, hope you understand. Today Fuentes told me he has confirmed with San Martín plaza of the bulls that we will appear together. I am very happy and honored to be in the same cartel as an American girl novillero. By the way, have you seen on tel-evision, Chief Rojo said something about us on a talk show. He called us Hermaphrodites lesbians. It's stupid what he says. A lesbian is a woman who loves women. A Hermaphrodite is a person who is both a woman and a man. One must tell Red he is stupid, and if you want to insult slaughter daughters, that he use better care of a dictionary! See you in San Martín. Good luck to you. P.S. Do you speak Spanish? Kisses, Magalie Soubeyran.

Goring wounds are a surgeon's nightmare.

Unlike knife or bullet wounds, the bull's horn can be counted on being terribly dirty. To complicate matters, most goring wounds are multiple trauma wounds. A bull

223

rarely just hits you once. A matador prays that he or she does not get hit in the face, head, abdominal area, or the femoral artery in the leg.

Leg wounds are the most common injury. Everybody knows that if you get it in the femoral artery, you can bleed to death. Many matadors die that way. So you hope you get it in the vein.

Genital wounds are an occupational hazard. Sometimes it's a near miss—the trousers are ripped open and the matador's genitals are hanging out for the rest of the performance. The men (both in the audience and in the bullring) seem to embrace the concept. Worrisome if the genitals are actually gored, but that also happens and people have died as a result.

Abdominal wounds are bad news. Once the horn penetrates the skin, fat, and muscle layer and punctures a hole in the peritoneum, the membrane that lines the abdominal cavity, it will cut a triangular path of destruction through whatever organ it pierces—stomach, spleen, liver, intestines. Some matadors don't eat before going into the bullring. They believe an empty stomach reduces the risk of food contaminating the rest of the body if the stomach is pierced. Regardless, any penetration of the peritoneum means peritonitis—an infection that necessitates multiple surgeries. Peritonitis means longer recovery time, and may be fatal.

In college, Alex had borrowed a copy of *Gray's Anatomy* from a pre-med student. She photocopied a chart of the human body and carefully colored in the parts of the body that she would prefer to be gored in (if at all). There weren't many good spots.

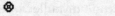

"I can't believe you haven't slept with him by now," said Nicky.

"He's my manager."

"So?"

"He's kind of like a relative. At least that's what I'm telling myself. I'm not allowed to think certain thoughts."

"Why?"

"You don't know what it's like to be me, to be in this world. It's like how you don't think about sex when you're in church, even if the altar boy is drop-dead hot. If you do the altar boy, you'd have to quit or convert to another religion."

"Since when did you become so religious?"

"Drop it, Nicky."

"I've been so hard up ever since I got pregnant. I can't believe it. No wine, no sushi, no sex. Just shoot me. I can just do anybody. I'll do Roberto."

"Well, come over here, I'll introduce you."

Roberto drove to El Puerto to meet up with a friend, Paco, and his girlfriend Ana. They were passing through town on a visit to see Paco's family.

"So, what's it like being in an American university?" asked Paco. Paco had been a *novillero* together with Roberto, but had dropped out to work at his friend's Web company in Sevilla. "I'm so impressed you got in, not knowing English!"

"It's not a real university, it's just an art college for foreign students. If you can pay, you can get in," said Roberto.

"Still! Can you speak English now?"

"A little. I've been taking classes. It's hard when you're

my age. At my school if you can draw, you can pass, even if your English is bad."

"Really? You can draw?"

Ana said Paco was behind the curve. "Roberto is working on a graphic novel," she said briskly, ordering more tapas. She knew all about it from reading the fan discussion boards on *VirtualPeña*. Paco asked her when she became interested in bullfighting. She retorted that she was not, but *VirtualPeña* was addictive. She added that she supported women in any kind of activity that men didn't allow them in, even though she taught yoga, was vegetarian, and opposed the *corrida*, and yes she was a bundle of contradictions, and did the men at the table have a problem with it?

"But I love graphic novels!" said Paco. "Really? You can do that? Awesome! What's it about?"

Roberto smiled and shook his head, reaching for the wine. "What else can it be about?"

"Oh, man, I love it!" said Paco happily. "It's about your bullfighting days?"

"No, it's about Alex mostly."

"Oh." Paco's face fell.

Ana added, "He doesn't support women in the bullring. He couldn't do it, and he hates to see women do it."

"But why about *her*?" wailed Paco. "It would be better if it were about you!"

"I can't draw myself for my graduation project. That would be ridiculous. I need a subject."

"Can I read it?" asked Ana. Roberto remembered that she worked for a small publishing company in Sevilla that put out popular novels. "I'm quite interested in Alejandra Herrera. I believe she's the first American woman to become a matador. I like her. She's not a wanker like the English guys who try."

"Sure, I'll scan some pages if you give me your email."

She wrote it out for him on the back of his sketchbook. "You want them too?" Roberto asked Paco.

Paco shuddered and shook his head. "Nah, just tell me when you write your memoirs. That'd be way more exciting!"

❁

Alex turned on the television. Spanish music videos. Shakira was licking someone's face. She changed the channel. German porn. An actress was dressed as a grandmother, holding her boobs to the camera. She turned off the television and threw the remote angrily into a pile of laundry. She had never felt more alone and depressed. She thought about calling Shelly, but it was dinnertime in Austin. She didn't want to interrupt. And if she called Shelly after and dumped on her, Shelly would go to bed worried, and that was just about the worst thing to do to someone who was trying to mother her from long distance.

She went on the Internet and tried to download a movie. *Your subscription does not authorize you to download a movie from your geographic location. Please call customer service for assistance.*

A long hour crawled by. She got out of bed, found a rubber band, tied up her hair, opened the window. She was on the second floor of a nineteenth-century country house. There were miles of cold, dark country all around and no street lamps.

Nobody would see her.

Still wearing her thin white flannel pajamas, she put her foot on the ledge and climbed up to the roof. It was still winter. It hadn't rained recently and the tiles were bone dry.

She sat on the roof, shivering, counting stars until the horizon grew suddenly pale with dawn.

"Did you use my car?" asked Roberto, appearing in the greenhouse where she was doing stretches.

"When?" asked Alex.

"I don't know, I thought I had a full tank of gas."

"Sorry. I'll go fill it up now." She got up.

He looked suspicious. "How did you get my keys?"

"I stole the extra set from your gym bag."

"Where did you go?" He followed her as she jogged out onto the garden path.

"Nowhere. I can't sleep most nights. I drive round and round the estate in circles. I look at the bulls and blast your playlist in the car. Nice sound system. I'm glad you ditched that rental."

"You can't drive my car around the farm! You'll scare the animals! They're used to seeing only the foreman's jeep. Fuentes has had cars destroyed by angry cows."

"Oh, don't worry. They're used to me. By now."

"The mud—"

"I'll hose it off." She grinned suddenly. "You know what would be really cool? If a bull ran at your car. Imagine what the side would look like. You can resell that car for top dollar on eBay, like a work of art. *Ferrari Attacked By Toro Bravo*. Some American banker would buy it."

Roberto said abruptly, "That's it. Give me my keys. I'll fill it myself."

There was a small patio with iron tables and chairs outside the hospital café in Sevilla. It was cold; there were fewer people out there.

Sofia scrutinized him when he brought their coffees.

"You don't look like Juan Carlos. You don't have his reck-lessness. Your father does, though." She leaned forward suddenly. "How do you feel about Alex hurtling out of America like this and demanding to be taken seriously as a matador? Why didn't you stop her?"

"I don't think I'm in the position to stop anybody from doing something they want to do, even if I don't want to do it myself."

"You don't want to do it anymore?"

"No."

"Then why did you come back?"

"I would come back for any friend who's been in an accident like this."

"You didn't come back to fight?"

"No, of course not," said Roberto quickly.

"How long are you back for?"

"I don't know, a few weeks. Until Alex gets better."

"Do you want to be her manager?"

"I don't know."

"If you are serious about coming back, and you want to help Alex, you should manage her. A lot of people in San Martín want this, as you know. The mayor told me the other day. We had lunch. He said he has been in touch with you."

"Yes, he was a big help. He got her licensed to fight in San Martín."

"The whole town has gone mad after you quit bull-fighting. They'll do anything to have you come back, even support an American girl matador. You're the only claim San Martín has these days to the bullfighting world." Sofia lowered her voice. "If you manage Alex, I will pay you."

"No, and no." Roberto shook his head.

"I still have Pedro's money, I don't spend much. I have been saving it for Alex. I don't want her to be a matador, but if I don't spend it on her now, she might die in the bullring, and I don't have any other children or grand-children to give it to." She named a sum.

"Sofia, I won't take your money."

"I have discussed it with your mother. I got her to agree."

"No."

"You could use it for your university fees."

"No. I can work, I'll find a job."

"Cristina said you can't work in America because foreign students are not allowed to work much. Visa laws," said Sofia stubbornly.

"You can earn money under the table."

"As what? A waiter? Why, when you can be paid as a manager for a matador?"

"I won't take your money, Sofia. It's not right. Alex's American sponsor will pay me something. That's enough."

"I want to help Alex."

"So do I."

Sofia stared into her coffee for a long time, then she looked up. "Please help Alex, Roberto. Even if you won't let me pay you. Juan Carlos and Pedro always helped each other. They wouldn't have been so successful if they did not have each other's friendship."

Roberto said soberly, "You needn't worry. I will help Alex. We owe it to your family."

"I'm so afraid she will die in the bullring just like Pedro. Roberto, she's the last of the line. Her father, Angel, died when he was Pedro's age. It's enough to make anyone superstitious. I don't want to outlive all of them."

"Sofia, Alex was only injured this time because she tried to help the younger *novilleros*. She's good at keeping out of danger otherwise. She has genuine skill. You just haven't seen her. I have faith in her. I wouldn't help her otherwise."

Sofia shuddered.

He said urgently, "The hospital in San Martín and the infirmary in the ring are very good. Don't worry. It's not like the old days. We live in different times now, Sofia."

"You'll make sure she gets good bulls, right? Not murderous ones."

"I promise you, Fuentes' bulls have a great reputation, they are easy for her. She works well with them."

Sofia breathed in deeply, making a face. "Oh, the bulls, the bulls, always the bulls! I thought I was done with the bulls until this nonsense started up again. It is not in my fate, Roberto, to have a normal family life. When I was your age, I had just married Pedro, I thought we would have many children and grandchildren. But we only had Angel before he died. And Angel only had Alejandra before *he* died. And now Alejandra has gone back to the bulls, despite all my efforts. Our family is destined to die out."

"That's what my mother says about us." Roberto managed to smile.

"Cristina and I have a lot in common. But you have left the *corrida*, you have seen the light. You're going to be normal, right? Get a university education, get a proper job, marry a nice girl, start a family. Do it for your mom."

"She's mad at me for leaving bullfighting."

"She'll learn. I'll talk to her. She doesn't know how lucky she is." Sofia got up briskly. "Let's get back upstairs. We never had this conversation. I am going to stay away from this business from now on. My nerves just cannot stand it. But if ever you need my help, you must call me. Don't hesitate."

"I will."

Antonio drove in one weekend to visit them.

"I have a problem with your octopus recipe," he told Rojo when he got out of the car in the driveway. Rojo was in his tracksuit jogging around the perimeter of the estate. "I did it exactly the way you said to on TV. It doesn't work."

"Did you tenderize it first by slapping it against the wall?"

"No. Do I really have to do that? I don't want to make a mess."

"It's not my fault if you skip a step," said Rojo airily, jogging away.

"Where are my matadors?"

"Training ring, where else?"

Antonio found Roberto leaning against the barrier, watching Alex intently. They both grew quiet as Alex prepared for the kill.

When it was over, Alex came up to both men expectantly. Blood was all over her training suit.

Antonio was visibly impressed.

"You're too tense," said Roberto.

"No shit," said Alex, wiping the sword.

Antonio clicked his tongue in impatience. "You know, you almost had me there, I thought I was seeing a great *torero*, then you open your mouth."

"I am what I am. Take it or leave it."

"You don't even pretend to comply," said Antonio.

Alex said impatiently, "No I don't. It is what it is. It's *my* life I'm risking. I do it the way I want."

"You're lucky. That was a good bull," said Antonio, watching as they took it away. "Fuentes is generous."

"He's got too many. They're being sent to the slaughterhouse," said Roberto. "We got him drunk and negotiated a good price."

Alex asked Antonio, "What did you think of my passes? Tell the truth."

"It was very good, matador. If only you can be that good always."

But Roberto was shaking his head. "You're too tense, it affects your performance. You need to have more grace, more lightness, more effortlessness. It's not a nice picture, the way you do it. It doesn't give the observer a feeling of lightness."

"Okay?" said Alex, struggling to follow.

"Don't be defensive, you can't learn if you won't accept criticism," said Roberto.

"Lightness? What do you want, ballet?" she retorted. She thought she had done pretty well; she was on a winning streak.

"Ballet isn't that far from the truth. It's an art, Alex, not a sport," said Antonio. "Don't forget that."

"Are you clenching your jaw the whole time?" Roberto reached out and touched her face, feeling with his fingers. "Antonio, did you see it? You know what I mean?"

"Yes, you had it too when you were a boy," said Antonio. "I made you chew gum, remember?"

Alex opened her mouth wide and shut it again several times, testing the tension in her jaw. "Chewing gum, huh? The secret of Roberto de la Torre's success?"

"Oh, there are many mysterious methods, hasn't he shared them all with you?" grinned Antonio.

Roberto said, distracted, "The fact of the matter is that there are no precedents for training women matadors."

"Hell, I'd chew gum," said Alex, swigging from a large bottle of mineral water. She poured the rest of the water over her face. "You going to town tonight? I'll go buy some gum. Whatever it takes."

They drove with Antonio to downtown Cadiz for dinner, after which they said goodbye to him. Roberto stopped by a children's candy shop with Alex.

"Not *bubble* gum," he said at the cashier, glancing at what Alex held in her hand.

For the next three days, Roberto trained with Alex in the ring, barking at her, correcting her posture, and then, when another live bull was put before her, watching and wincing as she popped pink bubbles insolently at the animal.

"Can't say she's not relaxed now, can you?" said Fuentes, stopping by to watch.

She blew an extra large pink bubble at the panting bull, popped it, then shook the *muleta*, "*Hey, hey, hey, toro! Toro!*"

"It's not a circus act," said Roberto, shaking his head.

Rojo was delighted and caught everything on video-tape.

One evening, she drove Roberto's car to the edge of the estate. A group of mature, black bulls spotted the landscape. In the distance, a man rode slowly on a glossy brown horse. It was the foreman, checking on the animals. She used to think he was a bit uncomfortable around her, because she was a female *torero*. She tried to befriend him by showing that she knew her way around the ranch. During birthing season, she helped him search in copses and rocks when he suspected that a mother had hidden her newborn. She could tell when a horse had trouble with its hoof; she knew how to mix the cattle feed and get an orphaned calf to take milk from the bottle. It was only recently that she learned the true reason for his discomfort. He took her aside and said gently that while he appreciated the fact that she grew up on a ranch and wanted to help with small chores, he did not want matadors to get to know the animals too well.

"How could you kill him in the ring, if you had reared

him with your own hand?" he had said. "The calf must learn his role. You have to learn yours." After that, she kept her distance. Jorge and his family grew very fond of her.

"Hello, Jorge! How goes it?" She rolled down the window.

"Hello, Alex."

She didn't get out of the car. She was not allowed to approach the animals on foot. "What are you up to?"

"Just bidding six of my babies goodbye."

"Oh yeah?"

"They're being trucked to Bilbao tomorrow morning, long journey. I wished them luck."

"Are you going with them?"

"No. Do you know that I have *never* watched a bull-fight in a city bullring in my life? I can't stand it. To me their beauty is all here. It is here that they are full of vitality. I don't need to see anything else. The city has nothing for me."

"I understand."

He tipped his hat and cantered on.

Rojo, Fuentes' boyfriend, was a plump, thirty-something chef who had his own cooking show on Spanish television. On TV he pretended to be a trendy gourmet from Lima, Peru, but he confessed to Alex that he was really a Mexican American from a dull suburb of Los Angeles. He pretended to be Peruvian because the producers thought his real background was too uninteresting for television.

Roberto came downstairs one morning in the guest house and found Rojo opening kitchen drawers noisily.

"Hello, handsome!" said Rojo cheerfully, a bottle of olive oil under his arm. "Fuentes has gone to a wedding in Sevilla with his family. I'm so bored."

"Don't you call before you come over?"

"The door wasn't locked. Do you have some kind of jar opener? We don't have one in the main house."

"No."

Rojo opened the refrigerator. "Empty! This is a house of horrors!"

"We don't eat much," said Roberto disinterestedly, wishing Rojo would go away.

"Yeah, right. These kitchen scales are new. Does Alex bake?"

"She weighs what she eats now, it's getting close to the fight."

Rojo's eyes nearly popped out of his head. "What, like falcons? You have a hunting weight or something?" He stretched out a finger and prodded Roberto's upper arm admiringly.

"Just about." Roberto moved his arm away.

"Hey," Rojo leaned close to Roberto, "still sleeping in separate rooms?"

"Who wants to know?"

"*Why* is it that bullfighters only *pretend* they are sexually promiscuous, and yet they are as celibate as priests?" Rojo followed Roberto around the kitchen. "Do you seriously believe that if you ejaculate, it will sap your strength when you go into the bullring?"

"Why ask me? I'm not the one fighting anymore. Ask Alex."

"I wonder if it's the same with women—"

Roberto turned on the coffee grinder so loudly that he drowned out Rojo's incessant patter.

"—since they're on the receiving end, wouldn't it make sense that women matadors would be *strengthened* by sexual intercourse, then?"

Roberto reached for the bottle. "If I open this, would you leave?"

"Good morning, Alex!" said Rojo, looking up.

"Hi."

"You look awful."

"So do you."

"Want to help Roberto open my bottle?" asked Rojo coyly.

Roberto held out the bottle for her. She tried it.

"How many matadors does it take to open—" began Rojo.

"Shut up, Rojo!" said Alex and Roberto at the same time. Alex popped the top.

"*Olé!*" cried Rojo. "So do you want to listen to my latest sexual theory about women matadors?"

Alex looked at Roberto. Roberto said, "Say no."

"No."

"Do you always do what Roberto tells you to do?"

"He's my manager."

Rojo drew Alex close and whispered, "Have you been reading *VirtualPeña?* The gossip meter is turned way up."

"You read *VirtualPeña?*" she asked, surprised.

"And why not? It's the only way to find out the latest *corrida* news these days. It totally beats all the other *corrida* news sources now. The schoolgirl fans are crazy. They're literate, responsible, accurate, and super nosey. They're the best investigative journalists. They post about everybody's movements. Everything!"

"Do you post things about me?" said Alex warily.

Rojo looked guilty and tried to leave.

Roberto blocked his escape. "What do you post, you little spy? Are you *Roberto_LoverSOS?*"

"No! That's a psycho from America, I don't know who he is! I'm *FraggleRock*. You don't have any goods on me!" Rojo looked tearful.

"I suspected you might be *FraggleRock*," said Roberto

sternly. "Whatever that means. It sounds so perverse I knew it had to be you."

Alex looked between the two men, bewildered. "I don't even read *VirtualPeña*. You two pretend to be girls and get on it?"

"You can't complain!" pleaded Rojo to Roberto. "I don't reveal where we all are, but I post little things like what you guys like to eat, what car you drive, what brand of exercise clothes you wear, and so on. And I post recipes. And I've signed up for the big countdown to the videochat next week. Ask Roberto!"

Alex stared blearily at Roberto. "What videochat?"

Roberto checked his emails at the kitchen table. There was a long and polite inquiry from another journalist covering bullfights who had asked previously to see sample pages of his graphic novel. The man mentioned a publisher who was very interested in running a few panels of Roberto's work in a new anthology about tauromachy. Roberto folded the laptop under his arm and went upstairs.

"Alex?" He knocked on her bedroom door. It was past midnight. Rojo had thrown a big dinner at the main house for some friends of Fuentes; she hadn't joined them. These days she wouldn't eat regular meals. She was out in the fields with the bulls by day. When she wasn't fighting them in the training ring, she was walking around the ranch in her mud boots talking to the foreman's family and a local vet about bulls.

"Alex?" He wondered if she had stolen his car again and was driving around the ranch at night like a deranged insomniac. Suddenly, fear seized him. He tried the door. It was open.

The room was cold; the night wind came freely through the open windows. He looked out. Far from the light pollution of the city, the crisp spring night was a shower of stars.

"Look up," came a voice above him.

He was startled. "What are you doing up there?"

"I couldn't sleep."

"Did you take your pills?"

"I won't take sleeping pills. It would affect my performance."

"And not sleeping won't?" He set the laptop down and surveyed the wall. "How did you get up?"

"Get on the balcony. Step here. Climb up here."

"Would the roof hold?"

"No idea. I just try to step on the spine of the roof, not in the middle of it. Seems quite sturdy. There!"

"God, the tiles are cold!" he said, settling down next to her.

"What do you want?" She seemed a little disturbed by his presence.

He told her about the email from the journalist.

"So publish those pages," she said listlessly. "It's *your* graphic novel project."

"But it has you in it. I just wanted to make sure you were fine with that."

She said nothing.

"Alex? Why are you up here? What's wrong?"

Alex's voice was muffled; she had curled up and buried her face in her arms. She said resentfully into her flannel pajamas sleeves, "I have to go to grad school sooner or later. I can't defer another year. People would kill to get a spot; and here I am, not wanting to go. You have to go back and finish your art degree. You can't just help me forever as my temporary manager."

"That's true." He couldn't see her expression, but thought she sounded unusually depressed.

After they looked out at the utter darkness of the ranch for a while, she said suddenly, "Maybe you'll get a publisher for your graphic novel when you finish it. Wouldn't that be nice?"

"I don't think there's a question about that. The bull-fighting lobby is cranking out books and documentaries. They're making noise against Catalonia's ban on the *corrida*. I'm sure some small press somewhere will put out my book if I wanted to join the fray. But first we have to finish it."

"We?"

"You write and live it. I observe and draw."

"Will you draw this moment?"

He looked around them. The guesthouse was an old farmhouse that Fuentes had a local architect renovate and retrofit. The roof tiles undulating beneath them were dreaming of the coming summer and the hundred degree heat. But not yet. Not yet. "I'll try."

He made a mental study of the tiles by moonlight. They taught still life at his art school. The curves of terra cotta felt cool and sturdy beneath his fingers. How could he capture the feel of them? They were crisp and porous, like coral. Their surface was crusty with pale grey lichen and nubby with velour spots of emerald green moss. He touched the moss with his fingertips.

"Feels nice, doesn't it?" she said, watching him. "I like being up here. The mossy patches are comforting. They feel like the material babies' stuffed toys are made of."

Could he ever reduce all this to a drawing? Could he ever depict this very instant and how he felt sitting beside her?

In the dark, he said, "Aren't you cold?"

After a long silence, she drew a deep breath and stuck

out her tongue. "You can almost taste the salt of the sea from here."

❁

The numerous problems faced by the decline of bull-fighting in San Martín were the subject of a local radio talk show that all the cab drivers listened to.

Two men were having a heated debate in the recording studio. The *aficionado* was saying to the talk show host, "I mean, it is a ridiculous situation, is it not, for a girl, an American girl, to come here wanting to fight? And even more ridiculous is San Martín offering this girl a chance to perform in a bullfight."

"Desperate times call for desperate measures," said the talk show host resignedly.

"The perfect solution, of course, for San Martín—if they are listening—is this: if we have an aggressive, valiant cow, we don't send that cow to the bullring. We breed the cow with stud bulls."

"Naturally."

"It is the duty of the cow to produce excellent bulls for the *corrida*. It is not the duty of the cow to perform in the *corrida*."

"That makes sense."

"And since Roberto de la Torre refuses to fight, it is his duty to serve as the stud bull. San Martín should breed Herrera with De la Torre and produce a son, then maybe we can begin talking about grooming a new San Martín matador."

"You're killing me! But what if the child is another girl? Oh, we have a caller. Hello! What's up?"

The caller was a woman taxi driver who gave the *aficionado* an earful.

"But I'm not saying women cannot drive taxis," he

interrupted her. "Of course you can drive taxis! But being a *torero* is different. Surely you must agree there are some professions that are too dangerous for women?"

"That's what they said about women cab drivers!"

"To me they are two completely different matters."

"You better not get into my cab!"

❁

"Easy," said Alex, as he scaled up. "Fuentes said this roof is a hundred and fifty years old."

"What's that?" he pointed. "Looks like a wraith."

"Steam from Fuentes' jacuzzi."

"I didn't know he had one on the ranch."

"I tried it before. It's boiling."

"Well, it's freezing up here."

She chuckled. "Imagine jumping in there right now. Ice to fire. I'd go into toxic shock."

"I dare you."

She looked at him. His tone reminded her of their California road trip, back when they used to have fun. "You know, I'm really glad you are here. Thank you. You're a good manager. Even if you're just temporary."

"Good. I've never managed anyone before. I am beginning to appreciate what Antonio did for me all these years, running the bookings and contracts while I just focused on performing. So much work, just for one fight."

"Don't get too good at it, otherwise you'll become a professional manager."

"Don't worry," he smiled. "I always play the amateur. It gets us more things. I negotiate every one of your dealings by starting with the line *we have no money*. Goodwill gets us a long way, especially in San Martín. I'm sorry I can't get you into Las Ventas."

Alex shrugged. "I knew it wasn't going to be easy. I

talked it over with Tomas. I'd probably end up getting killed if I insisted on doing my graduation fight now and taking on full-grown bulls. Even if I were to survive that, there would be no turning back. I'd be stuck working with full-grown bulls before I could really make a career out of it and be good at it. I'd rather be a novice who sucks than a matador who sucks. At least I have an excuse." She darted him a look. "Please don't think I'm not being serious."

"I have never doubted that you are serious," he said quietly. "By the way, I heard about the testing today."

Fuentes had produced a mature bull for Alex to test in the training ring that morning when Roberto was in San Martín. The foreman had identified the bull, which was called Furioso, as having the proper personality for becoming a stud bull. They had wanted Roberto to test it, but he was away, and Alex quickly volunteered. Furioso, true to his name, was one scary creature. It would charge at anything that moved, even at a leaf spiraling down from a tree, the foreman had said. Alex tested Furioso in the ring and was knocked down several times. Fortunately, she escaped with minor scrapes. But what she achieved with the bull so excited Fuentes that he made her stop and rang up his friends on his mobile phone to come and watch. He even invited a bullfighting newspaper critic. An hour later, there were about twenty people assembled in the training ring, watching intently. Alex was caping the bull to shouts of *olé!* Someone even brought out a CD player and played some bullfighting music for an impromptu bullfight. It felt like a fair, happening in Fuentes' own back-yard. He was very happy that day and said Alex was a genius.

"It was crazy," said Alex. "I think the bull and I both knew what was at stake. I prayed that he would perform for his life, and he did."

"Did he pass?"

"Yes. He's one of the stud bulls now. I saved his life. He'll never be in a bullring. He'll just be used for shagging cows until he dies of old age."

"How nice."

"Today was *really* fun." She beamed. "I really enjoyed myself."

"It's great when it happens like that," said Roberto. "In a way I'm glad that you're not going to Madrid. The crowds want something different in the big cities."

"You mean the critics? I'm not afraid of them."

"No, it's not that. I mean the public. It's very different performing in a small town. They're slightly drunk, they're generous, usually it's a public holiday, they are so honored you came to their town, they appreciate every little thing you do in the ring. They know how hard it is, they take nothing for granted. They may not know something you are doing is technically excellent, they may not know how to describe it, but they are spontaneous, and even if you make mistakes, they love you for trying. I really miss being a *novillero* sometimes, in smaller cities. It is only under those conditions that I truly feel like what my grandfather must have felt like, back in those days. I'm jealous that you're just starting out."

"Fuentes said I was lucky that I could even get to perform in San Martín. Is it true that the bullring might shut down?"

"You know that it's funded by the city council, right? Ticket sales alone aren't enough for our kind of bullring. The city's had to cut down on spending on things like fairs and the *corrida*. Even before the recession, the number of bullfights was going down anyway all across the country. God knows where or how the younger generation of matadors would get their training."

"Well, I'm starting to get excited about San Martín, no matter what Rojo says he's been reading online."

244

"What has he been reading online?"

"Lots of *aficionados* booing at me."

"Well, it could be worse. They could have just given you the cold shoulder. At least they are irritated enough with you that they are wasting ink on you. We don't even have to pay the news critics, they just run inches on you for free."

"They *pretend* to analyze my work, but really it's not about me. It's all about them."

"Don't pay attention to them. They're not in San Martín."

"I don't. Anyway most of them seem to have the mental age of seven-year-olds. Most of their criticism involves the frequent mention of the word 'balls'. Half of them are very concerned that I don't have any. The other half calls me a butch lesbian. I'm going to act even more girly just to irritate the hell out of them. Today I posted a ton of girly stuff on my fan page on *VirtualPeña*. I said I love Hannah Montana, teddy bears, and OPI nail polish."

Roberto winced. "Don't get baited. Don't read the bullfighting press. I never do."

"I won't anymore. It's hard not to. Rojo is forever reading me the latest gossip."

"I'll have a word with him."

"Don't worry. I can take it. I have nothing to lose." She rose to her feet stiffly.

"Where are you going?"

"I'm going to jump into the jacuzzi."

"In your clothes?"

"I'll accept your dare." She was already nimbly climbing back down to her room. He heard her clattering downstairs, then running across the lawn. For a few minutes he couldn't see anything, then a shadow crossed the pale blue light and the white steam. She had the foresight to bring a towel and a bathrobe for getting out after, but at the edge of the pool she hesitated. She lingered for such a long time that he got bored and decided to go down.

"Coward," said Roberto, when he got there.

"It's really hot," she said, putting her foot in. "It'll really hurt."

"That's the point."

"I'd get sick."

"Nobody gets sick from a hot tub."

"I don't want to get sick, it'll affect my performance."

He said, "Don't do it then."

"I dare you."

"I dared you first."

"You go!"

"You can't dare someone after they've dared you!" he said, outraged.

She just stood at the edge, shivering, going, "Shit. Shit. Shit."

"You can't resist a dare, can you?"

"No, I never could. You've found my Achilles heel." She walked round the little pool, arms folded in a non-committal posture, peering in hesitantly, as if deciding the angle of approach.

He pushed her in.

"It's all arranged by date," Fuentes said proudly. "If you watch one, please rewind it and put it back exactly in the same spot. This section is all clips of bulls only. This section is bulls and matadors."

Fuentes had amassed a large library of videotapes of famous bullfights. After watching Alex perform with his stud bull, he finally decided she was worthy of admission into his private library at the ranch. It was a little room on the top floor with a wood-burning fireplace, where he kept all his Manolete posters, stuffed bull's heads, and other bullfighting knick-knacks.

"You watch clips of only the bulls?" asked Alex in wonder.

"Yeah. Well, I started with watching the entire bullfight, but over the years, I find the bulls more interesting, so I had my video guy make me videotapes only showing the bulls, cutting out the matador shots. It helps me understand my animals better."

"You're so weird, Fuentes."

He looked annoyed and tried to think of a proper answer, but she had pounced on a tape. "My grandfather's fights!" she cried.

He showed her how to work the many different remotes on his complicated television system. They watched the first fight together on a large-screen TV.

"Genius! He was a genius!" cried Fuentes as Herrera executed a series of beautiful passes. "Oh, the stars were perfectly aligned that day. I would have given my left arm to be there. Maybe a finger. Okay, a little finger."

"He was such a small man. So ordinary-looking."

"Oh, but such balls. Such balls!"

"Do you have Herrera's *faena* from Granada in 1957?"

"Yes, you can fast forward. Oh, wait, what's that? That's the famous one. Stop, stop! That's the one where De la Torre gets gored."

Alex looked behind them to make sure the door was closed. "Roberto has never seen it."

"You want to see it?"

Alex stared at the older man. "Should we watch it?"

"It's up to you. I've seen it. De la Torre is gored and Herrera goes in and finishes his bull. Thus began the curse. Maybe you shouldn't see it. It's unlucky."

She stopped the tape and the static came on, roaring in the quiet room.

They both slunk downstairs guiltily.

"Watching porn videos again without me?" demanded Rojo from the kitchen.

❁

SEVILLA — These are dark times indeed. Having written so many columns about the bullfighting ban, I have decided to change direction this week.

I was invited to a testing of a stud bull yesterday on the esteemed Fuentes ranch. The matador testing the bull was Alejandra Herrera. There are three things that are interesting about Miss Herrera, 21, besides the fact that she is a woman.

First, she is the granddaughter of Pedro Javier Herrera. She is first to admit the importance of this. She said to me that we would not even have met but for her last name. Second, she is an American, from Texas. In recent years we've only heard of interest in bullfighting from the usual assortment of Northern European wankers — models, actors, journalists, bankers, lawyers, novelists and other rubbish gawkers from England, France, Germany — who are in it for the glamour and the danger more than anything. In my past columns, dear reader, you recall I have lampooned them and my good colleague Ernesto Muñoz has drawn his fair share of cartoons on this subject. Having failed in extreme tobogganing in St Moritz, these poseurs try our national festival on for size. In one of my past columns I have remarked before that during my generation, we have not had many lunatics from North America and theorized as to why. But now we finally have one, so I was curious to see her.

At the testing, the bull is black, named Furioso (548

kilos). It is a mighty specimen, and Fuentes had high hopes. Furioso charged easily, as all Fuentes' bulls do. But he had a few tricks up his sleeve which she was able to overcome. Her recent training in Sevilla (with the great artistic director Alonzo Aguirre) must have undoubtedly helped her style. On this point, see my column last month about why matador schools should not accept women students. It is not that I am sexist, but there is no point for them to complete the training and graduate because there are simply no openings in the industry for them. The schools are just making money off their empty dreams and must be criticized for doing so.

I have not yet watched many women in this line of work. In fact, this is the first time I have ever watched a *torera*, as I usually do not bother to attend their bullfights. I am sure my female readers will forgive me for saying this, as some of them might even agree, but I find it hard to get over the unnaturalness of it. I do not like watching women who are clearly women, dressed like men. It's ugly. Sometimes Miss Herrera betrayed her youth, and scolded the bull petulantly in a high voice. It is very unbecoming and far from dignified. Where a normal matador would urge a bull, and do so retaining his grace and nobility, in a woman you cannot help but think she is merely flirting with it.

Furioso was eventually not killed because they decided he had enough spirit to become a stud bull. I am told that Miss Herrera drops the bull every time when executing a kill, but I have not witnessed it for myself. The work that I did get to see was technically sound, but not yet completely exciting, and not really by the book. I have a vague feeling that she thinks being a *torero* is like being a professional fencer or an Olympic athlete. During the testing, she was dressed in the black and lime-green sports clothes of her American sportswear sponsor, Milou, which brought a very curious modern air to the whole affair.

I asked her if she, like many Americans, became drawn to bullfights because of the writings of Ernest Hemingway. She replied that the only Hemingway book she had ever read was *Old Man & the Sea*, "in junior high", and it was "so boring" that she never read another. She is completely unselfconscious about history or ritual. She does not care about tradition, the *peñas*, or bullfighting critics.

Her manager must surely be one of the youngest on record — no other than Roberto de la Torre, 21, who pulled out so suddenly from the *corrida* last year. Their ages when added together do not even amount to the age of an ordinary bullfighter's manager. Many have speculated as to why De la Torre consented to be her manager, so I shall not go into that here.

What's remarkable is that the city of San Martín, where the Herrera and De la Torre families are from, is staging a charity bullfight for Miss Herrera during Easter week. It is an ultimate indulgence on the part of the city, aided by Francisco Alvarez, the impresario of the local bullring. This bullring has lost money five years in a row, and the city is struggling to keep it open with ever-declining public funds. The final lineup of matadors and *novilleros* is still uncertain as most *toreros* understandably don't want to be in a fight with her. Yet, the fight is heavily advertised on social networking sites. It is almost certain that those who buy tickets would not be *aficionados* in the strictest sense of the word, but are just young people — perhaps all female — interested in watching something trendy — without any understanding whatsoever of what they are watching.

I told Miss Herrera that unfortunately, no self-respecting bullfighting critic, myself included, would attend or cover her bullfight in San Martín. She replied that volunteers from *VirtualPeña*, a social networking site, would report it live via Twitter, a Website that is very popular in English-speaking countries but not in Spain. It is not clear who will read this amateur reportage. The blind leading the blind: is this the "future" of the *corrida*?

" 'Miss Herrera' my ass," said Alex, when Rojo showed her the column. "Notice he calls Rob 'De la Torre', but I'm 'Miss Herrera'. Well, this Miss Herrera ain't going to be sitting by the kitchen fire making patchwork quilts."

Rojo licked the tip of his finger and touched her glee-fully, making a sizzling sound.

Antonio rang. "Did you see the column?"

"Yes," said Roberto. "At first when I read it I was quite glad that he even chose to write about Alex. Many people read that column. It didn't seem that bad. But when I re-read it, I started to get really pissed off at the little insin-uations. And when I read it a third time, I had to go for a very fast drive on the highway."

"Did she read it?"

"Are you kidding? She's bought every single copy of the paper."

Roberto plugged in the laptop and adjusted the Web cam. "You ready?"

"Sure," said Alex, distracted. She had a bad dream the night before. She dreamed she was gored and died in the San Martín bullring infirmary. In her dream, she wasn't afraid of death, just afraid of having to apologize to Sofia and Shelly and Tomas and Roberto. She could not bear leaving people behind traumatized. That morning she got up and wondered about saints and the utility of praying to them. She printed out a small image of Saint Joan from off the Web and snuck a small candle from the kitchen drawer. She was ambivalent about religion most of her life, but this was what matadors did. They went in the chapel before the bullfight. After all, bullfighting began before there were therapists.

"Hey, you were the one who started all this," said Roberto.

"Huh?"

"You got me hooked on this Web-chatting, SMS-ing, this stuff. So pay attention."

"No, no, this is good, this'll be fun, let's go live." She tried to smile.

His cellphone began buzzing angrily. It was Rojo.

"Yeah, we're ready. Alex is having cold feet," said Rob, glancing over his shoulder. Before he finished speaking, she had leaned over and clicked on the mouse. The videochat was on.

Roberto, having done many interviews, was a natural on television. He sat next to her on the bed and introduced her. The message board began filling up with dozens of messages. There were 60 people online. By the time Roberto finished his introduction, there were 127, then 276, then 392.

"Who are these people?" asked Alex curiously. "Are they all high-school girls?"

"I'm sure there are some guys."

The questions kept coming.

"Why do you want to become a matador?" asked Roberto, repeating a question that came up again and again on the scrolling message board.

Alex said nothing, just stared at the video screen. She began to smile as she read the messages.

"Alex?"

"Because I can."

He went on to the next question that popped up, "What do you think of Pedro Herrera's style? Are you going to copy it?"

She thought for a long time before answering, staring off camera.

"Alex?" he pushed his knee against hers.

Alex said finally, "I'm not sure I can, but I do like it very much. He was a brave man. He was quite little, though — he was shorter than me."

"How much do you weigh?"

Alex laughed. "Fifty-five kilos. Who wants to know? I'm not the bull."

"What's your favorite brand of clothing?" asked Roberto.

"Milou. Actually I'm paid to say it, they are my sponsor. I'm wearing their sweatshirt. Do you like it?"

The message board erupted with pleas for her to stand up and show the sweatshirt, which she did. She did a full turn, laughing. She pulled on the hood to show the opening for a ponytail at the back.

"Should women matadors wear something different other than the *traje de luces*?"

"Absolutely," said Alex. "I'm designing my own with Milou. It will be very cool."

Roberto stared, "You are? *What* are you doing again?"

Alex turned to him. "A new kind of *traje de luces*. It'll have new breathable fabric and is machine washable."

He looked at her incredulously.

"The traditional costume is very wasteful because once it is worn a few times, we have to give it away or throw it away because of the blood and the sweat and the muck.

Mine can be reused again and again. It also adjusts to your body temperature, so it keeps you warm in the winter and cools you down in the summer. Made of lycra and nylon. Cheaper, too."

Alex leaned forward again and tapped on the mouse. There were now 482 people online. "I'm sorry I can't read all your questions as they're scrolling faster than we can read them. What do I think of El Rivera? I think he is very good. But his style is different from mine. Who is my favorite matador? Pedro Herrera, my grandfather. Who is my favorite *living* matador? Roberto de la Torre. Why do I like Roberto's style?" She looked back at him and grinned. "I admire his stillness and his absolutely calm expression when the bull brushes past him. I have yet to master that face. What do I think of him as my manager? He is a very good one. Who else is in the San Martín bull-fight? Magalie Soubeyran is confirmed, I don't know about the rest. Will I kill all six bulls myself? Yes, if no one wants to be in the same show as me. Hello San Martín! Hello Madrid! Hello Granada! Cadiz, Sevilla — Paris. Wow, someone is watching from Lima. Hello Lima! Is there anyone from the United States? Look, it's someone from my school in San Diego! What was it like to be gored in Sevilla? You want to see my scar?"

Roberto interrupted and said that the videochat was drawing to an end and that people should post their last questions.

"Before we go," said Alex, "I would like to announce that Roberto de la Torre is going to publish a graphic novel, watch out for it. It's really good. It's about bull-fighting and I'm in it, so is he. Here is a page from it." She held up a piece of paper to the screen and put it close to the camera lens. "What's the title? We have not thought of a title yet. What's it about? I'll upload a page on the Face-book site for you all to look at. If Roberto lets me. Thank you all for your interest and goodbye! See you in San Martín!"

Roberto turned it off. They stared at each other.

"What was that talk about a new suit?" asked Roberto. "A modern suit? You know that's heresy. Your Milou contract didn't say you had to do this."

"They asked and I said yes. It was all done over email. Don't *worry* I won't wear it in a real bullfight. Yet."

"It was unprofessional, they should have asked me, I'm your manager," said Roberto, leaving the room with his laptop and a bundle of USB plugs and wires draped around his neck. "I would have said no."

"That's why they didn't ask you!" she called after him, in a good mood all of a sudden.

"What else do I need to know? Are you still fighting a bull, or is it some other kind of animal?"

"It's still a bull."

"See you in the training ring in ten minutes. I have something of yours to return to you."

It is no coincidence that the word we use in English to describe a passionate expert on any subject is *aficionado*. *Aficionado* comes from the Spanish word *afición*, and in Spanish it is used first and foremost to refer to the passion for bullfighting. The taurine world (for that is what it is called) is shored up by legions of snobs, of *aficionados*, mostly men, mostly middle-aged men, mostly Spanish, mostly Andalucian, with the odd British or American man let in from time to time, who—because of their outsider status—would grovel and wank about the honor, the privilege, of being privy to this closed world and produce tome after thick tome of English-language fan literature, most of which purports to explain bullfighting to philistines (like us), but often reads suspiciously like extended boasts of their cultural holidays and countless hours of man dates or "bromances" in hotels, pubs and bullrings.

Aficionados would not hesitate to declare that bull-fighting is one of the most complex subjects in the world. It behooves them to say this, so that we are intimidated, believing that we are seeking to comprehend something as elaborate as supercomputational neuroscience. Bull-fighting is a world of myth and superstition, attended to by many self-appointed high priests, who together have created an exacting, proprietary vocabulary and a pseudo-science, who would scorn tourists and amateurs who have not yet mastered the right words, the right attitudes, the right skills of appreciation, but yet, when forced to define what constitutes "right" and "good" and "best" in the world of bullfighting, would backpedal hastily and say "it depends, you know it when you see it, you have to know." *Aficionados* do not believe they owe anyone any explana-tion; as a result, other interest groups stepped in and explained their goings-on for the rest of the world. Because if you don't explain it, other people will do it for you, and you cannot complain if, in doing so, they take the opportunity to introduce their own politics in the mix.

Aficionados, moreover, are famously unable to articulate what makes a bullfighter a legend. Among the handful of good bullfighters, why is it that some have passed into immortality, and not others? They usually cannot tell us, because "you just have to know". If pressed, they would often invoke Lorca, the ill-fated gay Spanish poet, and say the best bullfighter is one redolent in *duende*.

What is *duende*?

Alex Herrera, at age thirteen, tried to look it up after hearing Tomas proclaim passionately about it. She read on the Internet the following posting:

Duende *is one of those things which if you have to ask what it means, you probably don't get it.*

"Wanker," she thought, re-running the Google search.

She read Lorca on the subject.

"It's the smell of a child's spit in the wind? That's really helpful," she thought, crumpling the printout.

She asked Shelly.

"Is it some religious thing?" said Shelly. "Sounds like one of those Catholic things involving child sacrifices. Like that Mel Gibson movie? *Apocalypto*? Don't get mixed up in it."

She asked her literature teacher at school.

"I've always thought it was like *je ne sais quoi*. Something indefinable. Ask your Spanish language teacher."

She asked her Spanish language teacher, who was from Mexico City.

"Ah, *duende!* It is a ghost! A little ghost that scares children. Or a little creature. Like, an elf."

"An elf?" asked Alex, exasperated.

"Yes, that."

Why would a bullfighter have an elf inside him?

Tomas came home from the livestock show that evening. Alex asked him.

"No, no, no," said Tomas, laughing and shaking his head impatiently. "Not an elf. It is a feeling."

What kind of feeling? Alex liked hard, tactile facts.

"Listen. I have been thinking hard about you becoming a *torero*," said Tomas. "I think that *duende* is what is going to save you. I have been talking to my bullfighting friends about one of the woman bullfighters in Mexico City. We think she's great because she has *duende*. You see, if you have *duende*, it no longer matters whether you are young or old, or even if you are male or female. The true *torero* embodies the spirit of *duende* in his or her performance. You get into this zone, where you just do it, so effortlessly, so dangerously, that we, in the audience, feel it in here," he indicated the pit of his stomach.

"You mean you like watching bullfighting because it makes you sick in the stomach?"

"Well. Kind of. You see, Alex, we go to watch the bull-fight because we are incomplete people. We have this yearning, and the experience we get from a person risking his life artistically, beautifully, and dangerously, is what completes us. It is the job of the bullfighter to fill this missing space up for us. That is his responsibility."

Shelly interrupted them. She was taking out the garbage and paused at the kitchen door. "I'm trying to get her to be in the 95th percentile of the SAT, and you're filling her head with crazy talk."

"I think it makes sense," said Alex slowly. She went back upstairs to write stuff down in her diary. There was a large gaping hole in her. It had been there for as long as she could remember. Being in front of the bull filled up that hole because there was no room to think of anything else. It made sense that completing herself in the bullring allowed other people to complete themselves too.

Perhaps that was what *duende* was—a blank that would be filled.

Her first initiation into Spanish traditional culture was a failed experiment.

When Alex was ten, Shelly took her to flamenco dance class as part of a Mexican American cultural weekend. All the other girls she knew loved that class. Alex found that she disliked flamenco dancing immensely. It embarrassed her deeply that her culture created this dance. It seemed so corny and fluffy—just a bunch of finger-twirling booty shaking. She did not like using her body that way. She was always athletic, she played tennis, she swam, she ran. She could not express herself in flamenco, she revolted against it with every molecule of her body. She lounged in the back of the room and scowled while the other girls clattered their shoes loudly, clapped and whirled to the beat of the music from the stereo. The music! The *paso doble* was heroic, military; its proper place was in the gritty grandeur of the bullring, she thought. Not here! What perversion to use it this way! To use it to dance with a boy! Eeeuuugh. She cringed with the self-consciousness of a pre-teen. She itched to seize a *muleta* and a sword and show them a thing or two. Finally, she begged to be taken home. The teacher thought Alex was ashamed of her cultural roots and did not think very highly of her.

Shelly, especially, was disappointed with her lack of enthusiasm. She felt strongly the responsibility of bringing up this child and engaging her in her culture. They had a huge fight about this. Alex stormed upstairs to her room and Shelly went to a movie by herself to calm down.

"She's just afraid," said Tomas later that evening. He came into her bedroom and looked at her walls, where she had pinned posters of bullfights and bullfighters.

Alex said, "Is Shelly afraid that I will get hurt by the bull?"

"She's afraid that even if you train in San Diego, you will never become a matador, that I'm just encouraging you towards something that will never happen."

"But didn't you say that what was important for a *torero* is not what happens after, but what happens before, and during, her training to become one?"

"So you're saying if you never become a real bullfighter, you won't cry?"

Alex pondered. At that age, she had yet to form a view about the rate of return on time investment. "But why won't I become a real bullfighter? I like the bulls and the cows. I like caping them. I'm not afraid of them. I know how to deal with them. And I like it. It's the only thing I like. More than tennis. Well, I like tennis, but it's not as exciting."

"Rodeo?"

She giggled. "C'mon! They made me put on a safety helmet when I got on the miniature goat! It's the same helmet I have for riding my bike! It looks silly!"

"*Flamenco* dancing? Piano? Ballet?"

She shook her head, rolling her eyes. "I prefer bull-fighting. I love horses and swords and bulls. It's so much more fun. I'm good at it. You said so!"

Tomas looked into her eyes closely. "You are your grandfather's child. Very well. Let me call the bullfight-ing school. I'll have to explain it to your grandmother. I'll just say it's genetics. You have it. You have the little worm of *afición*. It's come down the ages, skipping your dad, and completely infested itself in you."

"I don't have worms!" she said, alarmed.

"It's just a saying, it's not a real worm." Tomas stopped at the door and turned. "There is no going back, Alex. Once we start this training, it's expensive, and we are going all the way."

She couldn't hear him, she was jumping up and down in excitement and going on the Internet to check on the bullfighting class schedule for the summer.

"You ready?" asked Roberto. "Stop checking your emails!"

She put down her phone. "I just forwarded you an email from Magalie Soubeyran. Ready for what?"

He had a small blue suitcase on the low wall by the training ring. He beckoned and opened it.

"Are they your swords?" she asked curiously, picking up one.

"No. They're Pedro Herrera's swords. My mom's been holding them for you. Sofia hid them all these years. She asked my mother to pass them on to you. Mom kept them because Sofia didn't want them in her house."

"Oh my God." Alex examined the lot. They were old and worn, the steel a burnished dove-grey.

"And these are Juan Carlos's. People would pay a lot for them." He grinned suddenly. "If you bankrupt us all with your matador quest, we could sell these as a last resort."

Alex held up the killing sword and stared down its length at an imaginary bull. "I can't believe I finally have all of them. I wonder what Grandpa would think."

"All right, let's practice. Come on. Use them from now on."

"You use Pedro's, and I'll use Juan Carlos'. Switch."

"Why?" he said, looking as she carefully re-arranged them.

"We'll reverse the bad luck. Instead of we both *die,* we both *live.*"

"I'm game."

"I need a sword boy. Would you be my sword boy?"

"Don't be ridiculous. We'll get you a proper sword handler."

"What about a manservant? Do I get a manservant, too?"

"You'll get everything. I'm arranging it."

"Can I have a massage therapist?"

Fuentes reached for the remote and turned up the volume

so that Alex could hear. "This is a famous news show in France," he said, approvingly. "Listen. It's interesting."

A serious-looking young man with funky glasses was interviewing Magalie Soubeyran in French, on a blue-gold sunny day, outside what looked like a crumbling grey bull-ring. Magalie was in a white and red tracksuit.

"What's she saying?" asked Alex.

"He's asking if Magalie has pets."

"*Oui, j'aime bien les animaux de compagnie. J'ai trois chiens.*"

The interviewer asked how Magalie could kill animals when she loved them.

"*Et vous mangez de la viande?*" Magalie turned the question back to the interviewer.

He wasn't vegetarian. He smiled broadly, "*Oui, mais —*"

"*Et les animaux d'une ferme, ils vivent quelques années, seulement pour être tués, pour que vous les mangiez, n'est-ce pas?*"

"*Mais on ne les torture pas —*"

"*Vous êtes si sûr? Vous devriez examiner les abattoirs.*"

The interviewer chuckled good-naturedly, and pressed on. How could Magalie bear the animal cruelty in the bullring, how did it make her feel to see the bull attack the horse, how she could steel her nerves to kill the bull? Magalie said she grieved deeply each time it happened. It was the grief and the terror that reminded her of the responsibility of being human.

So all this elaborate torture of horses and bulls was just a philosophical exercise for her?

"*Chacun a son rôle,*" said Magalie simply, squinting against the bright sunlight. "*C'est leur destin. C'est mon destin.*"

❀

Francisco, the bullring manager of the *plaza de toros* in San Martín, a municipality south of Valencia, issued the following press release:

The City of San Martín announces that for the Easter Fair it will hold a running of the bulls to benefit the bullfighting museum. The novilleros scheduled to appear are:

Joselito RODRIGUEZ "El PEPITO"
Magalie SOUBEYRAN
Alejandra HERRERA

With picadores.
With bulls donated by the ranch of Luis Ricardo Fuentes.
There are no more tickets. No press.

"Is it true that there are no more tickets for Sunday?" asked Silvio, ringing anxiously from his shop.

"I lied." Francisco lit a cigarette cheerfully. "I made it a national release, all the newspapers have it. Nothing gets them going except the words *No More Tickets*. I threw in *No Press* for good measure. They've gone insane. I had to turn off my cellphone!"

"But how will you sell tickets?"

"Are you kidding me? I haven't even released the tickets yet, I'm holding it back till the last minute; it feels like I'm holding back a bursting dam. I've got so many orders from San Martín itself that I have to hire extra staff this Easter. I've got *banderilleros* and *picadores* calling me wanting to work for free. It's the first time our bullring has ever had quality bulls like that. This will be the fair to end all fairs. The stars are all aligning. This will be magic."

✿

Sofia rang Francisco.

"But why not?" he wailed. "It was so hard to even find someone who wants to be in the same fight!"

She did not like Joselito Rodriguez. Nothing good would come of it. He was the boy who tried to kill himself —a brilliant bullfighter, true, but too young, and overly sensitive. The rumors have not yet died down that he was trying to commit "suicide by bull" and if anything unlucky happens she did not want her only grandchild to be in the same bullfight.

"But he's the only guy we can find to make up the third! Otherwise we would just have a bullfight with two girls! Even you would agree that's pretty pathetic!"

"Well, I won't go then. I can't bear to watch."

"Oh, come on!"

✿

Suerte, the word for luck, has a nice ring to it in Spanish. Everybody in the bullfighting world uses it liberally; every-body knows what it means. But it sounds so ambiguous in English. It sounds like luck could be good or bad. It sounds like the word "luck" as in "luck of the draw". But it is precisely the randomness, the luck-of-the-draw-ness of the bullfight, which makes it so perversely thrilling. There are so many factors that could sabotage the event. The weather—bullrings are open-air. Oh, don't even think of having it in an enclosed stadium, that's not the real thing. Rain is fatal; wind is also fatal. If you are flap-ping a cloth at a bull weighing over eleven hundred pounds, you want the cloth to be in the right place at the right split second. You hope there is no wind. You hope there is sun—hot, yellow, scalding, high-altitude sun that

264

makes everyone's costumes sparkle and gives you postcardy photos of *sol y sombre*, that wonderful *yin yang* of the circular bullring that is half in shadow and half blindingly brilliant. The defining edge of the shadow must be sharp and clear, like a properly starched crease on a uniform. Yes, you pray for that kind of sun, so that the audience would be aesthetically placated. But you hope it's not too hot. You don't want to be too hot, you don't want to sweat and drop the sword with your sweaty, wet hands or get too uncomfortable in your starched suit, which is about as comfortable as wearing a giant *piñata*. You hope the sand is dry so you don't slip and fall on your ass and get a horn in your gut. And you hope that there are no assholes — especially drunken assholes or worse, professional hecklers — in the audience that would shout the wrong thing at the worst moment and completely freak you out and destabilize you just as the bull is charging, which is *so unfair*, especially in those shitty towns where *anything goes* and people think nothing of shouting crude things, things that sometimes makes you want to just laugh and throw down your cape and march into the cool alley of the bullring into a taxi cab and just cab to a pub and get a cold beer and forget about it all. Yes, you are paid a lot. Yes, you are a rock star. But what is "a lot"? Because you are certainly not paid enough, *never* enough, to endure this sort of public humiliation *on top of* risking your life. Come on, let's put a number on it. Your manager certainly does. Is your life worth $10,000 per fight? $50,000? $200,000? $500,000? And as for in-kind payment, well you would love to screw one of those denim-assed girls right outside the bullring who are asking for you to kiss them, and you know they wouldn't mind, but you can't, really, because you are so terrified of losing your form or getting blackmailed or getting a disease or getting photographed by paparazzi or falling in love, and you are so superstitious

265

that you can't take any chances, any chances at all. Why not have a steady girlfriend? Well, who wants to be with someone who is always on the road and who might die or become an invalid tomorrow? Someone who is never around, never available, mentally, emotionally, physically. No, educated girls these days don't take this kind of shit. Face it. The simple fact is that you and the bull in that ring are the only two sexually-intact males in the entire bull-ring who are full of testosterone and aggression but who never get to fuck any females, on or off the ranch. Only the bull understands your predicament. You are too terrified to let anyone in past the high walls you have erected around yourself, and sometimes you secretly think you are mad. No amount of money can compensate for this kind of life. And after you pay everyone off, and settle all your debts, there is not much left over for you anyway that you can count on if tomorrow you have an accident and became disabled for life. To supplement your income, for a change of pace, you can do some modeling for extra money—especially if you are good-looking—but then your sisters, female cousins, and ex-girlfriends will start saying that you are secretly homosexual, as they have always suspected. So you are stuck in this bloody hot ring with the sand and the bull and the blood and the horses and the smell. The smell. It's a smell that never leaves you, no matter how many long hot showers you take after the fight. And best of all, you have nothing to look forward to, except a long night of motoring on the highway a few hundred miles to the next town, for *more of the same*.

"He's fallen asleep," giggled Alex.

"He's talked out," said Joselito.

"I've *never* heard him talk so much."

"It's that last bottle of wine."

"*I* drank the last bottle," said Alex.

"Then it must have been whatever shit they put in the pipe we were smoking."

"What the *hell* was in that pipe?"

"Beats me, but he did a lot of it. I don't think he's ever done a hookah. Man, he's usually so quiet and polite in public. I've *never* heard him talk so much shit."

Joselito Rodriguez got Alex's number from Antonio and rang them. He lived in Sevilla and decided to stop by Cadiz for a bonding experience. Alex, Roberto and Joselito met for dinner in downtown Cadiz and got on famously. At two o'clock in the morning, they went to another bar, then to a club, then to some Moroccan tea joint where everybody had a go at the hookah, then because there were so many cushions, what else could they do but end up sleeping on the floor and when the proprietor woke them up to sweep the place, it was dawn. They ended up in a café across the street playing *E-Faena 2* drunkenly while drinking coffee spiked with liquor to get rid of their hangover.

"High score!" crowed Joselito, thumping the table.

"Look again, loser," said Alex.

"What! How did you get 600 extra points?"

"You went into overtime."

"Shit. Rematch!"

"I'll take a break, my fingers are cramping. So, honestly, tell me, why are you fighting in San Martín?" asked Alex, stretching and yawning. "I thought you didn't want to have anything to do with us."

"I don't have a choice," said Joselito into his coffee cup. He pulled up the sleeves of his sweater. There were shocking scars along the inside of his arms. He had tried to kill himself by cutting his wrists. "I've got fewer bookings this season. I need the practice. My manager's got cold feet, everyone's afraid of having me in their fights in case I bring bad luck to them. People think that I will just fling myself in front of the bull and get gored. This is my best chance to prove that I can still do it. Even if I have to go with you and Magalie on the cards."

"I wish Roberto would fight."

"He's been out too long. Has he been practicing? Is he in shape?"

"This guy?" said Alex, prodding Roberto. "This guy can do *veronica* passes in his sleep. He says the less he trains, the more inspired his performance."

"Fuck, he's old school."

"Here's to old school. Let's not let him down."

"He's a good guy. We want him back. He shouldn't have listened to my sister."

"Your sister?"

"That's how I met Roberto. He's dating my sister. Was."

"Delfina? She's your sister?"

"Yep. They were an item for two years. That's how he got in touch with me after I got out of hospital 'cos my parents were hiding me from the public. He found me through her. He kept calling her and negotiating. Finally got my address from her. Drove to Sevilla to see me to convince me to join your San Martín thing."

"So what's the story between him and your sister?"

"She broke up with him because he was bullfighting."

"Ah." Alex said, sleepily, "I think I have reached that point where there is officially more alcohol in my system than water. Oh God, I feel so sick." She folded her arms on the table and buried her head.

Joselito ordered another round. "Delfina and I have different mothers. She went to England to study and came back all stuck up and anti-bullfights. She said England opened her eyes. When he quit bullfighting she began sending him emails again, I think she was hoping for a reunion."

Alex mumbled into the table. "He's got a girlfriend in California. Blond. Speaks Spanish. Think Gwyneth Paltrow."

Joselito stared. "Some people have all the luck. Plus you? Two American girlfriends?"

"*I'm* not his girlfriend."

"You guys aren't doing it?"

"No, we're both very repressed."

"You don't want to sleep with him?"

"I think I've done it so many times in my head, I don't remember if we actually did it or not for real."

Joselito collapsed, laughing weakly. He cleared his throat and adjusted his oversized, drug-dealer sunglasses on his face when he noticed people turning around in the café and glancing at him. They had hidden Roberto deep in the booth, and few people recognized Alex.

She raised her head and peered through her curls. "So you think he retired because of your sister?"

"Partly."

"Then I have undone her good work."

"You have indeed."

They toasted to each other, to the bulls, to the *corrida*, and to moral decay.

"Are you scared about the fight?" said Joselito, ordering another coffee. "Won't that be your first proper public performance? I still remember my first time. It gave me such a buzz to be in that ring with all those thousands of pairs of eyes focused on me. I was so excited I almost fainted."

"Of course I am scared," said Alex. "It's good to be scared. I want to go in there scared shitless. The more scared I am, the better I'm going to be."

"What are you more scared of, the bull or public opinion?"

"Everything. I'm scared of *everything*. And I love it."

"You know, I thought you were full of shit, when I first heard about you, but you're okay."

"Thanks."

"You pass my test. I'd do you if you weren't a matador. But you've joined the fraternity. I respect you."

"*Suerte*, matador."

"*Suerte*, matador."

Dear Roberto, are there more pages to your graphic novel? I would like to read more. Also, Paco has started reading it. I caught him. Now he says he wants the next few chapters, he says it's addictive. I think he has even forwarded it to some of his bullfighting friends. I tried to stop him but he said you wouldn't mind. If you don't want him to do that, you better tell him. He has no respect for other people's property. Before you know it, it will be all over the Web. Publicly, he and his friends pretend they are not curious about women matadors. But they secretly talk about you and what you are doing <u>all the time.</u>

P.S. If you don't mind I would like to show your pages to my editor at work. Even better if you can send me as complete a draft as possible.

— Ana Garcia

Dear Ana, I am mailing you the photocopy of the first book. I've finished drawing and writing it. It's not very thick, but it's close to the San Martín bullfight and we're starting to get busy. I guess I don't care what Paco does with it, if it helps Alex overcome any attacks in the press, and drum up interest in the San Martín fight, that'll be great. Alex can't afford a publicist, and Paco has always had a big mouth. As her manager, I would be concerned if they are saying bad things, but maybe as a woman matador it's better to be talked about than ignored.

— *Roberto*

❀

Alex had her bad days at the ranch.

She would read an interview, or overhear a male journalist comment sarcastically on the radio about her upcoming bullfight. They burned her with the ice of their disdain. They damned her on things that she could not change. They rated her performance way below male *novilleros* whom she knew were inferior to her. There was no justice. She was a woman, and an American. She was an outsider. She wanted to do something no one else she knew desired. No community would accept her — not back in Texas, not in Spain. She belonged nowhere. She was a society of one. On bad days, the bogeymen would gather around her and multiply noiselessly, all shaking their heads and opening their mouths in silent ridicule.

I should have been in the car with my parents.

Instead, she was condemned to die in a sealed cave, alone, without a flashlight. But in that cave there was the slightest waft of air from the outside, and there was a patch that was just a little lighter than the darkness around it. Was it an opening? Was that unlit stone, or the night sky? Was it a trick of the vision, or the weakest possibility of starlight?

Why would this fever not abate?

On good days, she felt invincible. She had to fight as if she was immortal, as if she was not flesh and blood, as if she had already been to Purgatory, spoken with the

Devil, and obtained advance assurance that she would never die. That was the only way Alex could face a full-grown bull while ten thousand people watched. And she felt, on good days, that she had been blessed, that she had already obtained this assurance. The only time she felt apprehensive was when she stood outside the ring, right before the fight. The moment she stepped on the sand she became calm. She had done it a thousand times. No, she did not think about accidents or death, just as one did not think about such things when one boarded a plane, or got behind the wheel of a car. There was a reckless legacy that she reached out her hands to claim, eagerly, because no one else did. There was the little curse that lived on inside her, which had by now metastasized into every cell in her body. She was genetically programmed to try. When she died, they'd cut her open and all would become clear.

I am haunted by Pedro Javier Herrera, my grandfather, a man I have never seen except on television.

"He came back, only once," said Sofia quietly, one evening when she was visiting Alex in the Sevilla hospital. "The day after he was buried, he was sitting in the living room. I was making breakfast and heard a noise. He told me that I had to let him go, and that he was very sorry. It happens, you know. You hurt so badly, that your mind plays tricks on you, you see what isn't there. My aunts all saw their husbands come back. My mother, too. They always come back, because we are thinking of them. A few days after the funeral, the feeling fades. Why, what do you see?"

Alex thought for a long time, trying to explain. Words were not her forte. Old feelings that were soft, glowing and round, in the pit of her stomach, tumbled out like chips of flint when she tried to put them into words. Finally, "Sunlight in an old stairwell. Footsteps, laughter, Spanish words, thick in the air, like garlands. I can't make out what they are saying, but we are all rushing downstairs to go to the *plaza de toros*."

"To see Pedro?"

"No. To see Roberto."

"Pedro, Angel, alive, watching Roberto perform? It has never happened."

"And I am going also. I am going into the ring. I am a matador."

"Impossible."

"As you said," Alex tilted her head back in the pillow, suddenly tired, "you hurt so badly, that your mind plays tricks on you. I have never felt so accompanied in my life. There is so much noise, so many voices, so much bursting light, all crowding into me, pressing against me, holding me, till my heart is full, it overflows. There is love, love, love. Then I wake up, in a cold, grey, empty country, on the other side of a great ocean, far away from you all. And I cried to be back in the dream."

She opened her eyes. She was still in bed. The San Martín fight was still weeks away. Her hands were cold, her pulse was still racing, her head was full of sunlight.

Someone was knocking on her door.

"It's Joselito," said Roberto, his cell phone still in his hand. His dark eyes were tragic. "He overdosed on sleeping pills."

"What!"

"Delfina found him in time and got him to the hospital. They're pumping his stomach. He'll live. He posted a suicide note on Facebook. Delfina saw it."

Moaning, Alex hurried over to her laptop.

He sat on her bed gloomily. They read Joselito's long and rambling suicide note online.

"What is he going on about?" asked Alex.

"It's a talk show. His girlfriend just broke up with him on television, on a live talk show." Roberto leaned over her shoulder and looked at the screen. "Open up another window, the clip's on YouTube."

They watched a two-minute clip of a sobbing Joselito as a model-pretty blond declared she didn't love him anymore and that she was leaving him. The audience *oohed* and *aahed*, then clapped as she walked tearfully off the set.

"He has had two bad seasons in a row. This just pushed him over the edge," said Roberto.

"*Why* is this on TV? This is so *trashy*."

"It's the talk shows. You don't understand. They love matador romances. Why do you think I was always so paranoid about the press?"

"Jesus, if a guy commented on my sexual prowess on live television I'll sue him, not kill myself." Alex began typing briskly at the keyboard, muttering. She looked at her search results on the screen. "Do you own a gun?"

"No." Roberto was startled. "Why do you need a gun?"

"He keeps talking about shooting himself, yet he takes sleeping pills. He's not serious about dying. If you really want to die, you don't tell 872 friends on Facebook *beforehand*. And if you did, you just shoot yourself right away, not lie around waiting for someone to find you."

"Maybe he couldn't get a gun. This isn't America."

"We need him to stop doing this. We need him for our *corrida*. I'm not going to have him die on us like this."

"Well, he hasn't died."

"Either way, this is bad PR. This makes us all look ridiculous. Find a gun. There's got to be a gun on this ranch we can use. I have a plan."

Fuentes had a lot of guns, but they were rifles for game hunting.

"Useless . . ." announced Alex, emerging from the rifle room into the bright sunlight. "Come on, let's drive to town."

"What are you doing?" cried Roberto, running after her.

"To sort this out," she said determinedly, zipping up her jacket. "Coming?"

In the car, she took out her phone, tapped the screen for the search program, and said, slowly and deliberately, into the mouthpiece— *"Gun, Laws, In, Spain."*

"Well?" he asked.

She kept reading the phone silently as he sped down the highway.

"Well, Alex?"

"Ah, screw it," she said impatiently, tapping the screen again. *"Toy, Stores, In, Cadiz, Spain."*

An hour later, Alex came out of a small toy and candy shop off the windswept town square in Cadiz. "You can get Hello Kitty," she announced. "But not a realistic-looking toy gun. This town sucks! I'd die in this town if I was a kid."

Roberto was sketching under a café awning with a cup of coffee. He yawned and looked out into the turquoise ocean across the plaza. "The waiter says there's a Toys R Us in El Puerto."

"Why didn't you say so earlier!"

"Are you sure you don't want Hello Kitty?"

"Come on!"

Three days later, Rojo was reading the morning paper in the kitchen of the main house when he heard the roar of a sports car up the driveway. He peeked out of the window curiously.

Alex. Roberto. And a bedraggled Joselito Rodriguez between them, his hands duct-taped together. The teenage matador was completely drenched and sniffing. His hair was caked in green slime.

"I don't even want to *ask*," declared Rojo when the three of them came into the kitchen.

Roberto pulled out his pocketknife and cut Joselito's bonds.

Alex went over to the cupboard and retrieved a bottle of brandy and a glass. "We had a bonding experience." She handed a drink to Joselito.

"Where's Fuentes?" asked Roberto, throwing a kitchen towel at Joselito, who downed the drink and blew his nose. "This kid's staying with us till Easter."

"What's your manager's phone number?" asked Alex.

Joselito dug his cellphone miserably out of his back pocket and handed it to her.

They were gossiping in the local San Martín *peña*.

"Who's Alejandra Herrera's American sponsor?"

"Some sportswear brand."

"Milou."

"They do something for the Olympics, no?"

"Who cares, we have a fight! Do you know how many small cities are jealous of us, being able to put this up, in a recession year?"

"Francisco calls it the *Fight Of The Millennium*."

"Did you see the bulls?"

"Oh, they're gorgeous. I was afraid they might turn out shaggy and skinny because of the rain this spring in Cadiz, but they're not too bad. Fuentes has good stock and great guys working for him."

"Ah really? I read a magazine article about his ranch. He says if there continues to be low demand for bullfights he might give up breeding the *toro bravo* and breed Kobe beef cows for his restaurants instead."

"Is he insane? I better talk to him."

"Did you hear about the swords? Sofia had them all along."

"What swords?"

"The swords of De la Torre and Herrera."

"What! They've been found?"

"My God!"

"Where did she keep them all these years?"

"How much do you think they're worth?"

"It must have been, what, fifty years?"

"Who told you this?"

"Didn't you read *VirtualPeña*?"

"That's for the little girls."

"Well, *El País* isn't going to tell you this kind of stuff anymore, so I read *VirtualPeña*. My granddaughter's a member."

"Did someone tell Hector that the lost swords have been found?"

"No use, the museum doesn't have money to purchase them for display."

"Is the girl going to use Pedro's swords?"

"Not only that — get this — she's got a *traje de luces* made from his old one."

"No!"

"Personally, I am not sure how I feel about this."

"It's a nice gesture. She respects tradition."

"This is worth seeing."

"What about Roberto de la Torre?"

"Not fighting."

"Still not fighting?"

"Somebody knock some sense into him."

"His father and him are not really talking."

"Did you see his graphic novel?"

"He has written a book?"

"No, a graphic novel."

"What does that mean?"

"Like a comic book."

"Like Superman?"

"No, it's about bullfighting, about how the girl trained to be a matador and how he helped her."

"What's it called?"

"*Robert y Alex*. It's not published yet, but you can find it on the Web. Ask your son."

"About training a girl matador, hmph! It must be very boring."

"It's quite nice, actually, easy to read, he says a lot of beautiful things about bullfighting that I have never thought of before. Big type. And if the words are too small, you can follow the pictures. Sometimes they're all pictures, he draws quite well."

"He's an artist now, eh? How do you know?"

"Don't you read *VirtualPeña*?"

Roberto's cellphone rang. He saw the caller ID.

Alex did, too. "Tell her."

Roberto picked up his phone while Alex turned down the volume of the television. He said calmly, "Hi, Delfina. How are you?"

The woman at the other end went on for a long time. Roberto flicked his eyes at Alex. "I have him. Didn't you get my email? No, he's fine. In fact, he's sitting here with us right now, eating popcorn. We're watching *Transformers.*" He handed the phone to Joselito, who was sitting on the couch in sweatshirt, sweatpants and socks. "El Pepito! It's your sister."

Joselito shook his head violently.

Roberto told Delfina, "He doesn't want to talk . . . Yes . . . Yes . . . Yes, it's on . . . No, I'm not fighting, I told you I was retired . . . Maybe, I don't know. Or I'll become a graphic novelist. I don't have to decide. I'm only twenty-one. Why, do *you* have a career?" He hung up. "She wishes us all to hell."

"She thinks she's so clever. She's studying for a PhD," said Joselito through a mouthful of popcorn.

"Did you know Alex's going to get an MBA?"

"That's what girls are good for, studying. *Ouch!*"

It was destined not to be.

The final call came an hour before the bullfight.

"Magalie's still stuck at the French border," said Joselito's manager to Roberto. "They won't let her through."

"Have they found out who's doing this?"

"Don't know. They're being searched as if they were criminals. It's a mess. I've been trying to reach Fuentes, do you know where he is?"

"Hold on, I'll transfer you," Roberto jabbed his phone impatiently. He had to hang up when he got into the hotel elevator.

He reached Alex's room and knocked sharply. His phone rang again, he turned the ringer off and resumed knocking. He looked for a doorbell. What the hell was she doing? Luisa, Alex's friend from Sevilla matador school, was supposed to be helping her change into her *traje de luces.* Instead, the door was opened by Paco's girlfriend, Ana. She was in exercise clothes. He caught a dark, musky whiff of incense. The lights had been dimmed and the furniture moved to one side. Alex and Luisa were sprawled face down on the carpet on pink rubber mats.

"What the hell are you guys doing?" he cried.

"Yoga," said Ana, shushing him. She closed her eyes and began a Sanskrit chant.

Roberto knelt beside Alex. "You need to get dressed!" he hissed.

"It only takes a minute. Calm down."

"It does not! The fight starts in thirty minutes, it's still ten minutes to the ring by car if there's no traffic. Would you hurry!"

The three girls changed position and contorted their bodies.

"I bet you can't do this," said Alex, her head upside down. "Ana's idea. You know she's a yoga teacher? It's very soothing. You should totally try it."

"But what is she *singing*?" said Roberto unhappily.

"It's a chant blessing the Earth and all the animals in it, including the bulls. She says bulls are special to Hindus, too, you know. We find it very meaningful. We are praying to the bulls I kill today, for their forgiveness. We wish them a good death, and if we die, we die a good death also."

Luisa darted a look at Roberto's confused expression and giggled.

The girls assumed a new pose. Ana finished her chant in a clear, high voice, raised her hands to her forehead and said, "Feel your breath circulating around your body, healing all your past wounds, all the places you have ever been injured. Ask yourself what you can do today to make yourself stronger and to heal those around you. Think of where they have been injured and how they can become whole." Ana opened one eye and saw Roberto wriggling in discomfort. She suppressed a smile and continued, eyes closed, "As you let your thoughts back in, feel your strength from the sun above you and from the earth beneath you. Be thankful for your family and for your community. Do what you have to do today, with power, responsibility and grace. Let us say *om*. *Ommmmm-mmmmm. Namaste*."

The girls got up and rolled their mats. Roberto turned on the lights impatiently, the bad news about Magalie gnawing at him. He stood around, waiting for Ana to leave.

"These Milou mats are great!" said Luisa. "I'm starting to like this yoga thing."

"It works, right?" Ana asked Alex. "How do you feel now? Better?"

"It helps."

Ana told Roberto that there being no precedent for preparing an American woman matador, that Alex had invented her own methodology after chatting with her on Facebook, and the girls had all agreed after deep consultation on the right chant for the bulls.

"See you all in the ring," said Ana, slinging her yoga bag over her shoulder and blowing Roberto a kiss. "I will pray for all your souls."

Luisa hauled the *traje de luces* out of the closet and began laying the individual pieces on the bed.

"You ready to talk now?" he demanded.

"Yes," said Alex, opening a bottle of mineral water.

"Magalie's not going to be here in time."

"Why not?"

Roberto noted that she seemed to take the bad news well. Was it the yoga? "The Spanish guards are not letting her through the border, they've detained her. There is no way she can get here in time, even if they drove two hundred miles per hour."

Alex's phone went *whoop*. She glanced at the screen absently to check the text message.

"So, get a chopper for Mags," said Alex.

He shook his head helplessly.

"Who is it?" she asked, disappearing into the bathroom. "The Mafia?"

"A lot of people in the industry do not want to see you and Magalie succeed."

Alex re-appeared. "Hey," she said gently, going around the suite and turning off lamps. "Can you light this candle for me?"

He calmed down a bit and lit it solemnly. At least he knew this bit. He was relieved that she still wanted to pay observance to the candle ritual. One tried all the gods one could, at a moment like this. The votive candle would keep vigil for her until she returned in one piece from the fight. The hotel maids knew better than to blow it out.

Alex said, "I love the smell of matches when struck."

They were now both whispering. The amber glow reminded them of church. "You want to light another one?" he asked.

"Nah. One's plenty. I'm not really that Catholic."

"More for luck. Even if you're Hindu."

She shook her head and smiled.

Alex placed the wavering light before pictures of Saint Joan and Saint Catherine. Each of them bore a large sword. Roberto would write in his graphic novel of this moment. He would record, in a beautifully-drawn, contemplative aside, that Alex was praying to powerful women saints, like he had always done before a fight, except that she was also a woman. Of course they would watch over her with especial care, he wrote. He imagined an invisible, powerful sympathy of which he could never take part, and was suddenly envious. It wasn't a boys' club after all. It was a girls' club, and one that made him feel a little insecure.

Luisa, after trying to maneuver around him, shut him in the bathroom so that Alex could change.

He paced around nervously on the shiny bathroom tiles; she heard him.

"Hey, don't sweat it," she called. "Joselito and I will kill all six bulls. And if Joselito ODs on his meds a minute from now, rush him to the hospital and I'll take on six bulls myself. Magalie's done it. I'm always prepared for the worst case scenario."

"The public paid to see three matadors," he called back.

"We *have* three matadors."

Roberto fumed. "Can I come out now? Your *cuadrilla's* arrived downstairs."

"Yes," replied Luisa.

He looked at Alex in the glittering red suit of lights and felt just the slightest stir of excitement and jealousy. All he could manage was, "Don't be late. SMS me if you need anything."

" 'Kay."

He wanted to embrace her tightly, but in the end he hurriedly kissed both women on their cheeks and left. In the elevator he realized wretchedly that he forgot to wish Alex good luck, but it was too late to go back upstairs.

The downstairs lobby was filled with glittering *toreros*. He saw Sofia arriving in the lobby, looking bewildered, with Silvio the tailor holding on to her arm. He caught a glimpse of Delfina — what was she doing here? To watch over her brother? She had gone from golden blond to platinum blond. He allowed himself the tiniest pinch of satisfaction in noting that the color didn't suit her. They avoided looking at each other.

Alex's team arrived — more students from Sevilla matador school, led by Ignacio. They were resplendent in their suits of light and obviously self-conscious and excited. Roberto went to talk to them. Hector from the bullfighting museum came to hug everyone and take photographs. Paco and Ana waved at him from afar. He waved back. Ana said something to her boyfriend, who grinned and took a picture of him with his camera phone. Alex's sponsor, Milou, sent an American PR lady with beet-red hair and chalky makeup. She had in tow a beefy, blond Australian videographer who kept trying to catch his attention. They tried interviewing people in English, but were waved away impatiently.

More chaos. Fuentes came running down the grand staircase to the lobby, his phone glued to his ear, yelling at someone to take care of Magalie's problem. He disappeared round the corner. Antonio was pacing around, a blue-blinking cellphone earpiece jutting oddly out of his right ear, listening intently to someone on the other line. When he saw Roberto, he beckoned urgently. He hung up.

"Okay, the situation is this," said Antonio tersely, his eyes scanning the room. "Magalie's team is driving back to Nîmes. They've had enough. It's final. No Magalie today."

Roberto's phone went *ping*. It was a message from Alex.

Mags just SMS'd me. She's given up.

Everyone was talking to Roberto at once.

A new message popped up from Joselito.

I am in NO SHAPE to take on 3 bulls.

Someone let in the *peñas* and assorted fans. Thankfully there was no press, as the San Martín bullring had forbidden them. Even if it didn't, the bullfighting critics had already made a silent pact to ignore the existence of the fight. It would be as if it never happened. The paparazzi came, however. They could always sell pictures of matadors to the tabloids. A veteran matador who had come to wish them well tried to talk to Roberto. At his appearance, they were both suddenly surrounded by photographers and a sea of women asking for autographs and kisses.

Roberto signed an old photograph of himself, his mind a blank. His cellphone rang, it was Joselito's manager, he did not dare to pick up.

The Milou people fought through the crowd. A microphone was thrust in his face. "Here we have the manager of Alex Herrera, himself a young matador named Roberto de la Torre, currently retired. Hello, Roberto, can you tell us a bit about what to expect today?" said the PR lady, beaming.

Roberto smiled into the camera and said a few stock phrases he had learned from years of observing his own manager. Due to his limited English, his replies were even more cursory than usual. Before she could ask another question, he felt a firm grip on his shoulder. It was Antonio, Fuentes and Rojo. The chef was all smiles and bore a large, cream-colored plastic garment bag.

The Twitter feed for the San Martín Easter bullfight was in Spanish, Portuguese, French, and English, and went something like this:

> *At the plaza de toros in San Martín hoping to get tickets.*
> *No more tickets.*
> *Say NO to bullfighting!*
> *I just got tickets.*
> *There are DEFINITELY no more tickets, don't waste your time.*
> *In San Martín, a small town, to see the American matador Alex Herrera who is from our college. Go UT!*
> *There are still tickets left for sun seats. Good luck on a day like this. You'd roast.*

Down with bullfighting! The only thing that will interest me is if the bull kills the matador!

My mother and I are standing in line at the hotel hoping to catch a glimpse of the toreros.

Does anybody speak English?

They're not starting on time.

Soubeyran's out. No Soubeyran. Spread the word.

DOWN WITH BULLFIGHTING I HOPE YOU ALL DIE BLOODTHIRSTY ASSHOLES!!!

Magalie Soubeyran has not arrived.

Only 2 matadors on the cartel — El Pepito and Herrera, you still want to queue for tickets?

How do you say I want the cheapest tickets in English?

It's so fucking hot in Spain!

HERRE-RA! HERRE-RA! HERRE-RA!

Spread the word, only 2 matadors today. Soubeyran cancelled.

Where are you in the line? Are there still tickets? Am I in the right line?

It is so crowded I can't even move.

Where do you get those programs that everyone is holding?

VirtualPeña Rocks! VirtualPeña T-shirts everywhere, I'm so PROUD!

Beautiful weather, we are lucky today.

Say NO to women matadors.

Where are you?

Say NO to the corrida.

There are no more tickets.

Alex Herrera = Non Compos Mentis.

Get your VirtualPeña armbands, 2 Euros! Outside Gate 2.

Where are you?

They're late. No Soubeyran. Damn, I've come all the way from Portugal to see her.

Has anyone seen Alex Herrera? Does she look hot?

Soubeyran's hot but she's not coming.

It's El Pepito v. Herrera. GO EL PEPITO! You are the BEST! Don't weep over Carmelita, she sucks!

Maybe he'll fall for Herrera. If that's allowed.

YOU R ALL MONSTERS! I can't believe in this day and age there are people queuing up to see the torture of a dumb animal.

Only 2 matadors. Confirmed. I heard the team talking in the lobby.

Are you guys here yet? I can't see you.

Aren't all animals dumb? Do you know Talking Animals? LOL. Don't interfere if YOU don't get it!

My mother's got a photo with Roberto de la Torre!

He's HERE??? Where are you?

Came to see Soubeyran and she's a no show. Standing in line to inquire about refund.

I xxxxx Joselito! You are the best! You are an angel from heaven! Please don't die before we sleep together.

Bullfighting is BULLSHIT!

Is the fight being cancelled?

Tickets are at 150 Euros. What a rip! That's not the face value I'm sure.

How do you get a VirtualPeña hat? Are they for sale?

Does anybody have extra tickets to sell? My sister can't get in. Willing to pay up to 80 Euros.

VIOLENCE ON T.V. AND VIOLENCE IN BULL-RING = DOWNFALL OF SPAIN.

Ayaiyaiyaiyai! ROBERTO is the BEST! Sizzle!

Hi, I'm standing outside the gates, where are you?

Are there tickets left?

Sitting in the hot sun, the fight is being delayed, but the ring is full and more people are pouring in.

What are we waiting for? When is it going to start?

It's disgraceful in this day and age. Another failure of the government.

It's 45 minutes past the hour and no one has arrived. This is

my first bullfight. It feels like a concert at the Rose Bowl. Except
the seats are squeezy. Luckily everyone is skinny here.

WE HAVE A CARTEL!

De la Torre has agreed to sub for Soubeyran.

What?!!!!

De la Torre's on. I'm going back outside to see if I can resell
my ticket for double the price!

Finally!

Unbelievable!

Live from San Martín Plaza de Toros: Roberto de la Torre
is fighting today. YES it is TRUE.

Crowds screaming at announcement.

Desperate to get in.

Final lineup: De la Torre, El Pepito, Alex Herrera.

HURRAY!

HURRAY!

He's BACK???

Rock Star! Rock Star! Rock Starrrrrr!

Torero! Torero! Torero!

A young woman who wants to kill bulls must be mentally
unsound.

There was no PA system in the San Martín bullring, so
the staff walked along the rim of the bleachers shouting
up to the crowd that there had been a change of matadors.
A huge wave of excited applause broke over the entire
bullring; screams and cat-calls. This was the first time in
a long time that the ring was filled up and every seat taken.

"Take photos, take photos!" gesticulated Francisco
excitedly to his staff. "We definitely have to put this on the
website. The photos on our website currently show a half-
empty ring! Swap them out now, don't wait! Call the IT
guy."

"We can't, he's here watching the bullfight."

"Francisco, I have *El Mundo* on the line for you, inquiring about a rumor that De la Torre is performing today."

"Put them on hold."

Streams of people continued to crawl up and down the aisles. It was Easter weekend and the town was packed with people from the outlying suburbs, all in a festive mood.

"Just look at this," said Francisco. "How can this be a supermarket! How can this be a DFS store! This is alive! A day like this makes my job worthwhile." Stepping back, he surveyed the scene and congratulated himself, wiping tears from the corner of his eyes.

VirtualPeña occupied a whole section, all wearing fuchsia pink hats and T-shirts with "VP" and a crown and shield emblazoned in the front in gold. They displayed a pink banner that said: ALEJANDRA HERRERA FROM YOUR FRIENDS AT VIRTUALPEÑA!

VirtualPeña had their own fighting song, it went something like this:

I had a little cat
My father won't let me keep him

I had a little pony
My uncle won't let me ride him

I had a little bull
My brother won't let me fight him

But I'm too old for dolls now
I'm too old for dolls now
I am a torero! I am a torero! (x2)

Each girl wore a tangerine-colored armband with the

name of their favorite matador embroidered on it in gold. The armband was secured with a Velcro tab and was designed to be ripped off and thrown down to their favorite matador. They were nothing if not creative.

"Perfect weather," said Hector, sweating, looking up at the cornflower blue sky. "Not a hint of wind."

"I checked the weather report, it might rain later," said the gentleman beside him.

"Nonsense, I won't hear of it," said Hector. "This is a historic day. Pedro Herrera and Juan Carlos de la Torre will protect us all, God willing."

"We have the right bulls, we have the right weather, now we hope we have the right *toreros*," said Silvio.

"Francisco's a bit worried about the hecklers."

The two men looked at a certain section where protesters were booing *VirtualPeña* and busily unfurling rude banners that said ABOLISH BULLFIGHTING and MURDERER.

"How did they get in? Are they from Madrid? Did they pay for tickets?"

"Not sure."

"If things get rough, maybe the kids from *VirtualPeña* would protect us. I mean, just look at them. What are they singing? Aren't they a bit mental? Do you think they would be so stirred up if Alex Herrera didn't appear on the scene?"

"I just think they like anything American," said Silvio, unwrapping a McDonald's hamburger that he had brought to snack on at the ring.

Sofia was on the phone. "Yes, can you believe it. I have not seen a *corrida* in fifty years. I've forgotten how hot it is . . . No, nothing has changed . . . Of course I am nervous. Do you want me to talk to you during, or call you after?"

"Who is it?" asked Silvio curiously.

"Roberto's mother, Cristina," said Sofia, hanging up.

"Is she okay?"

"Well, we were trying to figure out which is worse, being here or not being here." Sofia shifted her handbag on her lap. The seat was very uncomfortable for her, despite the weather-beaten leatherette cushion that she had rented. "I think I am going to throw up."

Silvio gave her the paper bag from his Happy Meal.

❁

"Hi, Mom." Roberto was in the crowded van, his face sticky despite the air-conditioning. It was only a few blocks to the bullring. It would have been faster and cooler walking, but he was always driven to the ring.

"Sofia already called me."

"So you heard."

"Yes. We're all stunned."

"It was last minute. They delayed the fight by almost an hour for me to get ready. How are you feeling?"

"Don't worry about me. How did you get a team together so quickly?"

"Fuentes had a backup plan in case a matador dropped out. Of course, he always thought it would be Joselito who would flake out. It turned out that I was always intended by him to be the substitute matador." He sounded resentful.

"It's for charity, Roberto. A great matador never turns down a charity fight. It's your duty."

"I'm not a matador anymore. No one has ever respected my decision to retire."

"If you wanted to escape from bullfighting, why did you end up on a bull-breeding ranch training a matador? If you don't want to hang out with smokers, don't carry a box of matches in your pocket. So, we were right. You came back."

"Well, it's different this time."

"How is it different?"

"I know Joselito and Alex. I'd be in the ring with friends. I've been her manager, I feel like I care more about the outcome now than when I was just doing what Dad told me to do. At least, the outcome of this one fight, anyway." Roberto looked up and saw the unmistakable rotund shadow of the ring over the traffic junction. The old apprehension washed over him. "It's been a really long journey."

"Dad wants to know if you can fight in Cáceres next month."

He had a sudden vision of long shadows over orange brick and shuddered. His voice hardened. "This is the only fight I'm doing. It's an exception. For Alex. We owe it to her family."

Cristina was silent. Then she sighed and said, "Good luck, son."

"I'll call you later. As usual."

"Thank you."

Joselito was in white and gold, which suited his bone-white complexion and blond hair. He was the shortest and youngest of the three, with large, tragic eyes and drooping eyelashes, like a spaniel puppy about to be euthanized.

Alex was in deep red. She was tall, long-limbed, athletic, and tanned from her past year in Spain. She was nervous and chewing on a stray lock of hair that had come loose. Luisa handed her a hairpin.

Roberto finally arrived, scowling. Flashbulbs went off. The passageway leading into the bullring was dim and full of murmurings of *picadores*, *banderilleros*, bullring staff, vets, team members, managers, horse handlers. He went towards the scalding white sunlight in the front of the corridor, where the others were waiting. As the most senior matador that day, his job was to act as the director of the performance and protect the junior matadors should things go wrong. It was a job that Roberto took very seriously.

"Hey," whispered Joselito.

"Hey," said Roberto, taking his place. Alex was the most junior matador and stood between Roberto and Joselito. She noted happily that Roberto had picked his royal blue *traje de luces* to go with her red suit. Perhaps it would really reverse the bad luck of Pedro and Juan Carlos. She had never seen Roberto up close in a suit of lights before. She dug out her camera phone and took a self-portrait of them both.

"Stop it. You can get our photos from the photographers," said Roberto under his breath, as flashbulbs continued to light up the dark passageway.

"You all right?" she asked.

"Yeah. You?"

"I've always wanted to run away and join the circus," said Alex, bending her knee and doing stretches. Her trousers glittered with gold braid. "It's hot as hell."

Joselito said, "I'm so glad you're showing up as senior matador, Roberto."

"Yeah, and I have to go first. Fuck you."

"I can't do THREE bulls today, I'm still on medication."

"Just don't give me shit to clean up."

"Oh, it's not *me* who would need cleaning up after."

Alex complained that she had been enduring El Pepito's insinuations ever since they arrived. He wouldn't even let up when they took turns praying in the bullring chapel. She accused him of trying to psych her out. Joselito said she should be glad he was even deigning to be in the same fight as an inexperienced female, and it was only because he needed the practice, his reputation couldn't be ruined any further and that he had nothing to lose.

"Yeah, yeah, how many times must I kowtow to you, El Pepito?" hissed Alex. "What do you want, a blow job?"

"Only one?"

"Would you guys stop?" said Roberto, rattled. "You're being disruptive. Can't you at least look the part?"

Alex apologized and thanked him for showing up for their fight.

He said resolutely, "I'm doing it for the public of our home town."

Joselito interrupted them. "We three are gonna have *such* a party after. Are there any good bars in San Martín? I don't remember."

"The answer is no," said Roberto, wrapping his arm around his floral ceremonial cape and shrugging his shoulders up and down. Sweat trickled down his temples. He had a firm look about him now, and seemed an inch or two taller. Alex darted a look at him and felt her tension dissipate. When it was her turn, he would be watching her from the sidelines. They had done it a thousand times at the ranch, gone over every move. She would not fail. *Some day,* she thought, *this guy is going to graduate me in the bull-ring in Madrid. Not today. Not yet.*

"Where's my grandma sitting?" she asked.

Roberto told her where to look when she was in the ring. He had a sudden urge to pick her up and hug her and tell her everything would be fine, but the sight would be ridiculous before the entire *cuadrilla*, so he looked askance.

Joselito asked Roberto, "Bet you didn't wake up this morning expecting to be here. You prepared?"

Roberto was an astronaut who had been launched into orbit many times. The danger had become routine. Yet he was always aware of the cataclysm inherent in the tiniest of sparks in an oxygen tank. The absurdity of it all was what he fought against in the past. But not that day. That day he finally had a reason to be in the bullring. He said, "I'll be fine. I know the six bulls best of the three of us. I knew them at the ranch, I studied them at the sorting when we were picking them for Alex."

Alex said to Joselito, "Why worry? This is kindergarten for him. He'll just be on autopilot."

Joselito grinned. "I'm not worried about *him*. Oh, and did I forget to mention that when it comes to your turn, you will hear the hecklers, they're gonna shout all kinds of shit at you because you're a girl; you can't be distracted."

"That's the one thing we didn't practice," said Roberto worriedly. "Torearing when people are shouting all kinds of shit at you."

"Oh, bring it on," said Alex, lifting her chin and adjusting her hat firmly with one hand. "As long as they don't throw bottles."

"Maybe they wou—" began Joselito, but Roberto told him to shut up.

The band began to play. Alex started forward, but Roberto and Joselito both reached out and stopped her. It wasn't their turn yet. The twin constables on horseback circled the ring, their orange-red panaches fluttering. Their sixteenth century costume, all black capes and white ruffles, made them look like the fat old burghers in Holbein paintings. They advanced slowly across the bullring to ask the president permission to begin the procession.

"My favorite part," murmured Alex. She leaned closer to Roberto, "I wouldn't be here if it weren't for you."

"Well," he looked embarrassed, "a professional manager, someone older, would have been better, but I tried my best."

"No, no, I'm not talking about the managing. I'm

talking about three years ago, if you had refused to meet me in Valencia, that first evening, I would have given up. Right there and then."

He stared at her, aghast. He remembered how impressed he was by her conviction that night. "You can't be serious."

"I am serious. If you had snubbed me, I was prepared to have a good cry, fly back to Texas and call it a day, and never think about bullfighting again." She looked resolutely at the crowd, adjusting her arm slung in the ceremonial cape. "Because of you, I went on."

Outside, the *VirtualPeña* girls burst into another round of their song, disrupting the band:

I had a little cat
My father won't let me keep him

Roberto remembered how brilliantly Alex fought in the rain, in the wind, at the ranch in Cadiz; the nights sitting on the roof together, sleepless and searching. He had drawn her over and over again in his book, always with a cape and a sword in her hands, marveling at her grace and ease, this strange creature that had been raised by itself in North America, solitary and rare, like an orchid in a bell jar that he was helping to plant back in the red dust and heat of this world. He remembered his early days of suspecting her motives, then later, much later, trusting her and feeling hurt and offended when she did not try hard enough, feeling her shame-faced disgust on the days when she failed so utterly, feeling a stab of envy on the days when the bull brought out the best in her and she reached wild, joyous peaks of inspired perfection that he —at this stage in his career—would no longer be able to attain. The *aficionados* of Alex Herrera were destined for startling pleasure and utter heartbreak. God help them, thought Roberto.

Yet, despite these peaks and troughs, he never suspected that Alex had ever wavered from her purpose. It was her steadfastness that he admired and that had led him here, on this Easter Sunday, to stand beside her, each of their grandfathers' swords in the hands of waiting handlers. It moved him deeply to think that all this might not have happened, and to think of all that had to happen to the men and women of their families, in the last fifty years, in order for this day to arrive. The thought filled Roberto with sudden, secret gladness. This would be a good day at the ring.

> *But I'm too old for dolls now*
> *I'm too old for dolls now*

"I can't make out what they're singing," Alex was saying to Joselito. "Can you?"

"Dunno. The president is gonna have to make them shut up. So disruptive."

Roberto wanted to say something meaningful to her above the noise. He searched for the right words. Outside the constables raised their large hats to salute the president.

"*Now* we go," said Joselito, winking at Alex. All the *toreros* in the procession crossed themselves and wished each other luck. They began to move forward.

"Talk to you later," said Roberto.

Alex smiled a half smile with the corner of her mouth. Together they walked out into the sun.

EPILOGUE

T HREE YEARS LATER.
Hector is carefully dusting a brand new stuffed
Fuentes bull in the San Martín museum of bullfighting.
He's even put a small color photo of Alejandra Herrera
behind glass.

Roberto de la Torre, 25, and Joselito "El Pepito"
Rodriguez, 22, now consistently rank above El Rivera, the
previously trendy young champion, in the matador rankings in Spain. The year before, Roberto graduated Joselito
in Las Ventas, in Madrid. Alex was so jealous that she
refused to come watch.

Antonio has gone back to managing Roberto. Every
season, Roberto refuses to fight, ends up fighting, and
makes good money, which he entrusts to Sofia Herrera,
Alex's grandmother, to invest. However, he has cut down
his schedule. He no longer fights during the off-season in
South America. He has also moved out of his parents'
house. For the other half of the year, he draws in a beach
house he has just bought in Galicia, whose remote location is secret from paparazzi and tourists. Apparently, you
can only get to his place on horseback. His mother is
astounded again by this move, which she considers highly
eccentric, but tells people resignedly that at least he is in
his own country. Paco implores him to do another graphic
novel ("about pirates"). Antonio predicts that Roberto will
not last a winter in Galicia. Roberto admits that it is less

sunny than what the real-estate agent had promised, that buying groceries is difficult, that the postman doesn't deliver regularly, "but there is Wi-Fi", which he installed at great expense. Alex worries he will become a recluse or shack up with some Galician chick out of boredom. She Skypes or emails him every day.

Roberto's mother Cristina, herself daughter of *toreros*, sometimes attends his bullfights with his aunts, uncles and cousins. She's the curly-haired brunette in a wheelchair. He has a special smile reserved for her whenever he walks out to the center of the bullring. She tries to smile back, but she always counts the minutes until it is all over.

These days Roberto's father prefers to watch soccer, alone at home, on TV.

Sofia Herrera has never gone to another bullfight.

Thanks in part to support from *VirtualPeña*, Magalie Soubeyran has graduated to professional matador status, but is often unable to get a chance to fight outside of her home country of France. Now that she is no longer a novice, she has an even harder time getting professional engagements. Alex has convinced her to practice yoga before bullfights.

Delfina, Roberto's ex-girlfriend, married her British economics professor. Her brother Joselito couldn't attend her summer wedding in Surrey because he was fighting bulls in Algeciras with Roberto. To irritate her, Joselito emailed her a photo live from the *plaza de toros*, of Roberto standing over a dead bull at the end of the *faena*.

Roberto broke up with his American girlfriend Megan, and still intends to complete his art degree during the bull-fighting off-season, though not in San Francisco. Alex forwards him emails of art programs in warm cities every time she comes across one.

Robert y Alex, Roberto's graphic novel, has undergone several reprints and is sold in comic book stores, bookshops and train stations throughout Spain. Younger *aficionados*, both male and female, now have something to read besides somber biographies of Manolete. According to a recent adult literacy survey, it is the book most read by prison book clubs. As a result of the book, Alex is quite well-known in Spain, but completely ignored in her own home country of America because it has not been translated into English, and probably never will be.

Once a year Roberto signs books in a large bookstore in Madrid, and the line goes around the block. Detractors of bullfighting are uneasy about matadors also being published book authors because they can no longer call them uneducated, ill-bred people who are poor role models for Spanish children. At Sofia Herrera's suggestion, Roberto donates his book income to San Martín school libraries, which are sadly in need of capital improvements. This further discomfits his critics. Alex suggests that Roberto declare his vegetarianism, to further confuse everyone, but he says unlike her he can't give up *jamon*.

Fuentes and Rojo are developing a chain of restaurants around the country, specializing in organic, non-GMO food. Given the declining demand for the Spanish wild bull, Fuentes is transiting his animal stock to free-ranging, domesticated cattle and pigs. Rojo is mad about producing Kobe beef and a kind of ham that is even more rarefied and expensive than the famous *jamon iberico*.

The San Martín *plaza de toros* has gone into receivership and is scheduled to be torn down at the end of the year, to be replaced by the fourth largest indoor shopping mall in the country.

Alex Herrera has obtained her MBA and is in her first year as a junior analyst in a famous consulting firm in Boston. Both Shelly and Tomas are relieved, but worried she wouldn't like the weather. Alex takes the Amtrak train to Washington DC occasionally to spend the weekend with her friend Nicky, who now has two babies. Alex no longer stands too close to the train tracks.

Joselito Rodriguez has not attempted suicide since meeting Alex and Roberto. He has a new girlfriend, a Russian model, but still believes that Alex owes him a blow job.

❀

RobT1988: *Hi you there?*

Alex picked up her phone.

AlexH1988: "Where have you BEEN?"

We're having big storms in Galicia. The roof blew off my neighbor's house. My Wi-Fi was down.

"Regretting???"

No. What are you doing?

"Still in the office. I'll be here all night. You're up early."

It's the first day of sun in a week. I'm going for a run on the beach.

"Argh! Some of us run on treadmills in basement gyms!"

You never come visit.

"Isn't that why you moved there? So no one can find you?"

What is it that consulting firms do, again?

"Working day and night to find out how our client can sell men more shaving cream."

What are you doing on Feb 8?

"I don't think that far, I just try to get through the week."

I bet it would be really cold in Boston then.

"Yep. Almost as cold as — erm — Galicia!"

Want to go somewhere warm?

She raised her eyebrows and typed, "As in a vacation?"

As in DE LA TORRE, EL PEPITO, HERRERA. Guadalajara, February 8.

"Whaaat????"

We're short of 1 matador.

She hesitated. She then typed briskly, "NFW."

Av. temp in February is 25°C. Hard, but not impossible to get them to agree. They liked what we did in San Martín. Anyway, it's Mexico.

Alex stared at the green balloon on the screen, reading the words over and over again. Tiny letters, big promises. Her fingertips grew cold and her heart began to race. She imagined him tapping his phone as the first dry day dawned on the coast of northwestern Spain, on the opposite shore of the same ocean. She got up abruptly from the table. She was on the twenty-eighth floor of a building. She turned off the fluorescent lights overhead. In the sudden darkness, the twinkling lights of the skyscrapers of downtown Boston came through the huge plate-glass windows of the empty conference room. She could see meager lumps of hard, semi-melted snow on the rooftops of smaller buildings, piled up and forgotten on ventilation shafts and fire escapes.

Then—another *whoop*. She glanced at the phone.

How can you graduate if you don't practice?

Then—

I dare you.

She leaned her hot forehead against the cold plate glass and began to smile at the slumbering city.

FIN

Acknowledgments

Alex y Robert has a long history. The idea originally came from Beatrice Chia-Richmond, a professional actress and director in Singapore. We had gone to elementary school together. After stumbling upon a bullfight in Madrid, Bea wanted to create a theatrical production on this theme. For years she could not figure out what the story should be. In 2008, she commissioned me to find the story. My work product could be in any form, of any length, "as long as it had Spain and bullfights in it."

It was an insane idea. I found both Spain and bullfighting alien and impenetrable. I'd never read a book about bullfighting or seen a bullfight, nor had I ever wanted to. The little I heard about it caused me to associate bullfighting with certain embarrassingly *passé* attitudes. For a year, I thought of polite ways to turn her down. But because we were childhood friends, I made a last ditch effort. I bought an air ticket to Spain. Eight days, three cities, and one gored *novillero* later, I found the story I wanted to write. The following year, I went back to Spain to finish it. For an animal lover and a Buddhist, the undertaking of this story has been an unsettling yet moving experience.

A novel is a work of the imagination, not a documentary. I have taken great liberties in depicting bullfighters and their world. There are already many non-fiction books documenting this subject. For those of you who want to know what bullfighting is really like, I recommend Garry Marvin's treatise on the art and the industry, *Bullfight*. If there are few women matadors, there are even fewer women writing in English about bullfighting. Sarah Pink's

303

Women and Bullfighting, and A.L. Kennedy's *On Bullfighting,* are invaluable precedents.

If *Alex y Robert* were a film, the credits would roll on and on. Many thanks to the patience, hospitality and generosity of these individuals. They run the gamut from those who deplore bullfighting to those who live and breathe it; from those who went above and beyond the call of duty to help me, to those who contributed in the most invisible of ways. This book is stronger because of them. Any errors, of course, are my own. Thank you all. This was truly an international production.

MADRID:

Álvaro Cabeza

Carmen Collar, *aficionado*

Atilano Collar, *aficionado*

Dr. Ruperto Casañas

Tomás Entero Martin, *ganadero y empresario*

Ganaderia Cuarto Carretero

Enrique de Juan

Rogelio Rodriguez

Jaime de Villota

Josele, *torero*

Victor, *novillero*

Jesus Mejia, *novillero*

Sergio Pulido, *novillero*

Ganaderia Monte la Ermita

VALENCIA:

Dian Gorelick, *aficionado*

Phil Gorelick, *aficionado*

Dr. Juan Antonio Canales Hildago

M + K

Hannelore Medina

SEVILLA:
Cristina Delgado Quiralte
Pilar Gómez-Plana, *aficionado*
Juan Nunez
Enrique Garcia, *aficionado*

LONDON:
Jen Hamilton-Emery
Emma Pitcher
Gautam Bhattacharyya
Rachel Holmes
London Literature Festival
Susana Medina

TOULOUSE:
Julien Campredon

SINGAPORE:
National Arts Council of Singapore

USA:
Bailey Korell
Jack Chang
Luis Berriochoa
Emily Gavin
Chiahua Pan
Rafael Soriano
Dr. Robert Mittendorf
Anne-Victoire Kountz-Bonnamour
Abha Dawesar
Maria Vaso Garcia

The book mentioned by Megan's father during the
Macbeth scene in Orinda is, of course, Nassim Nicholas

Taleb's 2007 book, *The Black Swan: the Impact of the Highly Improbable.*

The Japanese poet Basho famously said, "Go to the pine if you want to learn about the pine, or to the bamboo if you want to learn about the bamboo. Your poetry issues of its own accord when you and the object have become one — when you have plunged deep enough into the object to see something like a hidden glimmering there."

This book is dedicated to Beatrice Chia-Richmond, who made me go to Spain to see the bulls in the first place.

Wena Poon
Valencia, Spain

WENA POON is a Singapore-born American author whose work has appeared in newspapers, on radio and in film. Winner of the 2010 Willesden Herald International Short Story Prize in England, twice longlisted for the Frank O'Connor International Short Story Award in Ireland, and nominated for the Singapore Literature Prize and the Malaysia Popular Readers' Choice Award, Poon is the author of *Alex y Robert*, *The Proper Care of Foxes*, and *Lions In Winter*. She also writes a sci-fi action-adventure novel series, the first four volumes of which are collected in *The Biophilia Omnibus*, which was voted Best Book Gift of the Year by CNN Singapore. A graduate of Harvard University and Harvard Law School and a practicing lawyer, she lives in San Francisco and Austin.